NIGHT ON FIRE

ALSO BY DOUGLAS CORLEONE

One Man's Paradise

NIGHT ON FIRE

DOUGLAS CORLEONE

ST. MARTIN'S MINOTAUR ✴ NEW YORK

NIGHT ON FIRE. Copyright © 2011 by Douglas Corleone. All rights reserved. Printed in the United States of America. For information, address St. Martin's Press, 175 Fifth Avenue, New York, N.Y. 10010.

www.minotaurbooks.com

Library of Congress Cataloging-in-Publication Data

Corleone, Douglas.
   Night on fire / Douglas Corleone.—1st ed.
      p.   cm.
   ISBN 978-0-312-55227-5 (hardback)
   1. Lawyers—Fiction.   2. Arson—Fiction.   3. Defense (Criminal procedure)—
Fiction.   4. Hawaii—Fiction.   I. Title.
   PS3603.O763N54   2011
   813'.6—dc22   2011001290

First Edition: May 2011

10   9   8   7   6   5   4   3   2   1

For Jack & Jill

ACKNOWLEDGMENTS

Mahalo to my extraordinary editor, Kelley Ragland, and everyone at Minotaur Books.

For their friendship, guidance, and support throughout this past year, I would also like to thank Vincent Antoniello, Rick and Tabbatha Chesler, Denis Dooley, Joe and Andrea Gaydos, Chip Hughes, John Krusas, Marc MacNaughton, Ray McManamon, Stefanie Pintoff, Joel Price, and David Rosenfelt.

Thanks, as always, to my wife, Jill, for her infinite patience, and to my son, Jack, who lights even the darkest nights.

There is no such thing as justice—in or out of court.

—Clarence Darrow,
interview in Chicago, April 1936

PART I

WISHFUL SINFUL

CHAPTER 1

I'm about to get laid.

It's about time, too, because I've been chatting up this cougar since happy hour. It's now a shade past eleven and the dozen or so mai tais I threw back tonight are threatening to render my downstairs tenant utterly useless.

We're drinking at Kanaloa's, a small outdoor beach bar and grill at the Kupulupulu Beach Resort in Ko Olina, about a half-hour drive from Honolulu. This is where I live now; not at the hotel per se, but in a villa just a stone's throw away. Here's why.

"I'm *so* drunk," the cougar says as she sets down her eighth Tropical Itch.

Ko Olina is a 640-acre oceanfront property in the town of Kapolei on the leeward side of Oahu. The property once served as a playground for Hawaiian royalty, but now services a different sort—primarily upscale vacationers from the U.S. mainland and Japan who would gladly pay a few thousand dollars extra to avoid the hordes of revelers down in Waikiki. The cougar I'm presently pursuing is one of those few, though right now I remember precious little else about her.

"Mmmm," she purrs, tugging at the red silk tie I wore to court today. She's trying like hell to be sexy, I know, but at the moment it feels as though she's tightening a red silk noose around my throat.

Koa the barkeep winks at me as he watches the show—a performance he catches a good four times a week. He's smiling, too, because Koa was standing right there behind the bar when I met the cougar this afternoon. He heard her go on and on about how she was such a lightweight, such a cheap date. How I'd probably have her in bed by eight if I played my cards right. That would've worked just fine for me because I've got to be on the road at the scream of dawn, in order to make it back to Honolulu in time for a nine A.M. calendar call before Judge Matsui.

Down the other end of the bar a young lady in a stunning red dress lights up, and Koa excuses himself. This inevitably occurs once or twice a night, someone visiting the islands unable to comprehend why they can't smoke at a bar, even if it's outside. They can't seem to understand why people like myself don't want to choke on their secondhand smoke while casually sipping a mai tai under the clean evening sky. Fortunately, most smokers don't give Koa or the other bartenders a hard time.

This one does.

With a bewildered look on her face she stares up at the stars as though maybe they can explain.

"Please," Koa says to her. "It doesn't bother me personally, but it's the law. Both the bar and I can get fined."

"Whatever," she says. "If you get fined, I'll pay it. Just let me finish this one fucking smoke."

The man she's with appears embarrassed, his face tinged

red in the bleak light of the outdoor bar. When he rests a hand on his girl's shoulder she brushes it away like he's a mosquito.

". . . the fuck off me," she says.

She lifts her tropical drink off the bar and, carrying the glass in one hand, the lit cigarette in the other, she heads this way, making for the opening in the small iron gate.

As she passes us, I get a good look at her face and immediately reconsider my support of no-smoking policies.

Koa follows her behind the bar. "I'm sorry, miss," he calls after her, "but you can't take your drink beyond the gate."

She turns on her heels with a look that almost makes me duck, the drink in her hand now looking more like a lethal weapon than a refreshing rum-based beverage. "I can't smoke *inside* the gate, I can't drink *outside* the gate. How in the hell am I supposed to enjoy myself?"

Koa doesn't have an answer to this, one of life's greater mysteries.

She tosses the cigarette on the ground and as it rolls past my foot, I stamp it out with my shoe, hoping there isn't enough alcohol on my sole to catch fire.

She storms past us again, drink still in hand, and settles back down at her original spot at the end of the bar.

By now, everyone at Kanaloa's is watching.

Koa returns to me and the cougar and apologizes. But by the time he takes another drink order, the looker is again yelling something at her date. Something about him being a fucking liar.

"Can you believe those two just got hitched this afternoon?" Koa says to me.

"No kidding," I say, a small part of me dying inside because she's taken.

Koa motions to the shimmering stretch of sand abutting the

man-made lagoon across from the bar. "Right there on the beach, they said their vows," he says, mixing a piña colada. "Had about seven or eight guests."

"Going to be one hell of a honeymoon," I say, my eyes still glued to the couple. She's hotter than the Hawaiian sun, the guy not so much. But isn't that the way it always is.

After a good long gulp of her final Tropical Itch, the cougar finally caves. "Wanna come upstairs and see my room?" she says, loud enough for half the bar to hear.

Before I can answer Koa has already set down my check.

I glance around. A number of patrons have turned their heads in our direction. The rest remain focused on the show at the other end of the bar, the looker still going off on her husband, using a selection of words that would have made George Carlin cringe.

I slide my blue Bank of Hawaii debit card across the bar, trying not to look any of the half dozen waitresses in the eye as the cougar slips her hands into my suit jacket and proceeds to frisk me.

"Do you think I'm pretty?" she asks.

"Of course, baby," I say.

And she is. Even earlier—before my fourth mai tai—I thought so. Now, of course, it's dark, I'm dizzy with drink, and it's all I can do to see the signature line on the debit card receipt Koa's just handed me.

For some reason my eyes keep darting toward the other end of the bar, toward the looker and the drink she's holding, the only light surrounding her that of the full moon and flaming tiki torches, the trays of glowing blue martinis still being schlepped around by the staff.

As the band plays "Somewhere Over the Rainbow" for the ninth or tenth time tonight, I dip into my pocket for Koa's tip.

All I have is a crisp one-hundred-dollar bill, but he's earned it. In fact, if memory serves, Koa made the introductions, same as he does every night, boasting to the cougar about how I'm a big-time attorney, my name always in the papers, my mug constantly on TV. Hell, he's even TiVo'd some of my better clips in case I ever need help making the sale.

At the other end of the bar, the looker and her husband continue quarreling, battling the band for vocal supremacy.

Koa smiles and winks at me. "You handle divorces, Kevin?"

I fish a business card out of my pocket. "Give her my number," I tell him, setting my card atop his tip. "I don't usually go to family court, but for her I'd make an exception."

A *lot* of exceptions.

"*Liar*," the looker yells again, and smacks her husband across his face.

I wince and turn back to the cougar. "Wanna get out of here?"

She nods, an intoxicating smile playing on her lips. I cast my eyes on the cougar as I drain the remainder of my mai tai, turning the glass bottoms up until the ice hits my teeth. Dark hair and big brown eyes, a body that could still stop traffic. I can't yet remember her name but that's not important, so long as I keep calling her "baby" and recall a few personal facts. Now that I'm staring into her eyes, some of those facts are starting to come back to me.

The cougar hails from some small city in Arizona, I think. Maybe Arkansas or Alabama. Possibly Alaska, though I doubt it. She's either a freelance journalist here on assignment or an editor here on holiday. Something to do with books or magazines, something in print. She has a dead father or stepfather, a sick mom somewhere in the Midwest. Or maybe the Middle East. A younger brother—*that* I remember—a good-for-nothing drunk and gambler she hasn't spoken to in years. He sounded interesting, like someone I could shoot the shit with over a beer.

And, oh yeah, she's thirty-nine.

They're all thirty-nine while they're here.

CHAPTER 2

"Would you be a sweetheart and get me a bottle of water?" she says, rubbing my chest as I'm about to drift off to sleep. "There's a vending machine just down the hall."

There's also a sink in the bathroom and that's just where I head, ripping the protective plastic from the flimsy plastic cup provided for our convenience by the eight-hundred-dollar-a-night resort. Groggy and naked, I hold the cup under the bathroom faucet and spin the knob, waiting for the tepid water to spout forth. But all I hear is a soft swooshing sound and the cup and the sink remain dry as a bone.

I briefly consider just falling back into bed, but I don't feel like getting dressed and walking home. And I fear that's just where this will lead if I don't manage to snag the cougar some Dasani or Aquafina before the night's end. So I suck it up, slip into my boxers, and snatch two singles off the cougar's nightstand.

Then I head for the door. I'm only thirty-two but I don't recover from drinking quite as rapidly as I used to, and I'm concerned I'm going to be too sick to make it to court in the morning. My partner Jake Harper might be able to cover for me, but it's almost one A.M. and I have little doubt that he's drunk, too, probably still banging back glasses of Jameson at Whiskey Bar in downtown Honolulu, swaying to live Irish drinking music with that girlfriend of his. I wonder briefly if I'll still be hitting the bottle as hard as he is when I'm sixty-seven.

After unlatching three locks I step out into the hall, shielding my eyes from the lights. I pad down the *Shining*-esque corridor lumbering like a George A. Romero zombie, not dressed but still dripping with sweat. The usual trade winds have been absent from the leeward side these days, and the heat is really starting to get to me. After only eighteen months in the islands, I'm already starving for a nice ice cold day of New York City winter. Maybe even a nor'easter.

Eyes half shut, I glimpse a sign for the vending machines and turn right, dismayed to find a kid of four or five dangling a wrinkled dollar bill in front of the Coke machine, apparently trying to decide which beverage best suits his palate, or which best complements the package of Drake's Devil Dogs he has waiting for him back at the room.

I sigh loudly enough for him to hear me, hoping he'll catch the hint. He doesn't. Doesn't appear to be the sharpest crayon in the box either. It's an awful thing to think, I know, but it's nearing one A.M. and I have to brave heavy H-1 traffic and the big hard Hawaiian sun in just a few hours, and someway, somehow, I've got to sleep off the half gallon of light and dark rum that is presently engaged in a race war in the pit of my stomach. So sue me.

"Need a hand, kid?" I say, trying to speed things along.

The kid looks me up and down, and I'm suddenly conscious of the fact that I'm not wearing clothes, that I'm standing in front of a preschooler in a pair of pineapple-pattern boxer shorts, asking the kid if I can lend him a hand. As a criminal defense attorney, I realize this is how you end up at a criminal defense attorney's door. Hell, this is how you end up on *Dateline*.

The kid shakes his head.

"Shouldn't you be in bed?" I say, then hope like hell that Chris Hanson isn't lurking around the corner with the "To Catch A Predator" microphones and cameras. I swear, NBC viewers, I didn't mean that the way it sounded.

"I'm thirsty," the kid says.

"So's the cougar," I mumble, "so let's get this show on the road."

"Huh?"

"Nothing," I say, motioning toward the vending machine. "Go ahead."

The kid turns back to the machine, still swinging his wrinkled old dollar. "Grandma got some soda from room service," he says, "but it tasted all oogie. I don't think there was any sugar in it. Grandma's a diet-betic. I just want a Dr Pepper, but look . . ." He points to his selection. "The red light is lit. That means it's all out."

"Maybe they have some Dr Pepper on another floor," I suggest.

He stares up at me as though he'd forgotten I was standing here, his messy brown hair falling into his eyes. Looking at him, I almost feel sorry for the kid. Almost.

"Will you come with me?" he asks.

I shake my head. "No can do, kid." I move toward the machine with my own two bills and notice the red light is lit over the Dasani bottled water, too. The luck just keeps on coming. "On the other hand," I say with a sigh, "I'd be more than happy to."

The kid holds out his grubby paw and I grudgingly accept it, escorting him to the stairwell to avoid the elevators. In the stairwell the echoes of our footfalls ricochet off the cement walls like stray bullets, his Sunday shoes clopping like a pony's, my bare feet slapping against the stairs like a wet seal's flippers. On the next landing I catch our reflection in the glass case that houses the fire extinguisher. A tiny kid and a tall nearly nude stranger holding hands in an empty hotel stairwell at one A.M. This doesn't look good for anybody. If someone spots us, I'm off to jail. Me with my pineapple boxers, reeking of rum and cougar sex, promising a preschooler a refreshing Dr Pepper from a vending machine on a lower floor of a tropical beach resort.

"Sorry about the way I'm dressed, kid," I say as we approach the door to the fifteenth floor of the Liholiho Tower.

"Oh, that's okay," he says. "I heard some girls saying you looked really warm in your suit before."

I pause, my hand on the door handle. "What's that?"

"Downstairs in the lobby," he says. "I saw you before, talking to some old lady."

"Hey, kid, she isn't *that* old."

He shrugs. "Anyway, while you were talking to the old lady, some young lady was talking about how you looked really hot in your suit," he says, "and her friend said she'd like to help get you out of it."

"Is that so?" I say, smiling. I open the door to the fifteenth floor. "Hey, how old are you, kid?"

He holds six fingers in the air. Then he says, "Four."

Smart kid.

As we move down the hall toward the vending machines I warn the kid not to make any noise, then realize that if Chris Hanson's around, I'm only getting myself in deeper and deeper. This transcript's apt to buy me four to six years at the Halawa Correctional Facility, at least.

"Here we are," I say, thrilled to see not a single red light on the machine, not by the Dr Pepper, not by the Dasani. "And it looks like we're good to go."

The kid rushes up to the Coke machine and tries to push his wrinkled old dollar bill into the slot. The machine spits it back out.

"Let me try," I say, plucking the bill from the kid's tiny hands and smoothing it out against the wall. I slide it in. This time the machine swallows it down.

The kid's eyes light up.

"Okay," I say, holding out my hand. "Now one more."

The kid shrugs, looks up at me as though I just spoke to him in Mandarin Chinese.

"You don't have another single?" I say. "No change?"

The kid pulls out his pockets like an elegant hobo. An old gum wrapper flutters to the floor but nothing else. "Grandma don't have no more change," he says. "I threw it all in the fountain downstairs with the fish. I had to make a bunch of wishes."

I sigh. "Ya know, a bottle of Dr Pepper is two bucks," I tell him. "A bottle of Dr Pepper from a vending machine is two bucks in every hotel in the English-speaking world."

He shrugs his shoulders again, then eyes my left hand and the two bills I'm squeezing into my fist.

"All right," I say, moving toward the machine. I slide in one of the cougar's dollar bills and allow him to select the Dr Pepper.

The bottle tumbles downward and lands with a thunk. The kid reaches his hand in and shouts, "Thanks!"

"Sure, kid," I say, glancing from the single I have left to the two-dollar price tag below the Dasani. "Let's go."

We head back upstairs. There are eight rooms down our end of the hall, four on each side, each with an adjoining suite. The kid's room is just next door to the cougar's, but the kid's room is adjoined to the last room on the left, not to ours. The last room on the left has a baby blue garter hanging from the door handle. Looks like I'm not the only one getting lucky tonight. Though, of the two of us, I *am* the only one who gets to sneak out the door come morning.

I bid the kid good night and tell him to keep our little soda mission a secret. Or at least not to mention the pineapple boxers.

He nods his head and walks toward his room. I turn and hustle down the hall to pay a visit to the ice machine.

When I return to the cougar's room I pull her key card from the pocket in my boxers meant for condoms. I quietly open the door and step inside.

The cougar's sitting up in bed, her arms wrapped around her toned, tanned legs. "Well, that sure took you long enough," she says.

I nod and douse the lamp she'd turned on above the desk.

"Where's my water?" she asks, holding out her hand with indignation.

"Here, baby," I say, placing a thick melting cube of ice in her palm. "Suck on this."

CHAPTER 3

I'm dreaming.

I know I'm dreaming because I'm back in New York, at the jail on Rikers Island, sitting across from a former client named Brandon Glenn.

Thing is, Brandon's been dead nearly three years now.

An alarm suddenly sounds. The jail is on lockdown. I jump off my metal folding chair and race toward the door but it's locked. Of course it's locked. It's always locked during attorney-client meetings with a prisoner.

When I spin around, Brandon Glenn's slumping off his chair, falling to the cold cement floor. I hurry around the table to help him, but by the time I get there there's no saving him. A shank juts out the side of Brandon's neck, blood gushing like a geyser all over my new Tommy Bahama sandals, my toes turning a deep and gruesome red.

I drop to my knees, force a soundless scream for help while trying to cover his wound with my suit jacket. My thoughts instantly flash from rescue to culpability. After all, it's only the two of us in this tiny sealed tomb, the room is locked from the outside—and somehow I know my prints are all over the shank's bloodied handle.

As I rise to consciousness I realize the prison alarm is just an alarm clock, maybe the loudest alarm clock on earth. Lying on my stomach I feel around for an extra pillow, place it atop my head, and try to smother my ears.

When the cougar begins clawing at my back I realize this is no alarm clock. It's a goddamn fire alarm, the kind of fire alarm even the dead could hear. I reach for another flat, lifeless pillow and tug it down hard over the first.

The cougar's growling something at me.

". . . time is it?" I shout.

I peek out from beneath my pillowed teepee and glance at the window. It's still night, no light spilling in at all. My eyes flutter toward the digital alarm clock, which reads two-twenty something, the last digit blacked out by one of my socks.

Quickly I take inventory of myself: pounding head, burning stomach, a mouth that tastes like rum and coconut suntan lotion. So, nothing out of the ordinary.

The cougar meanwhile is on her feet, slipping back into her sundress, shouting at me to get out of bed.

"No way," I say, lowering the heavy lids of my eyes.

Fire alarms, they go off all the time. Like car alarms, only louder. I've been putting up with this shit since my first semester at URI, some jacked-up resident advisor constantly chasing me naked out of the freshman dorm. Drills they called them. Drills held in the dead of night just to get the girls outside in their underwear, nipples instantly hardening under white cotton tank tops in the brisk New England air. Gossips loitering with their binoculars ready to report the following morning on who is sleeping with whom. Dorms, hotels, condos, apartment buildings, it's always the same. Always a prankster, some joker or toker higher than an elephant's eye blowing bong smoke up at the ceiling. Never is it a bona fide emergency.

Well, almost never.

The cougar smacks my bare back so hard that it stings. "There's a *fire*," she shouts.

I groan. "How do *you* know, baby?"

"Because there are *flames* out in the hall and there's *smoke* coming in under the door," she yells. "And *stop* calling me baby!"

That gets me up. Still in my boxers, I'm out of the bed and by the front door in a few rapid heartbeats, checking the handle for heat.

My hand sizzles for several seconds before I yank it away and yelp in pain. Yeah, it's hot. Hellishly hot. And even from a few feet away I can see the flames licking the peephole I'm too frightened to approach with my face.

I turn and glance toward the sliding glass door to the lanai, but we're sixteen floors up and cougars can't fly. As far as I know, neither can lawyers.

There is one more exit in the room, a door that leads to a door that leads to the adjoining suite. By the time I raise my singed hand to point to it, the cougar is already there, the first door open, checking the second for heat.

"It's cool," she says, frantically trying the handle. "But it's locked."

I edge closer to the front door, squint my right eye and catch a glimpse out the peephole. The hall is now filled with thick black smoke, and it's nearly impossible to see anything. But the smoke appears to be billowing from the left, and the suite adjoining ours is to our right. If we can get through that door, we might just have an avenue of escape.

In the distance I hear sirens, but for us it's too little too late. If we're going to survive, we're going to do so on our own.

My mind racing, I rush to the heavy wooden chair pushed under the room's lone desk. With some effort I heave it onto my right shoulder and run full speed toward the locked door, trying to break through. The chair crashes into the door, splintering in my arms, the impact striking me full force in the chest. When I rise to my knees, my torso is bruised and bloodied, and I'm entirely out of breath.

And fresh out of ideas. The fucking door didn't budge.

I push myself to my feet and search for my suit pants. The room is quickly filling with smoke. Ducking low, I spot the pants rolled up in a ball on the tiled floor of the kitchenette. Down on hands and knees, listening to the cougar scream, I crawl toward the pants as fast as I can.

When I reach the pants I fish around in my pockets for my Bank of Hawaii debit card. I finally find the card in the last pocket left to search. With the blue piece of plastic in hand, I rise to my feet and hurry back toward the locked door adjoining the suite.

Fortunately I've done this before, only this time my hands are shaking and I'm trying like hell to continue holding my breath.

I slip the debit card in and maneuver it near the lock, but nothing.

"Hurry," the cougar shouts as though I'm taking my sweet goddamn time.

I slide the card in and out, back and forth, up and down, trying to catch the lock. No good. I yank the card back out, draw in a lungful of smoke and choke, my heart pounding hard against my chest.

As the smoke in the room thickens I stare down at the debit

card, my eyes stinging, sweat pouring down my cheeks. "You got me into this fucking mess," I mutter to the piece of plastic, "now you get me the hell out."

I glide the card back into the crack and guide it toward the lock. Finally the familiar feel of the latch giving way. I twist the handle and the door swings open. I grab the cougar's arm and a moment later we're scampering through the neighboring suite, darting for the front door.

Before I open the door I check the handle for heat. Hot, but not nearly as piping as ours.

I peek through the peephole. Smoke, sure, but it's now or never.

"Stay *low*," I shout over my shoulder as I open the door.

We duck out of the room and into the hall, the alarm like a drill in my ears. The thick black smoke invades my nostrils, climbs up my nose and down my throat as I run. Trying to choke the life out of me.

I bolt toward the stairwell that the kid and I used before.

When the cougar and I reach the stairwell, I fling the door open. Then I turn back and take one last glance down the hall.

The kid.

Through the smoke I can barely see him, standing as still as a statue, tears raining down his face, a half-full bottle of Dr Pepper still attached to one of his paws.

"*Go*," I shout at the cougar, shoving her into the stairwell.

"What are you—"

Before she completes the question I'm hunched low, scrambling back down the hall toward the kid. He's coughing now, hacking as though he's been smoking Winstons the past half century.

I lift the kid, toss him onto my right shoulder, surprised that he's as light as air.

Breathlessly, I work my way back toward the stairwell, but the heat's too much, the smoke's filling my lungs. I begin choking and nearly collapse to the floor.

Instead, adrenaline pumping, I pick myself up and lunge forward.

"Stop, drop, and roll!" the kid's yelling in my ear. "Stop, drop, and roll!"

"I think that only applies if you're *on* fire, kid," I rasp.

Then we're in the stairwell, my bare feet again slapping against the stairs. Only this time there is an alarm screaming in my ears, and we're not on a mission for an ice cold Dr Pepper and a two-dollar bottle of Dasani. This time the clock's ticking and there's a damn good chance both the kid and I might die.

All right, Kev. We're down the first flight. My knees suddenly ache, the weight of the kid now taking its toll. Down another flight. Only fourteen floors to go. The smoke in the stairwell is getting thick. My lungs are about to give. Holding the handrail, I stumble down another flight. Thirteen more to go.

If I stop, I think, *I drop, and the kid dies.* Down another flight. *Keep moving.*

Another flight. Eleven to go.

Ten. *I can't breathe.* Nine.

Won't someone shut off this fucking alarm? Eight.

Almost there, Kev. Just seven more flights to go to get the hell out of this night alive.

CHAPTER 4

Outside, watching the flames dance, thick black smoke drifting over the Pacific, I listen to the kid screaming and crying for his grandmother, and I dread the worst. My eyes flick over to the ambulances every few seconds, though I know it's in vain. Anyone who is getting out has gotten out already, and there is no one alive and outside who meets Grandma's description. A sick feeling rises in my throat and I taste the remnants of rum, blended with smoke and bile. I nearly vomit at my bare feet but instead choke it back, keep my chin up, eyes focused, my hand resting gently atop the kid's head, trying futilely to douse the fire in his tortured imagination.

The kid told me amongst a rush of tears that he never made it back into his room after we bought him the Dr Pepper downstairs. The door was locked and he didn't have a room key. Silly of me now that I flash back to his outstretched pockets to think that one would have magically appeared. He knocked on the door but knew Grandma had long been sleeping. I think that maybe the soda she ordered tasted "oogie" because it was sprinkled with Bacardi light rum. And Grandma had taken her pills, the kid said. Her "Am-beans," he told me, the white oval tablets that never fail to put her down for the night.

Unable to reenter his room, the kid searched the hallway for me. Then he tried the stairwell, went down one floor and came back. He sat on the stairs for a while, sipping his soda. Figured someone would eventually come by and find *him*.

When the alarm sounded, the kid said, he immediately had an accident in his pants, peed all down his legs and into his shoes. I told the kid not to worry about that, told the kid that I did that, too.

There are thick gray blankets wrapped around us, courtesy of the Honolulu Fire Department. I've taken a few hits of oxygen and all things considered, I'm feeling sublime. The cougar's fine, too, just a tad shaken up. Standing next to me, the three of us almost look like a family. Which means, I believe, it would be a crime for me to sneak away and head home.

As police and news helicopters circle overhead, I turn and gaze at the swelling crowd of gawkers. Some are in their nightclothes, pajamas, nightgowns, nighties, even teddies. Some guys, like me, are still in their boxers or briefs. One's standing completely in the buff, a UPenn baseball cap covering his goods. Others are dressed in their day clothes—sundresses and aloha shirts, khakis and shorts. It seems some flocked over from the resort next door, others from the villas, town houses and condominiums that round out the rest of the Ko Olina community.

Through the chaos I eventually spot Koa. The bartender is standing by himself, entranced by the flames, his arms folded tightly across his chest. I wave my arm in an attempt to snag his attention but he doesn't see me. I call out, but with all the noise—the copters, the crowds, the still-sounding sirens—it's impossible for him to hear. Finally he tears his gaze away from the fire and searches the throng. I throw up my arm again and he sees me.

When he reaches us, he's leering at the towel-covered cougar standing next to me. Then he glances down at the kid, one eyebrow arched toward the sky. "Damn, you work fast, Corvelli. The two of you got one toddler already?"

Like most native Hawaiians, there's a slight hint of pidgin English in Koa's speech, such that his *th*'s sound like *d*'s, many of his *r*'s disappear completely, and "already" sounds a lot like *awready*.

"What are you still doing here?" I ask him, glancing at my bare left wrist out of habit. No watch, but I figure by now it has to be well past three o'clock. "I thought Kanaloa's closes at midnight on Tuesdays."

Koa half-smiles. "Nah, we just tell you that, Kevin, or else you'd never go home."

A few yards away flashes are going off. Not the occasional twinkle from a curious tourist, but a full-on barrage of shooting from every which direction, as though the four of us were standing on the red carpet in tuxes and gowns, instead of barefoot on the grass in towels and T-shirts. I shield my eyes against the glints of light, which until now had been aimed at the top two or three floors of the tower, hoping it's just investigators doing their jobs, looking for fire buffs, seeing who's lingering a little too long at the scene, who is a little less awed by the rescues than by the flames still creeping and crawling up the night sky. But I know that I'm wrong. I know that it's the goddamn media.

No sooner do I realize it than a tape recorder is aimed pointblank at my nose. The mikes can't be too far behind.

"Can you tell us what you saw?"

"How did the fire start?"

"Are you a guest at the resort?"

"Was anybody else up there?"

"How did you and your family escape?"

As I parrot "No comment," I slowly back up, dragging Koa, the kid, and the cougar away from the predators. My progress is immediately impeded by a large firm hand pressed against the middle of my back. The fingers move gradually up my stiff neck until they rest rigidly on my right shoulder. I turn and see the familiar though not-so-friendly face of John Tatupu.

"May I have a word with you, Mr. Corvelli?" Tatupu says.

Although I hold a good deal of respect for this particular native Hawaiian homicide detective with the Honolulu PD, he thinks I'm a sleaze, and I can't say it doesn't sting a bit.

I turn toward the media vultures and smile; saved by the dick.

"What can I do for you, John?" I say, moving with him away from the mob.

He flinches at my use of his first name. John and I are clearly *not* on a first-name basis. "Heard you were on the floor where the fire started," he says.

I arch my brows. "Really? Who told you that?"

"We're not in a courtroom, Corvelli. I get to ask the questions tonight."

"Fine," I say, stopping mid-moonlight stroll, turning my head up and squinting at a lit tiki torch at the edge of the beach. "If it's going to be like that, I refuse to respond."

"Rather do this downtown?"

"Are you asking me on a date, Detective? Because you sure as hell don't have probable cause for an arrest."

Tatupu rests his hands on his hips and tries again. "Look, I know you were with that woman over there." He points with his chin at the cougar ten yards away. "All I need to know to clear both her and you is exactly what you were doing when the fire started?"

"If memory serves," I say, "I was calling down to the front desk to request an extra Bible. See, there were two of us in the room and only one copy of the Good Book."

Tatupu sighs heavily, a long and deep, defeated exhalation. I almost feel sorry for him. Almost.

"Look, John," I say, pulling my blanket tighter against the late night trade winds finally blowing in from the ocean. "There are sixteen rooms on that floor, eight down our wing. It's mid-July and the hotel's filled to capacity. That means there were probably at least fourteen people besides myself and my date down our end of the hall. Why not hassle them first, see what you can get?"

Tatupu looks me squarely in the eyes, his broad lips sunken on either side. "I would but from what I hear from HFD's search and rescue team, most of them are already dead."

As I amble back in the direction of the cougar and the kid, I turn and spot the honeymooners we'd seen arguing at the bar, now huddled in each other's arms, the young woman sobbing uncontrollably into her husband's chest. I sigh heavily, Tatupu's words echoing in my head. Property damage is one thing, even if that property happens to house some of the finest cougars to visit the Hawaiian Islands. Even had the big bad fire consumed my favorite beach bar, it was still something to watch, something to experience, something to tell Jake and our investigator Flan about in the morning at Sand Bar over a few a.m. mai tais. But now that people have perished here . . .

I do a double-take as I pass the newlyweds. The guy she's

with isn't the groom at all; he's someone else entirely. Suddenly it hits me: the newlyweds were on our floor, in the room adjoined to the kid and Grandma's. The door adorned with the baby blue garter. I take another glimpse, wondering why then the bride is fully dressed, decked out in the same red dress she wore earlier to Kanaloa's.

"Who was that guy you were speaking to?" the cougar asks, as soon as I elbow my way back through the crowd.

"Cop," I say.

"What did he want?"

"Just has some questions."

"Where did he say the blaze started?"

Before I can respond, it hits me like a brick to the back of my head. Who? What? Where? *When* is obviously next. That's right, the cougar is a freelance journalist. I'm sleeping with the enemy.

Suddenly the kid tugs on my blanket, nearly yanking it off. "Where's my grandma?" he shouts.

I kneel in front of him, offering a sympathetic look but no answers. Lying doesn't seem right, but telling the truth seems a whole hell of a lot worse. "The jury's still out, kid," I say.

The kid stares back at me, dumbstruck, tears rolling down his crimson cheeks. "What?"

As I fumble for another answer, the cougar kneels on the kid's other side, speaks softly in his ear. Whatever she's telling him appears to calm him, and I realize that whatever that is, it doesn't really matter now. Whether Grandma's dead or alive, the kid will have plenty of time to process the verdict. No need to send him into a state of shock just now.

I stand and stare at the long line of yellow fire trucks, recalling the big bright red engines that paraded down Willard Avenue past my own grandmother's house in Totowa, New Jersey, twenty-five years ago. They rolled by in the daylight once, maybe twice a year, lights flashing, firemen waving, tossing Blow Pops and Tootsie Rolls to the kids on the street. The parade held some kind of purpose, I'm sure. Maybe to commemorate Memorial Day or Labor Day or the Fourth of July. Something like that. All I remember now are the lights and the candy—and my grandmother at my side, holding my hand, preventing me from running into the road, boarding one of the trucks, and leaving my childhood behind forever.

Koa says, "I'm going to take off, Kevin." He rests a hand on my shoulder, drawing me back to the present. "If they get this inferno under control before it reaches Kanaloa's, then I guess I'll see you tomorrow."

I nod my head, my attention drawn to a dark-skinned African American man slowly approaching us with a pad in his hand. He's wearing a bright yellow jacket, the big bold black letters HFD no doubt printed on his back. He is still a few persons away, taking statements.

I slip through the crowd toward him, not quite anxious to answer questions but to ask some. Well, one to be exact.

"Excuse me," I say, when there is a break in the conversation.

The man holds up one finger, not the offensive one, so I wait while he finishes taking the woman's statement.

The men in yellow are dispersed now throughout the crowd, seeking those individuals with cameras and video recorders first. Investigators are all around, scanning the crowd, observing the observers with binoculars and cameras and video recorders of their own. This is potentially an arson and homicide investigation. Gathering evidence early on is crucial.

A few minutes later the man in yellow steps over to me. "Name?"

"Kevin Corvelli," I say, grudgingly. "C-O-R-V-E-L-L-I." Frustrating as it is, I know he won't answer my question until I answer a few of his.

"Are you a registered guest at this resort, Mr. Corvelli?"

We go through the whole spiel, from how many drinks I consumed at happy hour to how and when I took the cougar back to her room and did the dirty. Then we finally get to the kid.

I tell him the entire story.

"Pineapple boxers?" he says.

When I'm through, the investigator, who has identified himself as Darren Watts, tells me to hang on a few minutes. Watts steps away, puts his radio to his lips, and says something I can't quite make out. Then he vanishes into the crowd.

I stare over at the cougar and the kid, heart in my throat, the sick feeling in my stomach growing more intense by the second. Wondering how the hell the kid's going to handle this.

I swivel my head, a little dizzy from the stress. The looker is still in the middle of the crowd, bawling into some other guy's chest. A sick horrible thought, the type we all experience but never admit to, flashes in my mind: *Hey, Kev. Looks as though she's single again.*

I push the thought away as the investigator Darren Watts returns, one of those you-know-what's-coming looks on his face.

"I'm sorry," Watts says quietly, looking past me at the kid, "but I'm afraid the child's grandmother didn't make it."

CHAPTER 5

"Kid's name is Josh," I tell Jake.

My law partner and I are sitting across from one another in our conference room, his Zippy's bacon and egg breakfast strewn across the expensive mahogany table as though a bomb just went off. Since Jake was gracious enough to cover for me in court this morning, I don't say anything. Besides, I can tell he needs the grease. Poor bastard's hungover as hell.

"Kid's mother, Katie Leffler, drowned in the Pacific behind their North Shore home just a few weeks ago," I continue. "Middle of the night. She'd been working on a second bottle of Pinot. Apparently decided it was a good time for a dip. Current took her. Her body was discovered on the rocks the next morning."

Jake whistles, a morsel of overcooked bacon soaring in an arch across the table. I take a deep breath and hold my tongue.

"Grandma was here on the island to collect the kid," I say. "To fly him back to the mainland. Nevada or New Mexico, I think."

"No father?" Jake says.

I shrug and try to keep the emotion from my voice. "According to the kid's great-aunt Naomi, the father has never wanted much to do with the kid. He's a confirmed bachelor, a bit of a ladies' man, and the kid apparently cramps his style." I watch Jake shovel a plastic spoonful of runny eggs into his mouth. "Anyway, Mom and Dad never married, but she stayed here in the islands so the kid would have a father nearby. Clearly, things didn't work out the way she intended."

"How did she wind up here in the first place if the family's from the mainland?" Jake asks, taking a cautious sip from his coffee.

"She was attending UH," I say. "Majoring in marine biology. Quit as soon as she got knocked up and moved out of the dorms, rented a small home up North Shore."

"And the father?"

"The dad's former military. Joined the Army right after high school in Charlotte, North Carolina. Transferred to Schofield Barracks here on Oahu a few years later. Apparently left the Army in 2003 to avoid the Iraq War, but remained in the islands and took on odd jobs. Think he fixes cars for a living now."

"Even with the mother and grandmother both out of the picture, the dad still doesn't want the kid?"

"Aunt Naomi is going to bring in a family lawyer to have a talk with him, but she's not holding her breath."

"A shame," Jake says.

I lower my eyes. *A shame.* Just saying the words is enough to clear our consciences of just about anything. So long as we express our disapproval of a horrendous situation, we're off the hook. I see the kid now, trembling and white with shock, with not a single human being itching for the pleasure of watching him grow up, and all I can say is, "It's been known to happen."

Jake sets his cup of coffee down and stares up at me. Before he can speak, I glance out at the Honolulu skyline and change the subject.

"So the fire . . ." I say. Everything I know about the blaze is splattered on the front page of the copy of the *Honolulu Star-Advertiser* resting on the chair beside Jake, but I elaborate nonetheless. "Nine confirmed dead, five in critical condition at the Queen's Medical Center, including two firefighters. Police and Fire haven't released anything yet as to cause."

Jake pushes his plastic container away from him. "According to the paper," he says, wiping his mouth with his sleeve, "some witnesses say they heard an explosion. You hear anything, son?"

"I was passed out on rum," I tell him. "You could've fired a cannon across the bow of the bed and I wouldn't have woken up."

"You're a lucky man."

I grimace, wondering why the hell people always tell you how lucky you are when you narrowly escape a tragedy. I could have lost all four of my limbs, one of my ears, half my jaw, but so long as I were still breathing, albeit with the aid of a Saab-sized ventilator, some son of a bitch would still come by and tell me how goddamn lucky I was. No, I wasn't lucky, not last night. If I were lucky I wouldn't have been at the resort in the first place. I would have been home, spread out on my Egyptian cotton sheets, my windows open, a cool breeze blowing in, with my ten-year-old Maine Coon cat Grey Skies curled up at my feet.

Jake lifts the newspaper off the chair and sets it on the table. "Some are thinking terrorism," he says, squinting down at the print.

"Some are always thinking terrorism," I say. "It's the new Journalism 101. Scare people, boost ratings, boost sales."

Jake runs his hand through his ever-thinning white hair. Seems to me he ages a month every week.

I sit back, cross one leg over the other, and gaze out the colossal conference room windows, swallowing the view. "Thanks for covering for me this morning," I say without looking at him.

"No worries," he says.

"So how did it go in court?"

Jake shrugs. "Son of a bitch is charged with his fifth DUI in as many years and still has the balls to accuse *me* of smelling like booze."

I don't say anything but I can smell Jake from here, yesterday's poison gushing out of his pores like the BP oil spill. "Rough one last night?" I ask.

"Had a long bout with Mr. Daniels," he says, turning his head toward the ceiling. "Used to be we got along just fine. No more, it seems."

"Jack Daniels, huh? I thought Alison hates Jack. What happened? You two finally run Whiskey Bar out of Jameson?"

"No Alison last night," Jake mutters. "Just me."

I swallow hard, knowing damn well Jake desires me to ask and pitting it against how little I want to. If I don't fill the silence immediately, he's going to launch right into a monologue, I know. Not going to wait very long for my prompting. And once Jake starts talking, well . . .

"Her and I," he says, "we've been on the rocks the past few days."

Too late, I think. *Here it comes.* I might as well direct the conversation because I'm going to hear about this one way or another. At least if I ask, I'll earn some points in the friendship department, maybe get him to cover for me again in court tomorrow, in case I decide to head back to Kanaloa's this afternoon to tie one on.

"Sorry to hear that," I say. And I am. Without Alison I've little doubt that Jake would have already drunk himself to death. "What's going on? She leave you?"

Jake looks up at me with watery bloodshot eyes and bites down on his lower lip. Jake first met Alison Kelly, a forensic scientist with the Honolulu PD, last year during our first trial together. I'll be damned if he didn't ask her out while she was on the witness stand, testifying to the scientific credibility of lip print analysis. Since then Jake and Alison have done their drinking together as a couple, which, as any alcoholic will tell you, is the only cure for drinking alone.

"Other way around," Jake says, mid-sigh.

"You left *her*?" I uncross my legs and lean forward, absolutely shocked and barely trying to hide my surprise. What abominable offense could she have committed to have caused my partner Jake Harper to leave a gorgeous, smart and sexy, utterly understanding woman like Alison Kelly?

There is a long pause from his side of the table, as Jake puffs out his chest and refuses to swallow his pride. "She quit drinking," he finally says.

There is a light rap on our conference room door, then the familiar squeak that drives me bat-shit crazy but I'm still too lazy to oil. Our receptionist Hoshi pops her head in.

"Kevin," she says, "you have a call on line three. She says her name is Erin Simms."

I glance at Hoshi and tell her to please take a message, that I can't take any calls right now. I turn back to Jake, whose eyes continue to focus on the conference room door. I swing back around and find Hoshi still standing there, her hands clasped together in front of her as though in anxious prayer.

"I'm sorry, Kevin," she says in a small voice, "but I really think you should take this call. The woman on the phone sounds panicked, and she insists that it's urgent."

CHAPTER 6

Fifteen minutes later I'm in my electric-orange Jeep Wrangler on H-1 West heading up North Shore to a spot called Hidden Beach. It was the only place Erin Simms would agree to meet, and even then, only after I assured her it was the most private place on the island. She's frightened, she said, and from the sound of her voice over the telephone that was an understatement. She'd been watching the local news all morning, flipping across our three main local stations, and just now learned that she's been named "a person of interest" in the Kupulupulu Beach Resort fire.

Traffic is light, a far cry from the hell on H-1 heading into Honolulu on a weekday morning and the horror heading out from about four to six in the early evening. That's why I often try to leave my office on South King Street by three P.M. Well, that and because Kanaloa's offers a variety of enticing drink specials from four to seven.

Right now driving is fine, and I can almost enjoy the ride, with the soft top down and soothing Jack Johnson melodies pouring out of my speakers. Only I'm none too thrilled to be meeting a prospective client related to the Ko Olina resort fire. It's big news already, I know, not just on the local stations but on CNN, MSNBC, and FOX News. Last thing in the world I want right now is another press case, particularly one that's gone national. Jake and I have been content handling an array of drug, burglary, and assault cases of late. They pay the bills, my dark hair stays dark, and there is plenty of time left over to enjoy this island paradise.

But this Erin's voice sounded so desperate I couldn't help myself. Even as my brain begged my lips to say no, I was telling her that everything would be okay, that I'd meet with her, if not in my office then anywhere on Oahu that she wanted. It was only a few moments before my mind finally flashed on Hidden Beach.

Hidden Beach is a secluded spot few locals and fewer tourists even know about, a remote block of sand that can't be seen from any road. I was introduced to Hidden Beach by my first lover here in the islands—a beautiful, young Hawaiian woman named Nikki Kapua, whom I met while conducting witness interviews during my first homicide case in Honolulu.

I take the exit for H-2 and head north through some congestion in Wahiawa, relieved when I'm finally hit with the scent of fresh pineapple from the Dole Plantation. The northern part of Oahu remains rural, thanks largely to efforts opposing urban sprawl. With the mammoth Waianae Mountain Range on my left and the pineapple fields to my right, I could very well be traveling through America's agricultural heartland, were it not for the draw of the azure Pacific Ocean just beyond.

Ten minutes later I'm gliding through the beach town of Haleiwa, which is relatively quiet now but will be bustling with surfers come winter and the hulking North Shore waves that accompany the season. I bear left past Dillingham Airfield, gazing up as a stream of skydivers in rainbow parachutes drift by in a diagonal line overhead. Then I glance in my rearview mirror as I slow my Jeep for the last half mile. Very soon I'll be running out of road.

At the end of the pavement, I roll to a stop and shift the Jeep into neutral, then into four-wheel drive. Another glimpse into the rearview to make sure no one sees me, then I put the Jeep back into drive and press down slowly on the accelerator.

As soon as my tires hit dirt, I become anxious. Between the massive jagged rocks and the city-sized craters, I feel as though I'm navigating the surface of Mars. Even wearing my seat belt, my head smacks against the side window, and my right knee cracks against the steering wheel more than once. If you ask me, off-roading isn't damn near as exhilarating as the commercials would have you believe. And it's sure as hell not as safe.

I nearly flip the Jeep over as I strike a large boulder then mercifully level off. The Jeep's temperature gauge reads ninety-three degrees and I wonder just when we'll escape this infernal heat wave. Even in a light Tommy Bahama T and shorts, with a UH baseball cap protecting my head, I'm cooking like a kalua pig at a luau. I could use a dip in the cool Pacific. Come to think of it, a cold hard drink of Coke and 151.

There are, of course, no bars on the mile and a quarter of treacherous terrain between Farrington Highway and Hidden Beach, just a dozen or so old telephone poles and lengths of tall dense greenery, along with the majestic Waianae Mountain Range shielding us from civilization.

I jolt to a stop across from the pole marked 196 and throw the Jeep into park. I unhook my seat belt, fling open the door, and drop onto the rock-hard dirt, my size-12 sandals kicking up enough dust to make me cough.

I head toward the beach, taking in the sound of waves crashing against rocks. Even in the summer the ocean's choppy at this spot. During winter you wouldn't head up here without a suicide note.

On the steep slope of dirt and rock that leads to the beach, I remove my leather sandals so that I don't break my neck. But when my feet finally hit sand it feels as though I'm walking through fire, so I toss my sandals down on the beach and hastily step back into them.

I move toward the water, hoping like hell Erin Simms isn't here, that maybe I'll get lucky and she won't even show.

Who am I kidding? Corvelli and luck go together like peanut butter and arsenic.

And sure enough, there she is, peeking out from behind an eight-foot rock-face to my right like a frightened rabbit. I shield my eyes against the mad mean sun and finally get a good look at her.

She's long and lean, with a tight body and small breasts, a face that any straight guy could instantly fall in love with. Not all that exotic but rather plain in a strangely perfect sort of way. She's dressed down in fitted sweats and an oversized T, but she looks every bit as hot as she did when I first caught sight of her.

I bite my lower lip as it fully registers.

Turns out, today's prospective client is yesterday's fiery bride.

In other words, Erin Simms is last night's looker.

"They're looking for me," she says, her voice already cracking.

We're at the edge of the beach where sand meets ocean, and the tide is licking at our heels, occasionally splashing our calves. Our backs are pressed up against tall craggy rocks, so that we can't be seen from the dirt path.

"They think *I* started the fire," she cries.

I raise my palms in front of me and tell her to calm down, to keep her voice steady. I assure her that she's safe here, that she can relate to me everything that happened in a composed and comprehensive manner, and that our conversation is fully protected by the attorney-client privilege.

But it's no use.

"They're *after* me!" she screams. "The *police*. And I don't know what to do or where to go!"

"All right," I say, still trying to soothe her. "Tell me why. Why do the police think you started the fire?"

She's crying now, her lower lip trembling. Her knees are wobbling and I fear she's about to collapse. I try to take hold of her arm but she yanks it away the moment my fingers touch flesh.

"I don't *know*," she says, clenching her teeth. "I think the fire started in our hotel room."

"Yours and your husband's?"

She nods without looking at me, her eyes locked on the mountains behind us. Her mouth is open, drool pooling at the corners. She appears to be exhausted and parched.

My own gaze travels from her plastic sandals and worn sweats, to the cheap souvenir Waikiki T, then finally fixes on the fading scars up and down the taut skin of her arms.

"And your husband—"

"He's *dead*."

"Died in the fire?" I say, just to keep the dialogue moving.

She swallows forcefully and nods.

"But you weren't in the room with him," I add.

She shakes her head, her light shoulder-length hair clinging to her cheeks and neck from the sweat.

"Think carefully," I say. "Where were you when the fire started?"

"I don't know," she says all in one breath, her watery green eyes suddenly burning with confused rage.

"But you were alone?"

She finally looks me in the face, her lips contorted in an unspoken plea. "My husband Trevor and I got into this terrible fight."

I don't tell her that I witnessed at least part of the fray at Kanaloa's.

Waves of questions flood my head, from how many drinks she had, to what the argument was over, to why she's decided to go into hiding. But all of this, I feel, is premature because we don't even yet know whether this is a case of arson or simply a tragic accident that killed her beau. In which case we should probably be discussing a wrongful death suit against the resort.

I lean back against the rock. I'm about to tell her all this when I notice her blanche, her eyes darting toward the path, and suddenly she is kicking off her plastic sandals and starting to run. But there's nowhere to go unless she's a hell of a swimmer and thinks she can make it a few thousand nautical miles to Tokyo.

I gaze past the rocks and see six white SUVs marked *HPD* slide to a stop behind my Jeep, kicking up a wall of dust. Out spill at least a dozen uniformed cops and one lone man dressed in civvies.

Erin Simms had allowed me to hire her a trusted driver to take her to the end of Farrington; from there, she walked. So I don't know how the police could have found her, why they wouldn't have just stopped my driver on the road if they knew where she was.

Then I look long and hard again at my bright orange Jeep.

Shit, I think. *It was me. I was followed.*

Guns are drawn and I turn, see Erin stopped at the edge of

the water, her trembling hands held high in the air. She breaks for some bushes and the sky is suddenly filled with sounds you never dream you'd actually hear. At least not in real life.

"Freeze."

"Show me your hands."

"Don't fucking move."

Erin stumbles and falls flat on her face as she tries futilely to climb up an embankment. The cops swarm over her in a matter of moments. As they cuff her—one cop with the patented knee in her back—I see fresh blood dripping down one slender arm from a gash on her elbow. When they lift her up, I catch another bright red patch on her chin, crimson spilling down her neck onto her cheap souvenir T.

Guilt suddenly hits me like a shot to the chest.

The cop in his civvies slowly descends on the beach, his feet adorned in dark boots, his hands stuffed casually into the pockets of a pair of khaki cargo pants. His badge hangs from a thick neck, dangling over a broad chest. His T is a faded dark blue. Long before I can make out the face, I know from the stride and salt-and-pepper hair that it's my old friend Detective John Tatupu.

I move to intercept him before he reaches Erin, who is now doubled over, still bawling in her cuffs.

"How'd you know she'd contact *me?*" I say quietly when Tatupu is close enough.

He throws a glance in my direction as he sidesteps me. Then he reluctantly digs into his pocket and pulls out a small plastic evidence bag. Inside are the remains of a charred business card. The sun is in my eyes and I can't read it from where I'm standing. I don't have to read it, though, and Tatupu doesn't have to read it to me.

I already know the damned thing reads HARPER & CORVELLI.

CHAPTER 7

Foot traffic in front of the Honolulu Police Department on South Beretania Street is a hell of a lot more frantic than usual. That's because we don't see all that many homicides here in the islands. Twenty per year on Oahu, tops. Those are typically comprised of domestic disputes gone horribly violent, barroom brawls that were taken outside and finished with switchblades, and of course the occasional drunk driver whose misfortunes included a charge of vehicular homicide.

But last night nine people lost their lives, all in one shot, and the police are desperate to put this case to bed before fear strikes the U.S. mainland and Japan, and tourism takes a vicious hit. And the local media, well, they finally have something juicy to report. A busy news day in Honolulu usually means Dane Cook is in town or an ostrich escaped from the zoo. But this is *real* news. This is hot. Hell, if this incident indeed turns out to be arson, this was mass murder.

Erin Simms is being processed and I can't speak to her right now, but I feel responsible for her even being here, since it was my damned bright orange Jeep that led police right to her. So I'm going to stand out here and wait, as long as it takes, until they let me in to confer with my client. I glance at my watch. It's been seven minutes already. It's hot as hell out here, and truth be told, I don't know how much longer I can stand this.

I pluck my cell phone from my pocket and dial the office. I have Hoshi transfer me to Jake, who is still in the conference room, now working on lunch.

"Jake Harper," he says with a mouthful.

I fill him in on this morning's happenings and tell him where I am. "Get ahold of Flan," I say. "Things are moving fast. *Too* fast for an arson case. We're going to need to get our own investigation started right away."

Arson cases are rarely solved early in the investigation. Unless a dozen credible eyewitnesses see someone running from a burning structure with a lit torch, arson investigations are typically time-consuming and usually go on for weeks or months before a suspect is even considered, let alone apprehended. That Erin Simms has been picked up in this case in under twelve hours tells me one of two things: either the police are jumping the gun under pressure from the governor, or investigators discovered a mound of physical evidence linking Erin Simms to the fire.

"Any ideas what they have on her?" Jake asks.

I don't, but I'm assuming the worst. "You can bet it'll be on the news before it reaches me," I say. No way police and prosecutors are going to keep this case quiet. The governor is going to want tourists on the mainland to know it's safe to continue booking their stays in the islands, that the perp is behind bars and can't do any further damage. If they have any damning surveillance tapes, we're going to see them on national television long before we see them in discovery.

Jake eagerly takes the cue. "I'll run downstairs to Sand Bar," he says, "see what I can catch on CNN."

As I slap the phone shut, a sultry voice sounds from behind me. "Well, hello there, Kevin."

I turn, lower the brim of my cap over my eyes to thwart the sun. Then my jaw drops onto the boiling sidewalk and sizzles.

"Hey," I say, "um . . ."

The cougar smiles, her cherry red lips dripping with scorn. "Sherry," she says, barely parting them.

I nod. "Sherry." Of course, Sherry. "What are you doing downtown?"

"Same as everyone else," she says, motioning to the mob. "Getting the story."

"Didn't you say you were leaving for the mainland tonight?"

Sherry shrugs. "Change of plans." She points to headquarters, where a bevy of uniforms are gently shoving back onlookers. "This is big. There may even be a book in it for me."

I arch an eyebrow, purse my lips as though I'm impressed. "A book?"

"True crime," she says. "You know, Ann Rule type of stuff."

"True crime?" I shrug. "We don't even yet know whether a crime has been committed."

"Someone's been arrested."

"Could be a big misunderstanding," I volley.

"Not from what I hear."

I lift the brim of my UH baseball cap slightly, opening myself up to her. "What have you heard?"

Sherry shakes her head, her long dark hair swinging back and forth. No sign of sweat. "Quid pro quo, Clarice," she says. "You first. Would it happen to be that you're here in front of police headquarters because you're representing the accused?"

I smile, my eyes darting left and right to make certain none of the other hyenas have captured the scent. I lower the brim over my eyes. "Wouldn't I be *inside* headquarters if that were the case?"

"Not while your client is being booked," she says, smiling. "Not someone as claustrophobic as you are."

"Is that what I told you last night?"

"You didn't need to tell me, Kevin. I saw you move the closest barstool a good eight feet away from you at Kanaloa's during happy hour yesterday afternoon."

I glance at the line of people waiting to get through security and cringe. "All right," I say. "But the answer is no. Far as I know the suspect doesn't have a lawyer yet."

Technically, this is the truth. Erin Simms hasn't retained me. And I haven't agreed to take the case. She called me for a consultation, nothing more. That the consultation took place at the unconventional venue of Hidden Beach is of no consequence. What *is* of consequence is that no money has changed hands, no paperwork has been signed. Far as I'm concerned, I can walk away right now.

Just like you could've walked away from the kid and cougar last night, Corvelli.

Sherry tilts her head, decides it's time to play lawyer herself. "But you met with her this morning," she says. "That's what I heard."

I bow my head and concede the point, though chances are she's just fishing. "I meet with a lot of prospective clients I don't ultimately represent."

"They don't like you?" she says, a smirk playing on her lips.

"Can't *afford* me," I tell her.

Initial consultations at Harper & Corvelli are free. Unfortunately, the only legal advice I've thus far been able to dispense to Erin Simms is to remain silent. Not to utter a single word until we have the opportunity to meet again. No chats with Tatupu, no commiserating with her cellmate, not even a phone call to her mother or father or favorite uncle. "The only person you speak to," I called to her, as Tatupu gently tucked her into the back of his SUV, "is me."

"Your turn, Dr. Lecter," I say to Sherry. "What else have you learned besides the fact that the suspect met with yours truly?"

A flirty shake of the head, a wink, a weak half smile. "Too broad, Counselor. Narrow it down."

"Fine. How did investigators determine it was arson so quickly, when—"

"Mr. Corvelli!" The grating voice comes from directly behind me. It's instantly followed by another hand on my shoulder. Someone should have gotten the word out by now: I don't like to be touched with my clothes on.

I spin around. At first I don't recognize her. *Another cougar from Kanaloa's?* I take a good look at her. *Dear God, I hope not.* If it is, I'm quitting Koa's mai tais cold turkey.

Then I glance down at the pint-size human picking his nose at her side. He's holding a can of Dr Pepper with his other hand, and I realize it's the kid Josh from the hotel fire last night. Which means the woman standing before me is Great-aunt Naomi, Grandma's sister who has lived in the islands all of her life.

"Hi, Ms. . . ."

"Leffler," she reminds me. "Can't tell you how happy Josh and I are to see you again."

Behind Aunt Naomi the media is swarming someone from the Homicide Division.

From the corner of my eye I catch Sherry joining the fray.

"Same here," I say to Aunt Naomi. "How's the kid?"

"*Alive,*" she says, beaming. "Thanks to you." She looks down at him, swats his fingers away from his nose. "You are all he's been talking about since the fire."

"Well, it's been less than twenty-four hours," I point out, craning my neck to see if Homicide is releasing any new information to the press. "I'm sure Spongecake Square Bob will retake center stage any moment now."

Aunt Naomi leans in closer to me, her old-lady perfume flicking me in the face. "Mr. Corvelli, we just can't thank you enough for your courage and quick thinking last night. Maybe you missed your calling. You should have been a firefighter or something heroic . . ."

I smile, kind of. Shake my head. "I couldn't stand the heat."

"Well, Mr. Corvelli . . ."

It's all I can do not to box my own ears out. I stand there, staring into her tired face, tense, wanting to escape more than I did that burning hallway on the sixteenth floor of the Liholiho Tower of the Kupulupulu resort last night. I'm straining my mind, sorting through the excuses, when Aunt Naomi says something that truly frightens me to death.

". . . and so we were thinking," she says, "the boy could really use a man like you in his life. So maybe when you're not so busy, you can find it in your heart to spend a little time with Josh?"

An hour later we are all gathered in front of the Honolulu Police Station for a press conference. The alacrity with which the Honolulu PD has moved on this case is astonishing. And alarming. Folks on the islands ordinarily operate on aloha time, something that has driven me bat-shit crazy since I arrived here from New York City. Nothing here happens fast—and I mean *nothing.* It typically takes forty-five minutes just to purchase a pack of Stride gum at the local 7-Eleven. I can grow a full beard in the time it takes to get served a chicken Caesar salad at most island restaurants. Now, a few hours after the fire, we are expected to believe that investigators already determined the cause, named their suspect, had her arrested, and are ready to file felony charges.

And all of this under a national spotlight.

A spokesperson for the department takes to the podium and immediately introduces the Chief of Police, who is brand spanking new to the job. Started as chief just last week. In other words, he is someone with something to prove.

"My name is Chief Edward Attea," he says into a small microphone, "and I've called this press conference to announce that we now have a suspect in custody in connection with the devastating fire that occurred last night at the Kupulupulu Beach Resort in Ko Olina, in which nine innocent people lost their lives."

Attea has a mustache, trimmed neatly across a sincere face. A quick glance at his CV, which was recently posted in the *Star-Advertiser*, and it's easy to see how he got the job. The Honolulu Police Commission appoints the Chief of Police for a period of five years. The last chief wasn't reappointed because of city politics. Well, at least that's what *he* claims.

"The suspect's name," Chief Attea continues, "is Erin Simms. She is currently visiting the islands from the U.S. mainland. More information on her will be released in the coming days. We can inform you at this time that Mrs. Simms is to be charged with counts of arson and murder in the deaths of nine people at the Kupulupulu resort. As you all know, the names of the victims have not been released pending positive identification and notification of the victims' families. We can, however, confirm that one of the victims is the suspect's newly wedded husband, Trevor Simms of San Francisco, California."

Every hand in the media mosh pit rises at once, as Chief Attea bows his head and steps back from the microphone.

The spokesman steps forward. "I am afraid the chief will be unable to take any questions at this time."

The chief steps off the stage and wraps his arms around a teary-eyed female civilian, who I assume is related to one of the unnamed victims, if not Trevor Simms himself.

I'm in a daze, everything happening so fast I can barely breathe. It feels as though the sun is punching me in the back, beating every last bit of energy out of me.

I lift off my cap to wipe away the sweat. The moment I do, I hear: "Is that Kevin Corvelli?"

I pull the cap back down, push the brim over my eyes, but it's too late.

Someone shouts, "It *is*. Swing the camera."

The mob turns and trains its microphones on me.

"Word is, you were at the fire, Mr. Corvelli. Are you a witness?"

"Are you representing the accused, Erin Simms?"

"Mr. Corvelli, have police yet identified a motive?"

"Were you surprised by your client's quick arrest?"

"Have you had an opportunity to meet with your client yet?"

I draw a deep breath, lift the UH cap from my head. Sweat drips into my eyes, causing them to sting.

I take a step back, taking my time, wiping the sweat from my eyes with the sleeve of my T. Finally, I look into the cameras as they look into me.

"No comment," I say. Then I slowly make my way through the mob toward the station.

CHAPTER 8

"Thank you for agreeing to meet with us, Mr. Corvelli."

It's a few hours after the press conference, the sun already hiding behind the mountains, and we're in my office rather than the conference room because the conference room still reeks of Jake's bacon and eggs. I think Jake stowed the leftovers in the back of one of our mahogany bookshelves. Hoshi, with a respirator tied tightly over her face, is on the case. In forty-five minutes, if she hasn't yet found anything, she has instructions to call in HazMat.

"Of course," I tell Erin's stepfather, Todd Downey, from behind my cluttered desk. He's a thin man, somewhat frail for his age, appropriately melancholy under the circumstances. A surprising number of parents, step or otherwise, who sit across from me at my desk don't appear genuinely distraught at all. It's almost as though they are there on behalf of some stranger who they simply have had the misfortune to know. And it's not just the folks of the real bad seeds, it's just as often the parents of good kids who merely suffered some lapse in judgment, who fucked-up, bought drugs, sold drugs, stole, embezzled, drove drunk, got high and climbed a telephone pole in their Speedo, whatever. Those children, no matter their age, always deserve parents who are at least willing to try to understand. After all, we all fuck up sooner or later.

"We don't know where else to turn," Todd Downey says.

"Well," I say, "that's why I do what I do." That and I was too chickenshit to follow my boyhood dreams to Hollywood.

I glance at Erin's mother, Rebecca, who hasn't yet said a word. Rebecca was clearly once as beautiful as her daughter, a cougar in her own right, even today. Smooth skin, eyes like green-blue marbles, hair as silky as any model in an Herbal Essences commercial. She may have had a facelift, I don't know. Maybe Botox. Whatever it was, it's one of those oh-so-rare cases where it actually worked, preserved to a sufficient degree the beauty that once was.

I lean forward on my desk. "Let me begin by telling you we don't have a whole hell of a lot of information on your daughter's case just yet. Nothing more than what you've already read in the papers and seen on TV. In the coming hours and days that will change. But for now, aside from a brief lecture on criminal procedure, all of the facts are going to be coming from your side of the table."

Todd Downey nods. "Understood."

I typically dread meeting someone's parents—a client's, a girlfriend's, a friend of a friend's, it doesn't matter. It's something I try to avoid at all costs. I just can't look them in the eye and smile while I'm imagining the ways in which they fucked up their child. Because they all have in some way or another, and I can't help but want to get them on the witness stand. To delve into the deepest, darkest recesses of their minds until I get them to admit the things they refuse to admit to themselves.

Following Chief Attea's press conference I had only a few minutes to speak in privacy with Erin herself. She was in no state to provide me with any relevant details, so I simply reiterated what I told her this morning on Hidden Beach: Exercise your right to remain silent and speak only to me.

Now I'm left to gather what I can from her parents. So I pull a yellow legal pad from my top desk drawer and ask them to tell me what I need to know.

"Where should we begin?" Todd Downey asks.

We're going to be here until dawn if I have to stop and answer stupid questions every three minutes, but it's been a long day for them too, so I let this one slide.

I click open my blue Pilot G-2 05. "How about at the beginning?" I suggest.

All so typical. "Normal" is the word they use, but "normal" infers that any other type of relationship, any other road to wedlock, or cohabitation for that matter, is *ab*normal, and I can't accept that. But the relationship between their daughter Erin and her beau Trevor was *tres, tres* typical. A one-year courtship, give or take a month, followed by a one-year engagement, give or take a week, and a destination wedding-honeymoon on the gorgeous tropical Hawaiian Island of Oahu. Typical. Traditional. *Tres Americana.*

What was *a*typical, of course, was the death, maybe murder, of their son-in-law on their only daughter's wedding night. And, as I am just now learning, the afternoon that immediately preceded it.

"There was a . . ." Dad pauses, searches for the word, not for my benefit, I can tell, but for his wife's. ". . . an *indiscretion*—"

"Oh, for shit's sake, Todd, just say it." Rebecca shuts her eyes and clenches her fists as she spits these words out. When she reopens her eyes, they're wet and angry and fixed on me. "Trevor fucked one of the bridesmaids," she says. "Erin learned about it just minutes before the wedding."

I lift my pen, put the tip to the yellow page, and scrawl *a woman scorned*. I turn the pad upside down on my desk. There's our motive.

"The bitch confessed it to my daughter," Rebecca says, "after Erin was already in her wedding dress. Said she slept with Trevor on his boat in San Francisco Bay just a little over two weeks ago."

At least now I know what they were arguing over at Kanaloa's.

"They said their vows," Todd says, "to save face, I guess. But Erin hadn't decided what she was going to do after that. She told her mother and maid of honor she needed a few days to think things through. She and Trevor had at least decided to stay in separate rooms during the honeymoon."

"But she retained a copy of the room key to the honeymoon suite," Rebecca says, as though she has read my mind.

I flip the legal pad over and scribble *access*. There's our opportunity.

Motive + Opportunity is not a pleasant formula for our side.

There are a lot of other questions I have—about who else attended the wedding, how many guests were there for the groom, how many for the bride, who presided over the ceremony, who catered the reception, was there live music or a deejay—but now's not the time for all that. Because there's one issue that takes priority over all others. One I can't escape, as much I'd sometimes like.

Todd the Father now seems to have read my mind. "How much is something like this going to cost us?" he asks.

"Something like this," I say frankly, "between attorneys' fees and expenses, I would need somewhere between three and four hundred thousand just to start. Likely double that if this case goes all the way to trial."

I pull the phone near me, in case Todd decides to have himself a heart attack on my desk. But there's no myocardial infarction, just a deep breath and two misty eyes, a glance in his wife's direction.

"We'll have to sell the goddamn house," she says immediately.

Todd bows his head in resignation, and I feel a little like shit. I only wish I could be the type of lawyer you find in Hollywood movies, one that doesn't accept money, that is independently wealthy, and can take on an array of good causes for free.

"Okay," Todd says quietly to me. "We'll get you the money. I talked to my broker back in California this morning. We already have a buyer lined up." He pauses, his eyes tearing up. "Six hundred thousand," he says. "That's all we can get. Three up front and three at the start of trial if and when it comes to that. Is that fair enough?"

"That's fair," I say.

"We spent our entire savings on this wedding and honeymoon," he adds. "The house is the only asset we have."

I nod. "I understand." Though I *will* have our investigator Flan check this out first thing in the morning.

"But what about *bail*?" Rebecca says, her voice rising like the tide.

I shake my head. "Your daughter's charged with nine counts of first-degree murder. And she's already tried to run once. If bail is set at all, it will be set in the millions. In which case, the point is moot."

Rebecca begins crying, Todd trying to comfort her. Their daughter will be doing at least the next six to twelve months behind bars thousands of miles from home.

"All right," I say, standing up, still in a T-shirt and shorts. "I'll have Hoshi draw up the retainer agreement and have you sign it. If you can leave a deposit of ten thousand dollars I'll be at your daughter's initial arraignment tomorrow morning."

Todd nods his head.

"One last thing before you go," Rebecca says as I step around my desk. Her voice is now cracking like ice in a cup of hot coffee. "One last thing you need to know."

I stand silent, waiting for the shot like a prisoner on the firing line.

She glares up at me. "Our daughter has a history of starting fires."

CHAPTER 9

It's standing room only in Judge Sonya Maxa's courtroom for an arraignment that may last all of ten minutes, about which anyone with an inkling of sense or knowledge about the American judicial system already knows the outcome. As I routinely tell my clients: "There are rarely any surprises at arraignment."

As I move through the courtroom, I instinctively loosen my tie. The windows are open but there are few trade winds blowing in during the middle of July. I turn to the nearest court officer, a dark young man with three chins and no neck. "No A/C?" I say.

I get a shrug and a barely discernable shake of the head. "Broken," I think he says.

I set my briefcase down on the defense table and glance over at my adversaries on the other side of the aisle. It's a big day for them. The press is hungry, the public's out in droves. At least two nations are watching events unfold from either side of the Pacific. The prosecution today—"the *good* guys," as cable commentator Marcy Faith might say—are all sympathetic smiles

and handshakes, an aggrieved crowd of cops and deputy prosecutors leaning over the rail to console the victims' families.

Front and center in the gallery is the female civilian whom
Chief Edward Attea hugged following yesterday's press conference. Jake and I watched her on the news last night at Sand
Bar during burgers and beers and a brief arraignment strategy
session. Her name is Lauren Simms, Trevor's sister, and she's
irate and out for blood. And she is "dead certain" my client Erin
Simms, who now "shamefully shares the family surname," is
the party responsible for Trevor's death. Not to mention the
demise of eight other innocents.

Lauren Simms takes her seat directly behind the prosecutor's table. Still standing at the table is Donovan Watanabe,
decked out as always, today in a meticulous gray Pierre Cardin
suit. Dapper Don, as he is known in legal circles, is one of the
best in the business, not only here in the islands, I'd wager, but
in all fifty states. On top of that, he's respectful and open-minded.
In fact, if I hadn't purposefully doused Dapper Don with a cup
of lukewarm Kona coffee during our first trial together, I'd be
honored to call him my friend.

Dapper Don notices me staring and bows his head solemnly
in my direction. I return the gesture with a wink, then open my
briefcase and remove a half-dozen pages of notes I scribbled
down last night at Sand Bar. I'm assuming this is Dapper Don's
case, if not the head prosecutor's himself. Strangely, as good as
he is, I'm looking forward to facing Donovan Watanabe again.
Our first rematch since the Gianforte case.

Judge Sonya Maxa enters the courtroom from chambers. Silent, we all rise on cue and I'm reminded of church and the
mind-numbing Sunday mornings of my youth. Maxa is a stern-
looking woman to most observers, though it may be the long
flowing black robe, the bifocal glasses, or the reddish brown

hair chopped obscenely short and combed neat like an eight-year-old Catholic schoolboy's. But I've been before Maxa on previous matters, and she is one of the fairest jurists I have yet to come across.

"Have a seat," she says.

From the corner of my eye I catch the prisoner being led this way in shackles down the aisle.

Here comes the bride.

An image of Nikki Kapua flashes through my mind but I quickly push it away.

Once Erin Simms is safely at my side, I stand again, gently sweep aside her hair, and whisper in her ear. "This is just a formality. I'll enter your plea and we'll argue for bail, though as I've told your parents, bail will, in all likelihood, be denied. If not, it'll be set so high, Bill Gates himself would probably have trouble making it."

She starts to cry, and I ache a little inside. So I look away, back toward the prosecutor's table. When I do, my eyes cross, my mouth contorts. I'm utterly perplexed and I can't help but show it. Standing alone across the aisle now is a man about my age, approximately my weight and height. A good-looking guy with blond hair, sharp blue eyes, and a suit picked out for the cameras.

I swing toward the court officer standing behind Erin. "Hey, Perry," I say.

Perry's so big he could break me in half, but he's one of the gentlest human beings I've ever known. "New guy," he whispers to me. "Just came over from L.A. Got a hard-on for the media and says he plans on being the next head prosecutor soon as Frank DiSimone retires."

I frown. "No enemies in the office yet? No opposition?"

Perry shrugs. "You know how it is in the islands, Kevin—too

much respect, too little personal ambition. Guy like him figures he can fly across the pond and steamroll his way to the top. Hell of a lot easier to do that here than L.A."

The clerk calls the case. *"State versus Erin Simms*, Docket Number . . ."

We briefly sit again while the judge gets her file in order. It's a few moments before I catch my foot tapping against the floor. Then the clerk asks for our appearances.

L.A. rises. "May it please the Court, Your Honor, Luke Maddox for the State of Hawaii . . ."

I scribble the words *Luke Maddox* on my yellow legal pad and decide that I hate the name already.

My turn. "For the defendant, Kevin Corvelli . . ."

I waive a formal reading of the charges, sparing Erin and her family a few extra minutes of grief. Then Judge Maxa turns immediately to the issue of bail. It's a lost cause, I know. And we'll get another shot at it within two weeks, once Erin has been formally indicted on the charges. Though I don't expect circumstances to change between now and then, I tell her now in her ear that there is at least a chance at getting bail reduced if exculpatory evidence surfaces before the next arraignment. Chances are, though, that she will remain incarcerated through trial, and I don't want to get her hopes up too high.

"Maybe though?" she says.

"Let's see what happens over the next two weeks," I tell her. "We'll try."

Meanwhile the prosecuting attorney Luke Maddox is being heard on the issue of bail. He reveals little more than what the public read in this morning's copy of the *Honolulu Star-Advertiser*. That the defendant Erin Simms committed the offense in question over an affair had by her new husband just weeks before the wedding. Yada yada yada. He's holding back a lot, I can tell, but that's because he doesn't need a lot. Not for this. Erin is not going anywhere unless her parents can somehow cough up a few million in bail, and as we all already know, that's not going to happen.

As I watch Maddox go through the facts of the case, I decide that Maddox is probably just going to bat for DiSimone or Watanabe during this initial arraignment. This is little more than an exhibition game. No need to tire out your starters.

". . . and the defendant's Zippo lighter was discovered at the scene . . ." Maddox is saying. She had access, a key. She had more than motive. There is no question, Maddox submits, that the defendant Erin Simms is responsible for this heinous crime.

"As such," Maddox concludes, "the State requests that bail be set in an amount no less than six hundred thousand dollars . . ."

What? My head snaps up, my eyes bulge from their sockets like a cartoon coyote's.

". . . with the conditions, of course, that the defendant immediately surrender her United States passport, be confined to a home here in Honolulu County, and submit to wearing a monitored ankle bracelet for the duration of this case. Thank you, Your Honor."

Her Honor appears no less stunned than I am. My client is already displaying a confused smile on her otherwise despondent face.

Judge Maxa turns to me. "Mr. Corvelli?" she says.

I stand, staring down at my file, trying to comprehend what just happened. I glance back into the gallery, at the front row behind the prosecution's table, at the deceased's sister, Lauren Simms, and I think I understand.

"Mr. Corvelli?" the judge says again.

I shrug. "I apologize, Your Honor. Six hundred thousand dollars, it just sounds like an odd number to me."

The judge lifts her brows as though she agrees, but of course she is not putting anything like that on the record. Instead, she says, "Are you complaining, Counselor? Because I believe that number, as odd as it might sound, is exceedingly fair, if not generous to your client, considering the serious charges pending against her."

I open my file and stare down at the retainer agreement printed up just yesterday by Hoshi, and signed by both of Erin's parents. I know exactly what this bastard is up to, and there is nothing I can do to stop it.

So I make my prepared argument for an even lower bail. It's weak, I know, and I don't hit too hard with it for fear of losing credibility with the judge, with the media, with any prospective jurors who might be reading my words in the *Star-Advertiser* tomorrow morning.

I take my seat as the judge renders her unsurprising decision: "Six hundred thousand dollars with the requested conditions."

Suddenly I have one hell of a decision to make.

"Your Honor." Luke Maddox stands again as I'm about to pack up my stuff and quite possibly head to the mens' room to vomit. "There is one other issue I'd like to raise and be heard on."

Even Judge Maxa seems uninterested. "What is it, Mr. Maddox?"

"It concerns Mr. Corvelli's representation of Ms. Simms in this matter. We'd like to put the Court and the defendant on notice that the State will be filing a motion forthwith to have Mr. Corvelli's law firm relieved as counsel for the accused in this case, Your Honor."

Maxa frowns. "On what grounds?"

Maddox looks over at me. "On the grounds that the State

intends to call Mr. Corvelli as a material witness for the prosecution."

Behind us the gallery buzzes and Maxa instantly calls for silence.

"Mr. Corvelli was present at the scene of the crime," Maddox continues, "and we have certain proof that Mr. Corvelli has specific firsthand knowledge through his own personal observations in this case."

Swallowing hard, I stare back at Maddox with a look of contempt, laced, I admit, with no small degree of awe.

Fortunately, Judge Maxa simply sets a date for his papers, another for my response, and yet another for oral argument and decision. Then she slaps her gavel, adjourning these proceedings.

I rise, already steeling myself for the questions, for the cameras, reminding myself to stick to my mantra and not to begin grandstanding, not to go off on some self-serving tangent.

Head down, I turn and move like a bullet back up the aisle.

So much for "There are rarely any surprises at arraignment."

CHAPTER 10

"They're trying to push you out," Jake says, leaning against one of the colossal conference room windows.

I sigh. "It's bullshit. A diversion. Maddox is going to try to busy us with issues that have no relevance to this case. He's an L.A. lawyer; I know his game."

Jake shakes his head and takes a seat across from me. "It's not the motion to remove you that I'm talking about, son."

I knew this was coming. I avert my eyes, toss a glance at Ryan Flanagan who is staring down at his rough dock-builder hands, obviously preoccupied.

"Everything okay Flan?" I say. "I'm going to need your full attention on this one."

"I'm fine," he says, quickly masking his New Orleans frown. Divorced with two daughters who despise him, and an injury that's left him sucking down narcotic painkillers nine, ten times a day, Flan's probably not the best investigator in the islands. But I like him. And that goes a long way.

"Good," I say, "then let's mov—"

"Just that Casey showed up today."

As my mind works to process this, somehow Jake—brain three parts whiskey—picks up on it right away. "Your oldest daughter? What's she doing in town?"

Far as I know, Flan hasn't seen her, hasn't even spoken to her in years.

"She had a falling out with Lucifer," Flan says.

That's an easier one. Lucifer (née Victoria) is Flan's hellish ex-wife on the mainland.

"Casey's staying at a hostel in Waikiki right now," Flan adds, "but she's asked to move in with me."

I don't know what to say. I'm no good at this, this hand-holding, this comforting others during times of crisis, especially when it pertains to family. Seems the only time I'm able to aid anyone is after they've been arrested. Out of nowhere I find myself saying, "I've got to do something about my Jeep."

Jake folds his arms, asks me what I mean.

"The color," I say. "Too conspicuous. Led Tatupu right to our client."

When Jeep introduced an electric-orange Wrangler, I snatched one up, certain they were going to be the next big thing. Months later, I couldn't spot another one on the road, and Jeep discontinued the color the following season. Thus, I have what is perhaps the only bright orange Wrangler that Jeep ever made. In my line of work, it's not always a shining idea to stand out in a crowd.

"Our client . . ." Jake says. "Son, that's something we have to—"

I deflect Jake's latest objection by turning my head toward our investigator and saying, "What do you think about the Jeep, Flan?"

"Wanna sell it?" he says. "Casey's already hinting that she's going to need a car here on the island."

I shake my head. "I'm going to have it painted. White, like every other vehicle in the state of Hawaii."

I pick up the conference room phone and dial Hoshi's extension, ask her to check the *Paradise Yellow Pages* for a decent detailer.

"How will I know if they're any good?" Hoshi says.

"Call each of them," I tell her. "Whoever quotes the highest price, we go with them."

Jake and Flan crease their brows.

"You get what you pay for," I say.

Jake plants his palms on the conference room table and leans forward, raising his voice for, perhaps, only the second or third time since I've known him. "*Which* leads back to the issue of our representation of Erin Simms."

All right. There's no ducking this any longer. I bow my head, let Jake have his say.

"When I said earlier that the prosecution was trying to push you out, son, I wasn't referring to Maddox's bullshit motion to have you relieved. I was referring to the stunt Maddox pulled with respect to bail. That girl wants out of jail, and hell, I don't blame her. Her parents want her out, and I don't blame *them*. But we both know—and, apparently, so does the prosecution— that Erin's parents have only six hundred grand to put up, whether it's for bail *or* attorneys' fees. They can't pay both. And until you have a conversation with the three of them, I don't think you should be referring to Erin Simms as a client of this firm, or putting much of the firm's energy and resources into her case."

"If we walk out on her," I say calmly, "she's going to end up with the dregs of the Hawaii Criminal Bar. Someone like Mickey Fallon, or Russ Dracano, for hell's sake. That's precisely what the prosecution wants—some lawyer they can roll over without so much as an objection at trial. We can't let that happen."

"*We* don't have much of a choice," Jake says.

I take a deep breath and swallow hard. "Yes. We. Do."

The conference room falls silent. I've made my decision and now I'm ready to go to bat for it. Ready to defy my better judgments, to fly in the face of everything the great Milt Cashman taught me back in New York. Ready to tear up my partnership agreement with my friend Jake Harper and work out of my six-room Ko Olina villa if I have to. Ready. Able. And willing.

"We can accept her bail assignment," I say.

Jake nearly falls over. *"Bail assignment?"*

Yup. Bail assignment. Dirty words in our business. Just a filthy piece of paper signed and notarized, granting us ownership of the amount of bail put up, *if* and when it is ordered returned to the defendant by the Court. Meaning if and when there is a final disposition in the case. If and when the defendant has made all her court appearances, has been acquitted or tried, found guilty or not guilty, been remanded to prison or released unto the world.

In the meantime, so much could go wrong. A mistrial. An appeal that goes on for years while bail is continued. Or worst of all, an escape. In which case, the bail money is held indefinitely.

Jake's not pulling any punches. "Are you outta your fucking mind, son?"

In fact, I have *been meaning to see a shrink.* But for now I keep that tidbit between myself and the other voices in my head.

Jake throws his hands in the air. "Not-Guilty Milty would have the State revoke your law license if he heard this."

True enough. It's the first of Cashman's Ten Commandments: *Though shalt not take a case without being paid up front.*

See, not only is there a chance that we'd *never* see the money; there is an assurance that we wouldn't see a dime at least through the conclusion of her case. A minimum of a year in a matter like this. Meaning we'd work for twelve straight months while receiving zilch, zero as salary, while putting up expenses for experts and trial exhibits, not to mention our own already hefty overhead, out of our own pockets.

"Keep in mind, she *already* tried to run once, son!"

There's that, of course. And I'm no goddamn Dog the Bounty Hunter.

"And you're no goddamn Dog the Bounty Hunter," Flan adds.

I push my chair out and stand. "I've made my decision, gentlemen. Now you've got to choose. You're either with me, or you're with the terrorists."

CHAPTER 11

"We're in," Jake tells me when I return to the office from my two-scotch lunch at Sand Bar, "but we've gotta be able to handle other cases as well. We don't turn clients away, and we don't pour every available man-hour into the Simms case, okay?"

"Deal," I say, as I move through the reception area toward the conference room.

"And one more thing," Jake says, following me.

"What's that?"

"I reserve the right to say 'I told you so' when all this is over."

When we enter the conference room, Flan is sitting there, his chair turned toward the mammoth windows, his eyes set on the Ko'olau Mountains. Clearly he's still in a daze.

I tear a blank page from my yellow legal pad, crumple it up, and hurl it at the side of his face. Direct hit.

"I'm heading over to SID to request the file on the Simms case," I say. "Barb Davenport there is a doll; she'll give me everything they have right away, so we can get to work."

SID is the Screening and Intake Division of the Prosecuting

Attorney's Office. The division chief, Barbara Davenport, shocked me the first time I met her during the Gianforte murder case by handing me the full file with no hassle whatsoever. Kind as a Girl Scout, generous as a grandmother. Meeting Barb marked the first time I fully realized I was no longer practicing law in the Big Bad Apple.

Barb and I have had a splendid professional relationship ever since.

"Before I return with the file," I say, looking at Flan, "I'd like you to get down to the Kapolei fire station, have a talk with some of the guys. Spread some of that magical Irish charm and get some answers. I want to know how and why investigators determined this was a case of arson as quickly as they did."

I turn to Jake. "Head over to the Kupulupulu Beach Resort. Start with Maintenance and work your way up. I want to know why the sprinkler system didn't go off. And why I couldn't get my cougar a cup of water from the bathroom sink just about an hour before the fire."

Flan perks up. "Sounds like the water main was shut off."

I point to him. "If so, we should know today whether or not the valve was dusted for prints. If it wasn't, we've found our first hole in their case."

"How about the guest list for the Simms-Downey wedding?" Jake says. "We have that yet?"

"It's a short list. Erin's mother is e-mailing it to me today. Once I have it, I'm going to go over every name with Erin herself. Then we'll divvy the list up and begin interviews."

Flan's cell phone starts blowing up on his belt, and I give him a look. He knows how I feel about those things in the office, especially during a crucial meeting.

He silences the cell, then glances at the display. "Casey," he says, sighing. "I'll take this, then head right over to the fire station in Kapolei." He opens the phone, says "Hi, sweetheart," then he's out the conference room door and it's just me and Jake.

"You gonna be okay with all this?" Jake says, leaning back against a wall-length bookshelf. "I mean the media and all. Been a slow summer on the twenty-four-hour cable news networks. No presidential election, the economy's getting old. Betcha Gretchen Hurst and Marcy Faith are licking their chops already about this Hawaii hotel fire."

"They're like pit bulls," I say. "Ignore 'em and they'll leave you alone."

"Or maul you to death."

I shrug, glance at my watch. I want to make it to SID by two o'clock, catch Barb right after she returns from lunch.

I buzz Hoshi. "Have a name and number of a detailer for me yet?"

"Not yet," she says back. "But you do have a couple of guests."

"Guests?" I look at Jake, who shrugs. "Wanna give me a hint who?"

"Well," Hoshi says quietly, "one of them is about three feet tall. And he's picking his nose."

CHAPTER 12

As I move down the street I pull my Panama Jack Bermuda hat low over my eyes, not just to keep my retinas from burning, but also as part of a disguise. And not just because I'm still ducking the media. The real reason is that at my side is the little guy I rescued from the fire the other night.

"Are you a policeman?" Josh says.

He insisted on holding my hand; I insisted he not. So for the time being we compromised, his tiny claws now latched to the tail end of my suit jacket like a pint-size water-skier to a motor-boat.

"No," I tell him as we cross Richards Street toward the Prosecuting Attorney's Office at Alii Place. "I'm the opposite of a policeman."

The kid's aunt needed an impromptu babysitter and swore the kid had been begging for me. Why, I have no idea; I don't even enjoy the notion of spending time with myself. I'd been about to say no (hell no, to be exact), when Aunt Naomi dropped

a bit of a bomb on us, said she had an appointment with her on-
cologist.

I immediately lost my voice, and Jake said yes *for* me.

"You mean, you're a bad guy?" the kid says.

I shrug, loosen my tie against the heat. "That would depend
on who you ask. But no, what I mean is that I represent bad guys,
defend them in the courts."

"Like in a sword fight?"

"Sometimes," I say. "But usually we just use words."

"*Bad* words?"

"Occasionally."

"Why do you defend bad guys?" he asks.

"Well," I tell him, "so that I can eat, for one. Buy nice clothes,
keep gas in my Jeep, pay the rent on my villa in Ko Olina." I stop
short and the kid bumps into me. I straighten him up and get
down on one knee, careful my slacks don't touch the ground. I
think of Turi Ahina. "But also because sometimes bad guys aren't
really so bad." Then I think of Joey Gianforte. "And because
sometimes the policemen accuse people of being bad guys when
they really aren't bad guys at all."

The kid appears nonplussed. It's the same reaction I receive
from most adults.

"Hey, Mistah C!" I hear from up the street. "When did you
go and get yourself a keiki?"

"Speak of the not-so-bad devil," I say under my breath, as I
watch the big man waddle down the street.

Turi Ahina, one of the "bad guys" I represent, is one of the
best men I know. Technically speaking, he leads a life of crime,
selling ice (aka crystal meth) on the street, but he's friendly and
always smiling. He has something else going for him, as far as
I'm concerned: A few months ago, Turi saved my life.

"The kid's not mine," I say, maybe a little too defensively. I glance down and Josh is paying no attention whatsoever, just staring up the side of one of the tall buildings and picking his nose again. "Picked him up at a fire sale, you could say."

I wince. Bad joke. It's that same twisted voice inside of me that celebrated the fact that Erin Simms is single again.

"Oh, shit," Turi says. "This is the keiki you rescued from the blaze, brah? I read all about that shit in the *Star-Advertiser*. You one hero, brah!"

Turi claps me on the back so hard my Panama Jack hat falls off my head and into my hands.

"I think you inspired me that night," I say, referring with a wink to the night on the streets of Kailua when Turi put two bullets into a crazed gunman in order to save my life.

"Hey, that's what we do here in the islands, brah. We watch each other's backs, yeah?"

"You keeping out of trouble, Turi?" I ask.

He smiles, his big round visage lighting up the street like no sun ever could. "Actually," he says, "that's what I was coming to see you about. I got picked up for possession last night."

"No worries," I tell him. "I've got to head over to the prosecutor's office now, but I'll call you tonight. We'll meet up this weekend, get it all straightened out."

The smile grows even wider as he places a pudgy, sweaty palm on my shoulder. "T'anks, Mistah C. T'anks so much."

"Hey," I say, slapping the Panama Jack back on my head. "What are friends for?"

Ten minutes later the kid and I are standing, waiting in front of the receptionist's desk for Barbara Davenport at the Screening and Intake Division of the Honolulu Prosecuting Attorney's

Office. I glance several times at my watch, not recalling her ever taking this long to make an appearance.

When she finally does arrive, it's not with the same sweet old smile I remember.

"Oh, you don't have children, do you?" Barbara says, glaring down at the kid as though she already feels sorry for him.

"None that I know of," I reply. "This one's on loan from the dealer."

She asks no further questions of the relationship; I provide no further answers.

"So what are you here for today, Mr. Corvelli?"

Strange, I think. Just a few weeks ago Barbara Davenport and I were on a first-name basis. "Well, Barb," I say, trying to recapture whatever it was we once had between us, "as you may have heard, I'm representing Erin Simms. I'm here to request your file."

Barbara Davenport glances down at my empty hands. "Do you have a written request?"

"I never needed one before, Barb. You know who I am. And I've filed a Notice of Representation with the Court. The prosecution received a copy this morning at arraignment."

"Well," she says, shaking her head sternly, like my second-grade teacher did when I asked what cunnilingus was after watching a Richard Pryor special on HBO, "I'm afraid our policy requires a request from your office in writing."

I reach into my pocket and pull out a business card for Harper & Corvelli, Attorneys-at-Law. I turn it over, ask the kid for the red crayon he's repeatedly jammed up his nose, then scribble the words *File Please* on the back.

Barb's not amused.

"I'm afraid we require something a bit more formal than that, Mr. Corvelli. You can drop one by later today." Like a good soldier, she turns on her heels and stalks away.

I stand mystified for a moment, then ask the receptionist for her fax number. I scribble the number down with the red crayon on the back of another business card, then whip out my cell and dial our office.

"Hoshi," I say, "draw up a request for documents on the Erin Simms matter. You can use the language I used in the Gianforte case, because as far as I remember that's the last one I had to submit. When you're finished, print it out and fax it over here, 'Attention Barb.'" I give her the fax number.

"Sure thing, Kevin," Hoshi says. "When do you need it by?"

I glance at my watch. "Anytime within the next three minutes will be fine." I slap my phone shut and stuff it back in my pocket, suddenly seething. I'm sweating and light-headed, my hands feel clammy. I'm wavering and feel as though I might fall over.

"Feel free to have a seat, Mr. Corvelli," the receptionist says.

I want to be defiant and stand but I don't think I can. So the kid and I sit.

Almost four full minutes go by before I hear the ring of SID's fax machine. I take a deep breath and wait for the page to slide through.

Finally the receptionist takes it, reads it, walks it back to Davenport's office. Another twelve minutes pass before Davenport steps back out, paper in hand.

I stand.

"I received your request for documents in the *State versus Simms* matter, Mr. Corvelli," she says, handing the paper back to me, "but I'm afraid the file has already been transferred over to the Trials Division. You'll have to request it directly from them."

I swallow hard, try to keep my cool, the blood already rising up my neck. I know I'm turning red. "Very well," I say, "although you might have mentioned it sooner. In any case, whose attention should I address the letter to over in the Trials Division? Don Watanabe? Frank DiSimone himself?"

She shakes her head indifferently. "Neither," she says. "This case has been assigned to Deputy Prosecutor Luke Maddox. He's already come by and taken the file. You'll have to request a copy from him."

CHAPTER 13

Outside the prosecutor's office, I glance at my watch and sigh. Auntie Naomi's appointment usually lasts two hours, she said, which means that the kid and I still have over an hour to kill. If I were going to kill it alone, I'd kill it at Kanaloa's. But the kid's seventeen years underage, and I don't think his auntie would appreciate me driving him back into town smashed on Koa's killer mai tais.

I pluck my cell from my pants pocket and dial my office. Hoshi picks up on the third ring with a cheerful "Harper and Corvelli."

"Any luck locating a detailer for my Jeep?"

"Yes, Kevin," she says, paging through her notes. "I found one in Waipahu. Very high-priced."

I glance down at Josh, who's staring at his feet. "Nothing in town?" I ask. On Oahu, "town" refers to Honolulu. We islanders just loathe the word "city."

"You usually ask for something outside of town," Hoshi says, "so you don't have to deal with the traffic."

Maybe she's right. "I don't know what I want, Hoshi." I look down at the kid, two fingers now up his nose, one snaking each nostril. I dismiss the idea of walking him around town. "All right," I say into my cell. "Give me the address."

Back at my Jeep in the blazing heat, I strip off my suit jacket and toss it onto the backseat. Then I move around the vehicle and open the door for the kid, watching as he struggles to climb aboard.

"You always dress like that, kid?"

"Whaddya mean?"

What do I mean? Josh is wearing a mismatched jumpsuit that looks like it belongs to Paulie Walnuts on *The Sopranos*.

"Think your aunt would be okay if I bought you an outfit or two?"

The kid shrugs. "I dunno. But you don't have to. I don't care what I wear."

"Clearly," I say. "But it's not for you. If you're going to be hanging out with me during your aunt's doctor appointments, I need you to look presentable. Not like some wise guy who just stepped off the set of *Jersey Shore*."

I start up the bright orange Jeep. Maybe a stop at the Tommy Bahama outlet in Waikele to see if they carry anything in his size. But first to Waipahu, to this detail shop called King Kam Auto. Because I won't be able to quit checking my rearview until this electric-orange Jeep is a nice, inconspicuous white.

As I pull into the parking lot of King Kam Auto, the kid's eyes go wide. I tell him he can wait in the Jeep and show him how to control the radio and A/C, but I can tell he's not listening to a word I'm saying.

In the garage, grease monkeys are hunkered over or lying

under cars, working to the sound of some god-awful heavy metal music. No one pays me any mind, so I find my own way to the office.

Behind a small desk, cluttered with work orders and receipts, sits a young Hawaiian woman with a stick-figure body and huge breasts.

"Aloha," she says, distracted.

A strange greeting in a garage, I think, with drills going off, metal tools clanking off the cement floor, the occasional horn. But I give her an aloha back just the same.

"Interested in having my Jeep Wrangler painted," I say.

"Okay," she says, shuffling out from behind her desk. "Let me go get Mongoose." She turns just in time to catch me looking at her ass. Our eyes meet and she smiles. "Be right back."

But she isn't right back, isn't back for quite a long while, in fact. In the meantime, I alternate between glances at my watch and my Jeep out in the parking lot. Checking the kid, making sure he doesn't drive off with my wheels.

A copy of the *Honolulu Star-Advertiser* sits unopened on one of the worn green customer seats. Without touching it, I read the first page headline above the fold: HIGH PROFILE LAWYER COR-VELLI TO REPRESENT ACCUSED MASS KILLER IN KO OLINA RESORT FIRE

"Goddamnit," I mumble to myself. "Here we go again."

"Help you, sir?"

The guy called Mongoose stands about my height and walks with a bit of a swagger. A few days' scruff covers an otherwise handsome face and a once-white muscle shirt smudged with grease reveals a set of toned biceps colored with ink.

"Looking to get my Wrangler painted," I say. "Orange to white."

Mongoose nods, slowly walks me to the opening of the garage, then points to the Jeep parked about fifty yards out. "That yours?"

"Yeah." The kid ducks down just as soon as he sees me. Either he fucked up the radio or is playing some freaky game of hide-and-seek.

"That's no problem," Mongoose says, turning us back around. "Let's step into my office and I'll briefly explain the process, go over the costs, and give you an estimate on how long the job will take."

I follow him into a cramped room that reeks of oil and grease. Calendars float lopsided on narrow wood-paneled walls, pictures of scantily clad women on the hoods of various sports cars representing the months of the year. Still mid-July, and August isn't promising to be much cooler.

Thirty seconds pass before I begin to feel claustrophobic, sweat causing my white button-down to stick to my back.

"So," Mongoose says unenthusiastically, "the process goes something like this. First we prep the vehicle—tape, newspapers, paper mats to protect the windows, wheels, head and taillights, et cetera. That's more than half the work right there. Next we prime it. Then we paint it, probably three coats for a new vehicle like that, especially since we're going from color to white. Then, ten to fifteen coats of lacquer and it's done. It'll look like it just came out of the showroom."

I stopped listening somewhere around the word "prep," but I'm pretty sure I have the gist. "How long will this take?" I ask.

"Five, six days. A week at most. Whole job will probably run you about twenty-five hundred."

"Perfect," I tell him. "Let's do it."

Mongoose calls out to Justell—the girl with the huge breasts—who brings in some forms and replaces him in his seat.

"What's your name?" she says.

"Corvelli. Kevin Corvelli."

From the corner of my eye, I see Mongoose glance down at the *Honolulu Star-Advertiser* resting on the empty seat.

Justell seems oblivious. "Address?"

Once I supply her with my home address in Ko Olina, Mongoose points to the paper and says, "You the lawyer representing that chick charged with arson?"

"Yeah," I tell him. "That's me."

He whistles, low and long, lifts the paper and leers at the booking photo of Erin Simms below the fold. "She looks like a handful," he says. "Good luck."

I finish giving Justell my information, anxious for fresh air and some A/C.

I grudgingly shake Mongoose's hand and I'm out the door and in the parking lot, headed back to my Jeep. When I unlock the door, the kid finally pops his head up.

Climbing in, I ask, "What's with you, kid? Why were you hiding? You afraid of tits?"

"Nah." He shakes his head. "It's just that man you were talking to . . ."

"Yeah?" I say, turning the engine over, glancing in the rearview to back out. "What about him?"

"That's my dad."

I turn my head and stare at the kid. "No shit?"

CHAPTER 14

She opens the door in a pale yellow spaghetti-strap sundress that comes to a complete halt a full inch above the knees. There's the hint of a tan from her early days of summer in San Francisco, maybe another coat from her wedding day here on Oahu. But nothing too deep. Nothing like Nikki's caramel flesh, the bronze veneer that still haunts my sleep.

Erin's sandals are slip-ons with three-inch wedges, her legs bare and beautiful, smooth and thin enough to grace the cover of any New York fashion magazine. But for the ankle bracelet, you'd never know by the scene that I am here to discuss a homicide case. I could just as well be here at her Kaneohe house to pick her up for a late luau and drinks.

"Nice to see you again," she says.

These are words I rarely, if ever, hear from a client who is out of jail on bail. Inside, awaiting trial, it's understandable; the slightest interaction with the outside world, especially with your fearless advocate, is the only scintilla of hope prisoners come to rely on, the only reason for getting out of bed in the morning.

But for clients who are out, as Erin is, I'm more like the dentist. Sure, I might be a nice guy, but our interactions together aren't meant to make for a good time. When you're out, the last thing in the world you want to think about as a defendant is going back in. And for the client who is out on bail, the possibility of prison is really all that I represent. No dodging the fact you're facing serious, life-changing charges when I'm present.

I follow her inside, immediately soothed by the gentle breeze blowing from the palm-shaped ceiling fan. The sliding glass door to the lanai stands open, and my gaze sets on the breathtaking view of Kaneohe Bay, with the offshore island known as Chinaman's Hat resting smack-dab in the center. My first thought is, *This rental must have cost a fortune.*

My second is, *Who's paying the tab?*

We'll get to that. Right now the sun is rapidly dropping behind the mountains, and we've got a lot of ground to cover in the hour I plan on staying.

"Lemonade?" she says, motioning to a full pitcher resting on a silver tray on the coffee table. She lifts one of the two tall ice-filled Collins glasses standing beside the pitcher and pours.

I take the glass when she offers it. Anything to help combat this oppressive heat.

"Let's get started." I take a seat on the rattan sofa. She sits next to me, a red-orange splash of brilliance washing over her long, thin neck from the setting sun. I take a sip of lemonade, then set the perspiring glass down on a wooden turtle-shaped coaster on the coffee table. "I'd like to begin with the night of the fire," I say.

Erin first confirms what her parents told me: that a close friend, a bridesmaid named Mia Landow, held a heart-to-heart with her shortly before the nuptials. Just after Erin's up-do, while her maid of honor Tara Holland was zipping up the back of her dress.

"He fucked her," Erin tells me matter-of-factly. "Just seventeen days before our wedding."

"By 'he' you mean Trevor," I say in order to gauge her reaction at hearing his name. I'm already evaluating Erin as a witness, though I hardly ever put defendants on the stand. Although clients have the right to overrule me on this decision, I've never represented one who has. They've tried; oh yeah, they've tried. Many clients want to profess their "innocence" to the jury. Problem is, even jurors are smart enough to realize that just about any human being the world over would lie to save his or her own ass. When I tell clients this, they inevitably respond, "But I'm *not* lying." When I tell them that doesn't matter in the least, they become indignant. That's when I ask them if they follow their doctor's orders. "Of course," they say. It's then I have to remind them why they hired me. And if they still won't listen, well then, let them find themselves another defense lawyer. Because I don't like it when clients lose cases for me.

Erin supplies me with a noncommital nod. In that moment I realize that if I can get one confident heterosexual man to make it all the way to deliberations, I can score a hung jury. A big *if* in any courthouse in the United States. And given the apparent ambition and tenacity of Luke Maddox, nothing short of an acquittal will count as a win in this case because Maddox would try her again and again and again, I can feel it. Which means Jake and I would never see our six hundred grand.

"So your maid of honor Tara overheard Mia telling you all this?" I ask.

"Yeah. Mia asked Tara to leave but Tara sensed something was wrong and said, 'Not on your life.' Tara's like that; she's very protective of me. We've been best friends since junior high."

"How about Mia? How long have you known her?"

Erin shrugs, purses her lips and says, "Almost as long."

The real question right now, the one I don't dare ask, is, *Who did you immediately blame more for the betrayal? Trevor, the man you were about to marry? Or Mia, the so-called friend who knowingly slept with your soon-to-be husband?* Given that Mia stood in as Erin's bridesmaid even after her admission tells me I think I already know the answer. And the answer doesn't bode well for Erin's defense.

But it doesn't matter what went through Erin's head. What matters is how she responded, how she behaved, what others saw. More pointedly, what others will testify to.

"All right," I say, "how did you react?"

She actually rolls her eyes at me.

"I'm sorry," I say, unable to keep the irritation out of my voice. "Am I taking up too much of your time? Do you have someplace else to be?"

"No," she says in a huff. "It just seems like a ridiculous question." She shrugs her narrow shoulders, a single spaghetti strap falling free. "I did my fucking Happy Dance. What do you think?"

Sarcasm. That always plays well with a jury.

"I think that if you plan on answering questions like that on the stand, you can start picking out posters for your prison cell walls right now."

"I was *angry*," she hisses at me. "Devastated."

I nod but say, "Those are two very different things. If you were on the outside, if you were Mia or Tara or anyone else who observed you, how would you describe your immediate reaction?"

She thinks about it for a moment, but I can tell she doesn't need to. "Furious anger," she finally says. "Unbridled rage."

Might as well come right out with it. "Directed at whom?"

"Mia, of course." No pause whatsoever before she adds, "But mostly at Trevor."

"Why Trevor more than Mia?"

She raises her voice. *"Because,* if it wasn't Mia, it obviously would've been some other slut. If he could cheat on me with her, he could cheat on me with anyone. Mia's just a friend; I wasn't about to marry *her."*

I swallow some lemonade, wishing it were splashed with rum. "What specifically did you say or do in that room, in front of Mia and Tara?"

She licks her lips, her eyes pointed toward the ceiling, as she catches her breath. Slowly she lifts the spaghetti strap back over her tanned shoulder. "I threw a glass vase filled with Gerbera daisies," she says calmly. "It struck the mirror and exploded. Glass flew everywhere. I think Tara caught a small piece in her right eye."

"And you said . . . ?"

"I said I was going to fucking kill him."

I allow a brief silence to fall over the room. Nothing but the hum of the fan overhead and the sound of the waves washing onto the shore, while her words slowly sink in. It's a natural reaction, of course, and I'll make that point to the jury when and if this case goes to trial. But Maddox will tell it a different way. When the words leave his lips—when he extracts them from a witness on the stand—they'll ring in jurors' ears like a bell. These words will play like a threat, like a prediction, like a promise.

"What then?" I say.

Erin went ahead with the wedding, of course. Too many plans, too many guests, not enough time to process all this new information, and what would she tell her parents? They'd just blown their life savings on her dream wedding. No use either in confronting Trevor before the vows. Maybe this was his way of getting out of the wedding, maybe this was planned—by him, by Mia, an entire conspiracy. No, she wasn't going to let him out of this that easily. If Trevor wanted out, he'd have to file for divorce. And she'd take him for everything he had, the cheating cocksucker.

The ceremony went off without a hitch. It was held on the beach rather than at the small chapel wedged between the two colossal resorts because neither she nor Trevor was particularly religious. The bride and groom, and seven guests, had all been flown in from the mainland at her parents' expense. She hid the tears, buried the hatred and burning frustration she felt. Her mind was understandably whirling while she recited her vows.

"It's all on video if you want to watch it," she tells me. She rises to get me the videographer's card.

"I'll need the photographer's, too," I say, as she makes her way down the long hallway, the walls adorned with original tropical oil paintings from some local artist whose name stops at the tip of my tongue. This will drive me crazy for hours; fortunately, I have the artist's business card at home. She and I shared an evening together a few months back at her Diamond Head home.

When Erin returns she hands me a small stack of business cards, and I sort through them. Wedding planner, minister, florist, ukelele player, videographer, and photographer, all of them with local addresses here on Oahu. I pocket them.

Then it's back to business, back to the night of the fire.

The argument began the moment the newlyweds were alone in their honeymoon suite. Because of the heat, the wedding party had gone up to their rooms to change out of gowns and tuxedos and into more suitable island attire. Erin confronted Trevor even before he had his white tuxedo jacket off his shoulders.

"*You fucked Mia?*" she'd screamed.

Trevor was clearly caught off-guard and didn't have the sense to deny it. Instead he took the more practical approach, assured Erin that it was a one-time thing, that it didn't mean anything. It was a stupid, just fucking awful mistake, and it would never, ever happen again. "I love *you*," he told her. "That's why I married you today."

Erin made it known she wasn't satisfied with the explanation. Apparently she made it so known that another hotel guest—she assumes from the adjoining suite—phoned the front desk and told the voice on the other end that some young lady was having a conniption.

A few minutes later hotel security knocked on Erin and Trevor's door, asked whether everything was cool inside. Erin opened the door wide enough for one of the two security guards to poke his head inside. Erin calmly stated that her new husband was a lying, cheating, piece of shit and whoremongering prick. "But otherwise," she told him, "everything is fine." Then she slammed the door in the security guard's face.

After a half hour of futile attempts to calm her, Trevor finally went downstairs to the reception alone. Erin stayed in the room and vomited. Then she hit the mini bar with a vengeance, mixing a concoction that would have made Nicolas Cage in *Leaving Las Vegas* recoil in disgust.

Good and liquored up, looking as sexy as she could, twenty minutes later Erin went downstairs herself, trying to act as though nothing had happened.

"The reception is a blur," she says now, wiping at her eyes. "I spent most of the time alone at the bar. I remember dancing, but with Isaac not Trevor, and I remember once or twice falling down."

"Isaac?" I say.

"Isaac Cassel. Trevor's best man."

She doesn't know if she said a single word to Trevor during the reception, but she knows the party was cut short by unanimous decision. Everyone seemed to want to go their own way.

"The next thing I remember," she says, "is sitting at Kanaloa's with Trevor. I think I made a bit of a scene."

I keep silent.

"The bartender wouldn't allow me to smoke," she says, shaking her head. "At a fucking outdoor bar, can you believe that?"

I don't mention it's people like me who pushed for those antismoking laws to pass. If I'm going to die as a result of a vice, it sure as hell better be one of my own.

"Then I tried to step past the gate where the bartender said I could smoke," she continues, "and he stopped me from bringing my drink." She shakes her head in anger. "Finally, I said, 'Fuck it, Trevor, let's just go up to our room.'"

And that's just what they did. But according to Erin, she didn't stay very long, just long enough to get another visit from hotel security for causing yet another commotion. This visit went very much the same way as the first, she tells me, with the security guard getting an earful of venom, followed by a door in the face.

Twenty minutes later, Trevor passed out. Erin snatched her handbag and went downstairs with a bottle of Dom in a brown paper bag under her arm. Last thing she remembers before the fire, she was headed with the bottle in the direction of the beach.

"At some point earlier my mother reserved me another room and gave me the key," she says. "But I never made it back to the hotel."

"How about Trevor's room key? Did you have it on you when you left the honeymoon suite?"

She nods. "It was in my handbag, I think. I was carrying this cute little leather Fendi."

When she heard the alarm screaming from inside the hotel,

she snapped out of her drunk and stared at the twitching flames, the dense smoke rising unabated from the few open windows. She could tell the fire was consuming the top floor. She panicked, she says, and ran toward the hotel, tossing the bottle of Dom into some shrubs.

"What about your handbag?"

She shrugs. "I don't know. I must have left it somewhere because I know I didn't have it on me when everyone was gathered outside, watching the fire. To this day, I haven't found it and no one's given it to me."

I swallow hard, wondering whether the police have the handbag. The little leather Fendi reminds me too much of a certain pair of bright white Nike cross-trainers. A pair of sneakers owned by Joey Gianforte that were spattered with his ex-girlfriend's blood. These things tend to pop up. Typically at the worst possible time for the defense.

Behind us the moon is reflecting off the sea. I glance at my watch and decide it's time to leave. I take one last sip of lemonade and rise from the couch.

"One last thing," I say, flashing on yesterday's meeting with Erin's parents. "Have you ever started a fire before?"

She glares at me while grinding her teeth. "I don't understand what you mean?"

"I'm sorry," I say. "I'll rephrase the question. Have you. Ever started. A fire. Before?"

Suddenly she's on her feet and pacing, deliberately scuffing up the shiny hardwood floor. She stops briefly at an end table, opens a small ceramic box and removes a cigarette. "How *old* are you anyway?" she rants, a deep red rising steadily up her neck. "My parents said they were hiring the best. I was expecting some gray-haired old man who's been practicing law for forty years or so."

"My law partner has a few gray hairs left, if that helps."

Erin places the cigarette between her lips, strikes a match, holds the flame to the business end and inhales. "I think you should leave," she says, her voice suddenly soft, a thin stream of white smoke emanating from each nostril. "I need to talk to my mother. I mean, this isn't some kids' game. My entire fucking life is at stake."

"You're absolutely right." I dig into my pocket for a business card. "Do some research tonight. Find out who I am." I consider the rash of online articles covering my defense of Brandon Glenn, of the infamous photo of me, standing in the rain at his funeral. I take out my pen. "I've handled one homicide case since I moved to the islands. Defendant's name was Joey Gianforte." I jot Joey's number on the back of the business card and hand it to her. "Call him if you'd like a reference."

She takes the card without looking at it and frowns.

I turn from her and move toward the door.

"And the client before that?" she asks, as I turn the knob.

I stop, a light cloud of tobacco smoke enveloping my head.

"Can I get a reference from him?" she says.

"Sure," I say, without facing her. "But you're going to need a medium."

With that, I swing the door open and step into the sweltering Hawaiian night in search of a cold, hard drink.

CHAPTER 15

On little sleep, I'm at the office early the next morning, my head heavy, vision blurry, the lids of my eyes already threatening to close up shop and call it a day. But we received Luke Maddox's motion to have me taken off the case yesterday, so I'm at my desk with the papers in front of me, sucking down my second Red Bull.

I swivel my chair, pull up a WordPerfect document on my desktop, and fill in the caption for *State versus Simms*. Ten minutes later my fingers are hovering impotently over the wireless keyboard, my face washed in the glow of the kaleidoscopic screensaver, while I stare down yet another silver-blue can of energy drink.

"Hell with it," I say, reaching for the phone.

It's ten after six A.M. here in Honolulu, which means it's just after noon in New York. Not that time matters much to the legendary Milt Cashman.

Milt's always working, even when he's not.

"Speak," Milt barks when he answers his cell.

"Hey Milt, it's Kevin." I still feel a pang of loss when I phone my former mentor, even though on a personal level we were never particularly close.

"What gives?" Milt says. "I'm seeing your mug all over the news again. You representing that hot piece of trim that burned down that hotel in Hawaii?"

"Allegedly."

"What do you need?"

One thing I love about Milt Cashman, there's never any beating around the bush. No pretext. Friend or adversary, you need a favor you just come right out and ask and he'll respect you for it. Fuck the niceties, the quid pro quo, the tit for tat. Lawyers help lawyers whenever they can, and whoever doesn't want to play ball, well, fuck 'em. A lawyer refuses to extend Milt Cashman a professional courtesy and Milt will remember that slight forever. Because Milt will face that lawyer in another case sooner or later. And then he'll break the son of a bitch in open court.

"This prosecutor, some L.A. pretty boy, wants me off the case."

"Why?" Milt teases. "'Cause you're so fucking good?"

"That's my bet. Anyway, he filed a motion to have me removed on the grounds of conflict of interest."

"Sounds like what happened to me," he says, "on the Brandon Glenn case."

A lump forms in my throat, as I'm transported back to the day Milt asked me to take on the *People versus Brandon Glenn* matter. "It's a big fish," he'd said. "Sure you can handle it?" I had grinned like a schoolboy about to get his first hand job and nodded. He handed me the file and said, "Then go have some fun. And be sure to smile for the cameras."

Were it not for the Brandon Glenn case, were it not for his conviction, for his subsequent rape and murder on Rikers Island only days before he was vindicated, I'd still be in Manhattan sharing office space with my mentor Milt Cashman. Or, as the media refers to him, Not-Guilty Milty.

"It's a little different," I tell him. "The prosecutor says he intends to call me as a material witness. I was there at the resort on the night of the fire."

Milt chuckles. "Thought you said the prosecutors were human out there in Shangri-la."

"*More* human, I told you. This one's different. He plans on making a name for himself on this case."

"Hold on a sec, Kev." Milt hollers out to his secretary. "Candi, pull up the *Sigler* file, case where the DA tried to have me removed based on conflict and we buried him." He pauses, mumbles something to himself. "Better yet, Candi, fuck the *Sigler* file. Grab me *People versus Tagliarini*, 1998. The whole file."

"Tagliarini?" I say. A mob case in which our client was tried for murder and racketeering under the federal RICO statutes.

"Remember, Kev? When you first came on board, the fucking guinnea prosecutor tried to accuse me, a harmless Jew, of being a member of the mob. Said I was too close to Vito Tagliarini to try the case, had relevant information, blah, blah, blah. Same shit they pulled on Bruce Cutler in the John Gotti case."

It all comes rushing back. My first year of law school, my first days with the Cashman Law Firm in New York. I arrived after the motion had already been decided, but I remember leafing through the papers with a smile.

"Use this, Kev, and you'll toss the fucker on his head. Before we're done, they'll pull the bastard's law license. Let him open a tiki bar on the beach or some such shit. Better yet, send him the hell back to L.A."

The great thing about practicing law is that everything's already been done. Every argument's been made, every issue decided. You just have to find out where and when and by whom. Then you make the connections, no matter how tenuous, to cases within your own jurisdiction. You caution the judge that a ruling contrary to your position will result in her ruling being overturned. You persuade the Court not so much with your own tongue, but with the words of great lawyers and jurists past. That's where a connection the likes of Milt Cashman really comes in handy.

"Listen, Kev," Milt says now. "Bottom line: You convince the judge you cannot, under any circumstances whatsoever, be called as a witness in this case."

"And how do I do that?"

"Easy," he says. "You demonstrate that you don't satisfy one of the basic criteria for serving as a witness."

"Meaning?"

"You're fucking incompetent."

Red Bull pumping through my veins, I jump out of my chair and head down the hall to wait for the fax from Milt Cashman's secretary, Candi.

"Another rough night?" I say when I see Jake heading up the hallway. He looks like hell and smells like the men's room at the Bleu Sharq ten minutes after a cruise ship full of twentysome-things pulls out of port.

"Think I got the swine flu," he says.

I keep walking. With three cans of Red Bull jolting my brain, it's no time to get pulled into a verbal headlock by Jake. "How many bottles of Jack Daniels does it take to get you infected?" I mutter under my breath as we pass each other.

Jake grabs my left arm and spins me around. Suddenly I see what thousands of people must have seen in Houston bars and courthouses over his decades-long career: the anger, the hatred, the pushing away of life's defeats. Mad at the world and un-afraid to show it.

"Listen, Kevin," he growls, "I made my first court appear-ance before you could take a piss standing up. I won my first acquittal in a capital case, saved an innocent man's life, before you saw the inside of a schoolroom. So don't you presume to tell me how to spend my days *or my nights.*"

"Easy, cowboy," I say, my palms out in case he makes a move. I figure the situation with his girlfriend Alison Kelly has come to a head. "I just—"

"You just *what?*" Suddenly he's in my face, the odor of stale coffee so pungent I have to breathe through the mouth. "If you think I'm bringing this practice down, then draw up the disso-lution papers. We'll go our separate ways. 'Cause if I hear you mumble something under your breath again, you and I are go-ing to go round and round. And I don't care if you kick the hell out of me, 'cause life's been kicking the hell out of me for near sixty years, and I'm still fucking standing."

I stand still and silent, even lower my eyes to let him have his ground. "Is this about Erin Simms and the bail assignment?" I say quietly.

Jake turns without another word, pivots, and disappears into his office. He slams the door, knocking from the hallway wall my own twelve-hundred-dollar oil painting by that artist I slept with whose name I still can't quite remember. *Lilly something?* The bottom of the large frame hits the floor and the painting falls forward, landing at my feet.

Mandy? I turn and resume course to the fax machine. Come to think of it, the artist's signature must be on the front of the artwork. I'll have to take a look once Hoshi comes by to hang the painting back up.

CHAPTER 16

Stonewalled by the prosecutor's office again, I call it a day and climb in my Jeep at one thirty in the afternoon. Traffic on H-1 West is merciful this time of day, so I take a deep breath, sit back and try to enjoy the ride while listening to *The Very Best of The Doors*. But it's difficult to enjoy anything with Jake's dressing down still ringing in my ears.

The old bastard ambushed me with a murder case a day into my tenancy on South King Street last year, yet for some reason, I still seek his approval. I'm smarter, more clever and resourceful, think quicker on my feet, but still I look up to him. I'm a better litigator, a better lawyer, maybe even a better man in recent days. Yet as I press my sandal against the gas pedal, an atrocious lump develops in the pit of my stomach, the base of my neck begins to ache, and I feel as though at any moment I'm going to combust, hit the fuel tank, and cause my electric-orange Jeep to explode into flames.

Fact is, I owe Jake my career. If not for his roping me into the

Gianforte murder case, I'd probably be spending my days in traffic court, as was my original plan when I fled New York.

Pull it together, Corvelli. It's Friday afternoon and the next is going to be one hell of a week. Motions will be filed, the investigation on our end will begin with a fury, including tracking down and getting statements from witnesses, sorting through hundreds, if not thousands, of photographs, and trying to assemble some sort of defense. But for now I need to dull my senses, so I head to Kanaloa's to drink myself into the night.

When Suzie sets a mai tai in front of me, I push it away, ask for a Glenlivet on the rocks. It's an unusual order for an outdoor beach bar in the middle of the day, but I'm feeling too dark for rum. Dark, even with the sun pounding on my back, trying to penetrate my Panama Jack, even with the beach just behind me, even with girls in thin wet bikinis sitting on either side of me. I take a long, hard pull off the single malt scotch when it comes, open the top three buttons of my bright yellow Tommy Bahama shirt. I'm cooking out here; it's too fucking hot.

Baseball's on the flat screen in front of me, the Dodgers and Padres, but I can't seem to pay attention to a single pitch, the phone call to Milt now replacing the monologue from Jake in my mind. " *'Cause you're so fucking good?*" Was that a shot?

"*What do you need?*" Milt had said. Because I only call when I want something from him? Because Milt took me under his wing in Manhattan and I fucked up and left?

The Glenlivet slides smooth as silk down my throat and I take a deep breath, thinking about Josh. There was a message from his aunt on my voice mail this morning, but I ignored it. The kid wants to see me. And some part of me that I never knew existed wants to see the kid. But the part of me I'm more familiar with is too invested in this case, too invested in this client.

Every instinct in my being is screaming for me to run from Erin Simms, especially after all that transpired when I fell for Nikki Kapua. Still, I feel drawn to her, to her case, to her cause. It's as though I'm being held against my will and relishing some sordid pleasure every moment of my captivity.

"Everyt'ing awright?" Suzie says, staring at me. She's a sweetheart but I'm in no mood to talk.

I nod without looking at her, press my prescription sunglasses higher on my face. "What time does Koa come on tonight?"

"Oh," she says, glancing at her watch. "He'll be on at six, I t'ink."

I throw back the Glenlivet, slide the empty rocks glass toward the back of the bar. "Another, Suze," I say. "Please. And make it a double."

A few hours later there's a plate of gnawed Buffalo wings in front of me. I don't recall eating them and I sure as hell don't remember ordering them, but when I glance in the mirror behind the bar, I look like the love child of my bright orange Jeep and a fifth of scotch. I must have eaten them. That what's called in the law "a reasonable inference."

I remove my hat and sunglasses, hop off the barstool, and stagger around the corner to the men's room, where I intend to wash my face. Maybe pee myself silly while I'm at it.

I swing open the door, bypass the sink, and go straight for the urinal. I unzip my fly and let the good times roll, the bland restroom tiles doing some strange native dance on the wall in front of me.

The door squeaks open behind me, and my eyes instinctively dart to the mirror above the sink. *Look at this guy,* I think. Big and bald and as white as a wedding dress, with steroid-enhanced muscles bulging beneath a tight black T and denim jeans.

This is Hawaii, pal. No one wears black unless it's formal wear. And jeez, what's with the goatee? You flew to the tropics, bub, not back to the early nineties.

"Corvelli?" he says as I start to shake myself dry.

Dazed, I turn before tucking myself back into my fly. Big mistake, because next thing I know, his catcher's mitt–size fist is on a collision course with my face. He connects, and I'm sent flailing backward against the urinal, the porcelain striking me hard in the back just above the waist.

My body sinks to the floor and is rewarded with a black combat boot to the ribs. Then he grabs two fistfuls of sunshine, pulling me up by the collars of my Tommy Bahama shirt. I grip his bald skull, try with my thumbs to gouge out his eyes, but as soon as I feel the sweet, soft texture of eyeball, he swings me toward the mirror, grabs me by the back of the head, and hurls me face-first into the glass. The mirror spiderwebs at the spot where my forehead struck. But just as I register the blood on my own reflection, he has me by the rear of the head again, and this time when he aims my face at the mirror, he holds nothing back.

I hear glass shattering and see white-hot flames flickering before my eyes. My legs suddenly go out from under me, but not until my left cheek finally hits the cool tiles do I realize that I am about to experience the bittersweet mercy of passing out.

CHAPTER 17

When I come to, Koa is standing over me, holding a dirty bar rag packed with ice.

"Here," he says, trying to place it on my left eye.

I push his hand away, wave him off. "Put those cubes in a glassful of Glenlivet and bring it back stat."

Koa backs off a bit and points to my midsection. "First you're gonna have to put that away. This is a family place."

I lower my chin to confirm I'm still hanging out of my fly, then tuck myself back in.

"What the hell happened?" I say.

"If I had to take one guess, I'd say someone kicked your *haole* ass."

"Thanks," I tell him as I extend my right arm so that he can help me up. The question is, *why* did someone kick my *haole* ass? As I steady myself on my own two feet, holding onto the sink, my alcohol-soaked mind searches for the answer.

I turn and stare into the smashed mirror above the sink, ex-

amining the telltale signs around my mouth. It's as good an excuse as any. "I think maybe I ate that guy's Buffalo wings."

I'm standing in front of the sink washing off the blood and
Buffalo sauce when Koa asks if I need help getting home. "I can
call you a cab, Kev."

I glance at my watch. "Maybe in a few hours," I tell him. "For
now, just snag me a seat at the bar."

"No worries. Your Panama Jack is still on the barstool, saving your place."

From my seat at Kanaloa's, I gaze up at the Kupulupulu Beach
Resort and flash on the night of the fire. Before that blaze, everything seemed to be going so well; I had not a worry in the
world. A cougar, a kid, a client, and an ass-kicking later, and it
seems as though my entire life is about to cave in. Jake's all but
ready to bail on our partnership, and I can't say I blame him.
I placed us in a precarious financial position, and I still can't
really explain why. And suddenly I have a young, arrogant prosecutor gunning for me. Might be best for everyone involved if
Maddox wins his motion to have me relieved as Erin's counsel.
Problem is, I don't like to lose. And I sure as shit don't like to lie
down in the middle of a fight.

Well, in a physical fight, sure. But in a legal battle? Not my
style.

Suzie sets a mai tai in front of me but I don't complain. The
rum feels good going down, washing away the tangy blend of
blood and Buffalo wings.

My left eye is sore; I feel it puffing up, so I ask Suzie for some
ice. Fortunately, the sun is setting, the sky already a brilliant
purple-red. Soon night will disguise my injuries and I'll be a
new man again.

As the sky fades to black, Koa lights the tiki torches and Kanaloa's begins to overflow with tourists, most of them from the neighboring resort. A local band takes the small stage and soon we're somewhere over the rainbow again.

While Koa mixes tropical cocktails, the two of us begin bullshitting, just as we did before the fire. He asks me about the kid, and I tell him the whole story, how I reluctantly made a new best friend.

"That's a nice thing you're doing," Koa says, sliding a fresh mai tai in front of me. "This one's on the house."

I add, "I took in a stray cat last year, too, you know."

But Koa's attention has turned to the gate. Slinking through the entrance in a tight black dress is maybe the sexiest young woman I've ever seen, drunk or sober. She's followed by a motley entourage, and it strikes me that she's probably a celebrity.

"Who's that?" I ask Koa.

"That, Kevin, is Miss Hawaii."

I take a long, hard pull off my mai tai, then say, "I like her name."

Forty-five minutes later, Miss Hawaii and I are seated at the far end of the bar away from the stage.

"So, Miss Hawaii . . ." I say.

"You don't have to call me Miss Hawaii." Her smile lights up the night. "Call me Kerry, I told you. C'mon, you can remember that. Otherwise, it's Miss Naikelekele. Take your pick. But no more Miss Hawaii, all right?"

She's half native Hawaiian, she tells me, her father a Caucasian film director from Los Angeles. Whatever the blend, it's intoxicating, and tonight she's dressed to the nines, her long straight jet-black hair shimmering, the fire from the tiki torches dancing in her wide Polynesian eyes.

"So what do you do?" she says between sips of her Blue Hawaiian.

Before I can answer, Koa cuts in. "Kevin here is a big-time lawyer," he says, leaning over the bar. "Criminal defense." As though it's a mere afterthought, Koa picks up the remote and changes the channel on the flat screen behind the bar. KGMB News: Hawaii Now.

Luckily, with the band playing, the television is on mute, because sure enough, there it is, footage of me heading down the courthouse steps with my client on the day bail was set. Then I read the bright blue banner at the bottom of the screen: CORVELLI DEFENDS SUSPECTED KO OLINA FIRESTARTER.

Kerry gazes from the screen to the vast resort that's still operating, its Liholiho Tower without a top. "The fire here?" she says. "You're representing the woman accused of starting it?"

I bow my head once, waiting for Miss Hawaii's reaction, a lump forming at the top of my throat.

"That's so fucking cool," she says finally.

I breathe a deep sigh of relief. "Koa," I say, "one more round."

Two minutes later Koa sets the drinks in front of us and recites my favorite phrase after *not guilty*: "On the house."

CHAPTER 18

It's nearing noon, Monday, when Jake first reaches for his yellow legal pad. He snatches a pen and with a shaky hand begins jotting down a list of possible witnesses.

Flan slaps his cell phone shut before he reenters the conference room. He takes a seat and opens his file without a word about his daughter Casey.

The Law Offices of Harper & Corvelli are all business this morning. Jake and Flan have even been instructed to wholly ignore the various cuts and bruises on my face. I told them little about Friday's incident at Kanaloa's other than that it may be Buffalo wing–related. Neither man seemed terribly surprised, which is fine, because there's simply no time for further explanation. See, Luke Maddox finally gave up the Simms file through his secretary three hours ago, when I marched over to his office, cell phone in hand, forefinger poised over the speed-dial number for Judge Sonya Maxa's chambers.

"Ever work an arson case before?" Flan asks Jake.

Jake shrugs, shakes his head no.

Flan turns to me. I glance up, chewing my lower lip, and it's all the answer he needs. This is a first for us all. Anyone watching us sift through the crime scene photos—trying to make out the floors from the ceilings, the char from the carpets, the corpses from the furniture—would know it.

It's all so goddamn grotesque.

I push my share of the photos away for the time being, take a hit of Red Bull, and grab the pleadings. Pleadings, at least, feel familiar—ugly white pages declaring war, setting forth the crimes charged and sparing us much of the gory details. But the pleadings aren't going to be going before the jury; these monstrous photographs are. So I hold myself back from flipping each one over so that they're face down on the table. There's no hiding what happened at the Kupulupulu Beach Resort that night. There's only procrastination.

"Nine counts of murder," Jake says with a sigh, motioning at the complaint I'm holding.

"Eleven," I correct him. "Today's *Honolulu Star-Advertiser* says two victims died from their injuries late last night, one of them a firefighter. By this afternoon we'll be looking at an amended complaint."

"Waiving the prelim?"

"Now? You bet."

The preliminary hearing to determine whether there existed probable cause for arrest was something I originally thought we might win, considering the state's rush to arrest and charge Erin Simms. But learning this morning what the state has in the way of evidence has caused me to do a one-eighty. No chance of dismissal at the prelim. In fact, barring some miracle, this case is going all the way to trial.

"Here's what they have," I say, flipping through a report prepared by a veteran arson investigator named Inez Rios. "Point of origin is likely the far left-hand corner of the room, opposite the bed."

"How do they know that?" Flan asks.

"Point of origin is the area where they find the most damage. That's where the fire burns hottest and longest."

Jake leans forward. "How about the cause?"

I scan the next page. "Cause is listed as incendiary, simply meaning the fire was intentionally set, as opposed to accidental."

"How did they determine that?"

"Rios discovered an accelerant, specifically charcoal starter fluid at the point of origin. And there was a trailer leading from the point of origin to the bed."

Flan asks, "What's a trailer?"

"A trailer could be any material placed near the accelerant to spread the fire from its point of origin," I explain. "Could be gasoline-soaked towels or newspapers, even gunpowder. In this case, it was a trail of the accelerant itself."

"Why not just start the fire on the bed? That's where the victim's body was found, right?"

"Right," I say. "I suppose whoever started the fire didn't want to watch the victim burn to death. Or smell his burning flesh. This way, she or he could have turned and ran before the fire ever reached the bed."

"Maddox will use that," Jake says, "to show that the perpetrator knew the victim, couldn't just stand there and watch him burn."

"Maybe," I say. "Then again it's likely every suspect we come up with to cast reasonable doubt will have known the victim, too. I don't know how much further we'll be able to go than the guest list. Anyone outside the wedding party, we lose motive."

Jake nods. "Let's move on to the stuff that really hurts us, then."

I don't need to look at Rios's report to tackle that issue. "Ignition," I say. "Rios claims with a hundred-percent certainty that the ignition was a Zippo lighter found at the scene."

"Erin's Zippo," Flan says.

"Correct. That's their smoking gun. The lighter was hers, there's going to be no getting around that. It has her initials on it and I'll bet everyone in the wedding party has seen her with it at one time or another." I don't mention that I'd seen her with the lighter myself the night of the fire, when she'd been arguing with the victim at Kanaloa's.

Jake says, "Do we have an out?"

I shrug. "The usual. We can argue her handbag was lost or stolen that night."

"Weak."

"I agree. And a little too convenient. But it will also cover another vital piece of evidence."

"The key card to the hotel suite?"

"Bingo." Erin's key card to the honeymoon suite is missing. The key card wasn't discovered in the fire, and thus far—at least as far as we know—Erin's little leather Fendi hasn't been found either. The argument is simple: Erin's Zippo and passkey were both in her handbag, but someone else gained possession of the handbag between the time it was last seen with Erin and the time when the fire started. We don't yet know how long that window is; for that we'll have to hit the pavement. Obviously, the larger the window the better.

I turn to Flan. "We're going to need to learn everything we can about the victim, Trevor Simms. And not just what we can find out from the wedding party. Book a flight to San Francisco soon as we finish the interviews here on the island."

Flan nods.

"We're still waiting on the autopsies," I add, "but the ME's report on Trevor Simms is going to be key. I'm particularly interested in the toxicology findings."

Flan purses his lips. "Think he was so drunk he set himself on fire?"

"Hell of a way to suicide," Jake says, straight-faced.

I shake my head. "What I want to know is whether Trevor truly passed out from alcohol, as Erin suggests, or whether he was drugged."

Jake had no luck at the Kupulupulu Beach Resort last Thursday. Everyone from Maintenance on up provided the same response: No interview of any sort without one of the resort's lawyers being present.

Flan had even less luck at the Kapolei fire station. "You'll find everything in our reports," Chief Gary Condon said. "Now if you don't mind taking yourself someplace else, Mr. Flanagan, my men are understandably upset today, and no one's in any kind of mood for your questions."

Fortunately, we now know from discovery that the valve to the water main was indeed turned off, and that when it was dusted for prints the valve came up clean.

"Moving on." I pull a large manila envelope toward me. "Erin's memory is cloudy, so we're going to have to reconstruct her timeline from the moment she and Trevor left Kanaloa's to the moment she was first seen outside after the fire. No one has come forward with an alibi, so our only hope is that something was captured on camera. The prosecution has turned over hundreds of photos, and I suspect, if we do our jobs right, we can locate hundreds more from that night alone. Then there are the dozens of security cameras at the resort."

Flan pushes a stack of videotapes toward me.

I sigh, grimace at the daunting task before us. "Let's start with the photos, shall we?"

"Sure," Jake says, "but let's sort through them downstairs, all right? I'm awfully hungry. I could go for some kalua pig and Tater Tots."

I bow my head yes, knowing all too well that Jake isn't hungry. He needs a drink.

Damn thing is, so do I.

CHAPTER 19

"How is this woman out on bail?" the talking head with the platinum-blonde wig and bug eyes demands to know.

I turn my head away from the television above the bar and send some rum and Coke down my throat. I'm off the scotch today because I'm attempting to maintain a somewhat clear head for tonight, when I'm scheduled to meet Erin at her home—ahem, place of confinement—in Kaneohe on the windward side of the island.

"Well, Marcy," the quote-unquote legal expert says, "the Eighth Amendment of our Constitution guarantees—"

"Wait a minute," Marcy Faith snaps at him. *"Whose* Constitution? Hawaii's?"

"Um, no, Marcy, the U.S. Const—"

"Wait a minute. WAIT A MINUTE. Uno momento, por favor," Marcy bellows as I take a bite out of my cheeseburger and peek at the screen above Seamus's head. "You're trying to tell me that the Constitution of the *U*-nited States of America grants special privileges if you commit mass murder in the state of Hawaii?"

The legal expert grimaces. "Actually, no, that's not what I'm saying at all."

"Then just what *are* you saying? That the Kingdom of Hawaii has its own laws?"

"I'm not quite following you, Marcy."

"*Ha-wa-ii*," she yells. Her southern drawl is so grating that Seamus slightly turns down the volume even though Jake, Flan, and I are Sand Bar's only three patrons and we've asked him to keep the volume up. "More like Ha-*die*-ii. You won't see me on vacation with the twins on the island of Waikiki anytime soon."

"Well, Waikiki isn't an island, Marcy, it's a—"

Marcy's eyes nearly pop out of her bulbous head. "That's it! Someone cut his microphone, *pronto!*"

"Sorry, gents," Seamus says with his thick Irish brogue, snapping off the TV with his remote. "I just can't fucking take her anymore. I realize you three are the best customers I have, and that my bar probably can't survive without you, but I'd rather the pub go under and I live under a fucking bridge than listen to another minute of that crazy bitch."

"No worries, Seamus," I tell him.

He turns up the stereo and Marcy Faith's shrill voice is replaced by the soothing sounds of the Dubliners.

I've already been through the ringer on the national cable news, so I know what's coming—constant coverage, all of it bad for the defense. Indignant legal analysts who prefer the television studio to the courtroom, know-nothing civilians phoning in and calling for crucifixion or execution-by-stoning before the first witness takes the stand. Then of course there will be round-the-clock trial coverage, during which the American system of criminal justice will be praised and/or criticized depending on the day's events.

I don't give a damn what they say about me anymore. But the

fact is, a defendant who receives national attention from the media cannot take for granted that she will receive the same constitutional protections meant to afford all Americans a fair trial.

"Found a used condom in the backseat of my car," Flan says, a string of lettuce hanging out of his mouth. His daughter Casey has been living with him now for a week. "That and four parking tickets. I don't know what the hell to do."

"Give 'em to me," Jake says, popping a Tater Tot into his mouth. "I know a municipal court judge who'll take care of them for you."

"Not exactly what I meant," Flan mutters. "But thanks."

Jake pushes his plate away and continues flipping through the crime scene photos.

"I especially want to learn everything we can about Trevor's business dealings," I tell Flan, trying to bring us back on point. "Work with a San Francisco P.I. firm if you have to. And ask them to bring in an accountant, one who's very discreet."

"Sounds like I'm going to be out there for a while," Flan says.

"Just until you find what we need. Remember, this is coming out of the firm's own pocket for the time being, so work efficiently. Look fast, but look hard."

"Speaking of looking hard," Jake says, sliding one of the crime scene photos down the bar toward me. "What in the hell do you reckon this is?"

Flan studies the photo over my shoulder. "That's the floor in the hallway."

"Yeah," Jake says, licking his sun-chapped lips after taking a gulp of ice water. "But what's *on* it?"

"Burns in the carpet?" Flan suggests.

I lift the photo off the bar. "No, the circles are too perfect. Looks more like coins."

CHAPTER 20

When I arrive at Erin's home, scented candles are lit along a mantel, the flames flickering from the phantom sea breeze blowing in. Past her bare shoulder the sun is dipping slowly behind Chinaman's Hat in Kaneohe Bay. The calm waters are shimmering as though lit from below, creating a scene fit for French cinema. Only here there are no cameras, no crew, no audience. Just us and the reality of the situation. Her situation. So when she suggests the couch, I point to the dining room table. More room. There are files, I say. Photos and such. We'll need to spread out.

A grudging nod does nothing to mask her disappointment, and I suddenly wonder whether I shouldn't have brought Jake.

There's no mention of my cut-up face. She doesn't ask and I don't say. But for the first time I wonder whether the attack may be related to her case. It wouldn't be the first punch I've taken in my capacity as a defense lawyer. The first was delivered on the steps of the Brooklyn criminal courthouse by one of my own clients. The second I received during Joey Gianforte's homicide case here on the island.

I fold my hands atop the table. "The handbag is the problem," I say, searching her eyes. "Absent evidence your handbag was stolen, the prosecution is going to infer that you were in possession of both the Zippo and the key card the entire night." I unfold my hands, lean back, take a deep breath. It's nearly time for me to ask for the truth. "The Zippo was discovered in the room, so we know it survived. The handbag, however, may have burned up without a trace."

"What are you saying?"

I plant my elbows on the table and speak slowly so that she hears clearly every word. "First and foremost, I need you to be entirely honest with me. I don't want to waste man-hours searching for something that's never going to be found. The police won't do much looking, because the Zippo being in the room and the purse having disintegrated in the fire fits perfectly with their theory of the crime."

I watch her lips but they remain emotionless. Usually by now, the client is indignant, appalled at being accused of lying to her own lawyer. Erin simply shrugs her bare shoulders. "I don't know," she says. "Last I remember having my handbag on me was when I last left Trevor in the room."

I sigh inwardly. We'll continue looking for the little leather Fendi, hope that it turns up in the home of a known arsonist. But until it's found, we'll have to operate under the assumption that the handbag burned, the Zippo remained, and that the jury will likely believe that Erin was in possession of both in the moments before the fire started.

"Enemies," I say.

"What about them?"

"Trevor have any?"

"None that I know of."

"How about you?"

"Me?"

"Any enemies?"

She shakes her head as she stands, floats over to the end table, and rescues a cigarette.

I watch as she steps lightly over to the mantel, places the cigarette between her lips, lifts a scented candle, and holds the dark end to the flame. "No one on the guest list?" I say.

Erin inhales, exhales, shrugs as though the answer is of no consequence.

"No one who might have wanted to hurt Trevor?" I say.

Quietly, "No."

"No one who might have wanted to hurt you by hurting him?"

Again, "No."

"All right," I tell her as she sits, blowing smoke across the table. "Let's go over the guests one by one." I begin with Mia.

Erin insists that up until that day, she considered Mia a friend. Despite Mia's betrayal, Erin is unwilling to entertain the notion that she might have had something to do with Trevor's death.

"Tara?" I say.

"She'd never do *anything* to hurt me."

"How did Tara feel about Trevor?" I ask.

"Trevor? She thought he was great for me. They always got along as well as any best friend and boyfriend could."

"Tell me about Isaac Cassel."

Her lips turn up at the corners like a burning strip of paper. "He was Trevor's best man. Followed Trevor around like a puppy dog."

"That's all?" I ask because I know that's not all. This afternoon I saw photographs of Isaac and recognized him at once. He was the man holding Erin outside the hotel during the fire.

Not to mention the only man she remembers dancing with at her own wedding reception.

"What do you mean?"

"I mean, what was your relationship with Isaac?"

"Mine? Isaac and I were friends."

"And now?" Once I identified Isaac in the photographs sent over from the prosecutor's office, I immediately asked Flan to do a search, to find out who was paying the rent for this gorgeous Kaneohe house.

"Still friends," she says. "In fact, Isaac is the one putting up the money for this house."

She's either being forthright or clever, guessing at how much I know, trying to gain my trust. "Why's he doing that?"

"I don't know." She leans forward, lowers her head so that she has to lift her eyes to see me. "I'm sure the right answer is, 'because he knows I'm innocent.'" Her breasts press against the table, accentuating her cleavage. "But the truth is, Isaac probably carries a torch for me."

"You dated him?"

"Briefly. In fact, that's how Trevor and I met."

I consider how to phrase the next few questions. A query too blunt and she may experience a knee-jerk reaction, take the default position of any criminal defendant and lie, lie, lie.

"How long did you and Isaac date?" I ask. In other words, *Were you fucking him?*

"A few months."

"Was it serious?" *More than just sex?*

"I think for him it was."

"And you broke it off when you fell for Trevor?" *Does Isaac have a motive I can use to create reasonable doubt?*

"Around that time, yeah." She sets her lit cigarette, now just a butt, onto the edge of a ceramic ashtray and leans back, arching her body like a kitten just waking from a nap. Her pale green dress creeps up, but her legs are mercifully hidden under the table.

Still I feel the heat of infatuation rising up my chest, clawing at my throat.

An hour later a few questions remain. About Trevor's sister Lauren and her longtime fiancé. About Erin's parents, particularly about her mother and how she reacted when she heard the news of Trevor's infidelities. But I realize I can no longer stay.

Another of Cashman's Ten Commandments: *Thou shalt sleep with neither client nor witness.*

Last time I disobeyed that one, things all went to hell.

When she stands, the silky dress falls like a theater curtain over her form, and I decide that yes, indeed, it's time to go.

"Can I get you a glass of Merlot?" she says. "Because I certainly need one."

I shake my head. "I have to be heading out." I stand and try to prevent our eyes from meeting. "I have a date tonight."

"Oh, really?" It's the first time she smiled all evening. "May I ask her name?"

"Miss Hawaii."

"Nice name."

"That's what I said."

I pack up my papers and slide them into my satchel, failing for perhaps the first time in my life to place the contents of the file in their proper folders.

She steps around the table, just as I place the leather strap over my arm.

"May I ask you one more question, Kevin, before you go?"

I face her, and immediately regret it. Her eyes are merely inches from mine, and it takes a small moment for me to catch my breath. "Of course."

"I spoke with Joey Gianforte," she says. "Suffice it to say, I was very impressed."

"I'm glad."

Erin leans forward. When she speaks, her breath is warm and smells of smoke. "But Joey's is the only number you gave me."

"So?"

"So I don't know your track record back in New York."

I set my satchel down on the chair and stare into her eyes, the sun now all the way set, the candlelight soft, a light breeze blowing in from all sides. "Well, what do you want to know?"

Erin Simms is like the fire itself, something I should run from whether she started the blaze or not. In either case, she's my client and can burn me in every way imaginable. Besides that, she's vulnerable, was made a widow only a few hellish, hazy hours after being made a wife. Anything now but a curt good night would be unethical, immoral; it could downright damage her case.

She doesn't say another word, doesn't mention Brandon Glenn or anything else about my life and career back in New York. She simply stares up at me, her eyes steady, her lips pouting, all but begging to be kissed.

Only now do I realize that every action I've taken since the night of the fire has been leading to this moment. Taking her case, accepting her bail assignment, interviewing her here in her home alone, it's never been about money or justice. She's been my motive all along.

Our lips are nearly touching and I can almost taste the smoke on her tongue.

I want to leave. I *need* to.

But I can't.

I've already traveled too far down this path to turn back.

PART II

LOVE HER MADLY

CHAPTER 21

Flan and I wear neon orange hard hats as we traipse along the ravaged sixteenth floor hallway of the Liholiho Tower of the Kupulupulu Beach Resort. We were cautioned that the crime scene is a dangerous place, yet not the least bit discouraged to go searching. "By all means," Chief Condon told us with a mirthless smile, after speaking with Chief Attea of the HPD. "Just try not to fall through the floor."

We start by stepping into the rooms with the least damage, but even in these rooms that were spared the worst of the blaze, nearly everything is a dead, charred black. Flan carries a large Maglite and a lightweight Samsung DVD Cam that records all but the horrific odor. I hold only a list of names—the nine original victims—and a map of where each of them perished. We remain perfectly silent for all of the first twenty minutes, then it's I who finally feels the need to speak.

"This is the room we were in, Sherry and I."

The room is a blackened relic of what it was. Only now does it truly hit me how close we came to dying that night. For me, it was a second brush with death, the second in less than a year here in the islands. Maybe it's time to return to the relative safety of New York City.

Across the hall is the room where the Kenders died—Dean and Marlene, their children Dean Jr. and Missy. An entire family wiped out in a matter of minutes.

Next door is where the Wenecks met their end. Jared and Helen, a retired couple on the ironic mission of completing their list of "50 Places to Visit Before We Die." According to their daughter Janie, Hawaii was only number three on their list.

On the end, in the corner across from the Simms's honeymoon suite is the room where Marty Treese and Enis McLaughlin suffocated from the thick black smoke. Both Marty and Enis were married, but not to each other. They worked together, though—he a high school principal, she an American history teacher at his school. Both of their spouses were apparently shocked by the news, not only of their deaths, but of their infidelities.

We step outside Treese and McLaughlin's room and I can see that Flan is short of breath. I place a hand on his shoulder. "You all right, big guy?"

Flan nods yet appears anything but. Finally he sets down his equipment and bends over. Planting a palm firmly on each knee, he vomits onto the remains of the carpet. With the second violent retch, the hard hat comes tumbling off his head. I look away quick as I can, swallowing back down my own Red Bull and pound cake breakfast. My eyes instantly tear from the stench.

That's when I notice the pennies Jake pointed out in the photograph taken by the fire investigators. There are maybe twelve of them on the crisped floor in the hall outside Josh and Grandma's door. As Flan coughs and spits into his hands, I lower myself to my haunches to examine the coins more closely. Just a dozen or so pieces of blackened copper that could have fallen out of anyone's pocket in their mad dash to escape the hotel.

Leaving Flan to settle himself in the hall, I creep into Josh and Grandma's room. I realize instantly that the kid, too, would be dead if he hadn't had a hankering for the twenty-three mysteriously refreshing flavors found in Dr Pepper. It makes me weak in the knees. Never before have I set foot on such a crime scene. Never has the damage been so extensive and touched so many lives. Never have I represented anyone accused of such brutal carnage.

I wonder briefly what I'm doing here. How can I defend the person who most likely committed this abominable act? Yet the conventional answer arises almost immediately:

Where would I draw the line? One victim? Three victims? Eight?

Does the method of murder matter? Is there a "cruel and unusual" standard that can be applied to homicide just as it is to punishment? Should the age and gender of the victims be of concern? Should I only represent the killers of men and not women and children?

Where would I draw the line?

There is no line. In my profession one must never be drawn. Because if I can justify walking away from this homicide case, I can justify walking away from any. I'd be left representing small-time crooks and miscreants charged with misdemeanors and violations like shoplifting and pissing in public. That's not why I went into Law.

Then why did I?

"Because you're so fucking good?" Milt's voice resonates in my head.

But no. Were that the case I would have ended my career in New York, would have walked away from the law the day I received the phone call from the assistant DA on the Glenn case, telling me Brandon was innocent. Innocent but no less dead.

"*Kevin,*" Milt once said, "*some people are just made for this shit.*"

Right now I'm not so sure.

I back out of Grandma's room, coughing finally from the pungent odor of ruin, forearm pressed against my mouth.

"Flan, let's take a look at Trevor's room and get the hell out of here," I say, mid-hack. I've already retained a retired fire inspector to examine the crime scene, prepare a report, and testify at trial, if necessary. "Let's leave this to the experts."

Trevor's room is a whole new devastated hell. It's easy to see now how fire inspectors concluded so quickly where the fire started. In the rear of the room, on the wall facing the bed, I immediately find the infamous V, the burn pattern that indicates the fire's point of origin.

I look from there to the remains of the bed, the spot where Trevor burned.

Not Trevor, actually. Trevor's *body*.

We received the autopsy reports this morning. Toxicology tests turned up nothing surprising. Still the medical examiner Dr. Derek Noonan concluded that Trevor Simms was dead before the fire ever started.

This fire, as in many arson cases, was apparently set to conceal the crime.

This changes everything while changing virtually nothing. Erin Simms, the prosecution will say, killed her unfaithful husband Trevor first by stabbing him with a knife in the stomach. The knife has yet to be recovered, but the weapon is believed to have had a three- to four-inch blade with a serrated edge. The ME's report suggests that the perpetrator—

Suddenly the dead black room is spinning. A bright white border frames my entire field of vision, and a dull chime sounds incessantly in my ears. Faint here, I realize, and I may very well cause a cave-in on the fifteenth floor, unwittingly burying myself alive in the rubble. I need to get out of here, sure as I did the night of the fire. So I summon Flan and together we walk briskly back toward the stairwell.

Soon as I hit the stairs, I elbow Flan aside and start to run.

CHAPTER 22

"Missus?" I say.

Jake squints again at the page in his hand. "That's what it says here on her witness statement."

I finger the fading cut on my forehead, then the puffy yellow-green flesh just below my left eye. "She never mentioned she was married."

"I don't suppose you asked."

"Maybe she was divorced," Flan says from the other end of the conference room table.

"No, no." Jake sets the statement down and points. "Says here 'married.' To one Mr. Bruce Beagan. No question about that."

"Shit," I say.

"What are you thinking, son?"

"I'm thinking maybe I did something worse than eat that hick's Buffalo wings."

Jake grins. "You mean, like, maybe you fucked his wife?"

Flan says, "Maybe the Buffalo wings were just the last straw."

So Sherry is married. I try to recall a wedding band but I'm drawing a blank. *Did I even look for one? If I spotted one, would it have mattered?*

Or am I just like . . . ?

"Mia Landow," I say quietly. "She's the first witness I want to speak to. I need to know whether Trevor told her he planned on going ahead with the wedding. If Trevor lied to her to get her into bed, we have motive. Even if Trevor didn't lie to her, I want to know why she decided to spill her guts less than an hour before the ceremony. She didn't come clean just then because her conscience was killing her—she had an objective. And I think that objective was to stop the wedding."

"How about the maid of honor?" Jake says. "What do we know about her?"

I flip the page on my legal pad. "Tara Holland. Apparently, she's like an older sister to Erin, even though they're around the same age. Erin is convinced they've been friends since the beginning of time."

"You doubt her?"

I consider the question. "I doubt Erin on just about everything she says," I finally admit. "But I particularly doubt anyone who thinks they have the perfect friend. Loyalty only goes so far."

Jake shoots me a look. So does Flan.

"But if Tara Holland *is* as protective of Erin as Erin thinks," I continue, "then any motive that is attributed to Erin applies to Tara as well."

Jake says, "The same can probably be said of Erin's parents."

"Flan," I say, "I'd like you to interview Todd and Rebecca Downey separately. Tell them it's simply routine, but we have to surprise them with this, not give them any extra time to make sure they have their stories straight. Record the interviews.

Have them transcribed. Then we'll look for any inconsistencies. But whatever you do, Flan, be polite and be discreet."

Flan jots it all down. "Got it."

"Jake, talk to your pals in the police department. Glean any information you can about Trevor's sister Lauren Simms and her fiancé Gabe Guidry. Lauren is spending an awful lot of time with the other side and she's pretty damned convinced that Erin's our killer. I want to know why."

"I'll get what I can, son. But I've got to tell you, I've lost a lot of friends on the force since you came along."

I instinctively fix him with a stare. "Cops dislike a good defense attorney, Jake? I'm shocked."

"It's not just how good you are, son." A brief pause, then Jake's back to raising his voice. "It's how you do things. How you conduct yourself in *and* out of the courtroom."

"Jake, I . . ." I hold my hand up, hold my tongue. "All right, we don't have time for this. I've also got to hunt down Trevor's best man Isaac Cassel and have a chat with him. There's something more to his relationship with Erin than Erin's letting on."

"The best man had a thing for the bride?" Flan asks, as Jake continues to seethe.

"They were together before Trevor, and I don't think Isaac ever truly let her go."

"But if Isaac killed Trevor to get to Erin, he wouldn't let her go down for murder, right?"

Hoshi buzzes us on the intercom. "Kevin, you have a guest."

"Tell him to have a seat, I'll be right there." I turn back to our investigator. "Self-preservation is an incredibly powerful instinct, Flan. You can see that by looking into the eyes of just about any criminal defendant. Even as a motive for murder, self-preservation can never be underestimated."

Flan mulls this over.

"Besides," I say, "there's another scenario we have to consider. Unfortunately, this alternative scenario doesn't much help our client."

"What is it?" Flan says.

"That someone else murdered Trevor. And that Erin lit the fire to clean it up for them, inadvertently killing ten innocents in the process."

CHAPTER 23

"Where are we going today?" Josh says. "Back to Tommy Lambada?"

"Tommy Bahama," I tell him as I accelerate onto H-1 West. "But no, not today. Today I have something special planned."

I've thought a lot about the kid these past few days and I've come to a decision. There's no reason at all that Josh shouldn't get to know his father, even if his father doesn't fancy playing a parental role in the boy's life. I don't know how long the kid will be in the islands. Great-aunt Naomi's prognosis, I'm told, is terminal. Eventually, another family member will have to step in or Josh will be placed in a foster home. Either way, I'd say that Josh is most likely headed back to the mainland in the months to come. Twenty or thirty years down the road, I suspect both Josh and his father will regret not having had the opportunity to spend some time together, to get to know each other, for however briefly, as father and son.

When I pull into King Kam Auto in Waipahu, Josh is asleep, so I nudge him. "We're here, kid. Rise and shine."

Josh groggily lifts his head, then makes a face reserved for broccoli as he scans the garage. "I thought we were going to Hawaiian Waters Adventure Park."

"Not today." I help the kid off with his seat belt. "I have to drop my Jeep off to be painted and pick up a rental car across the street. Let's go."

Justell is seated behind her desk browsing a copy of *People* when we enter the office. When I clear my throat, she looks up and offers a smile. Then she looks down at the kid and her dark eyes widen. "That Mongoose's boy?"

I nod. Mongoose's legal name is Sebastian Haslett, and from the few accounts Flan and I collected over the weekend, not at all a bad guy.

"That's right," I say. "Thought I'd bring Josh along when I brought in my Jeep, maybe get the two of them a bit reacquainted."

Justell closes her magazine and makes googly eyes at the kid, but tells us Mongoose went out to lunch and isn't expected back the rest of the day. I sigh. There goes my plan to park myself at the bar at Chili's, while Josh and Sebastian enjoy a family reunion with some cheese fries and baby back ribs.

Justell picks up the phone and summons Sebastian's second in command, a young guy named Dominic, who appears in the office before Justell even hangs up the receiver.

"Can I do for ya?" He spits his words out so fast even a New Yorker like myself is briefly taken aback.

As I tell him about the Jeep and Sebastian's estimate, Dominic scratches his left ear and shoots a look at the kid, throwing him an uncomfortable smile. No question as to why this guy isn't at lunch—he's a hair over my six feet yet probably weighs a buck-twenty soaking wet. Food doesn't seem to be high on his list of priorities. When Justell hands him the paperwork I filled out last week, his fingers tremble so badly the papers sound as though they're being taken by the wind—although there is no wind, not so much as a breeze, I'm convinced, on the entire island of Oahu today. I'm dripping with sweat and cussing in my head Parker Canton, the ass-clown who calls himself a weatherman on one of the local stations. For some reason, Parker Canton thinks this killer heat is funny.

"We can do that, we can do that," Dominic says, before launching into the process that Sebastian's already explained.

Without hearing him speak a word, I could've told you Skinny Dom's problem. Before I took on Erin's case, I saw at least one of these guys in my office every week. I like small-time crystal meth cases, because the money's quick and easy and I generally don't have to worry about my client doing time. Just a stint in rehab. Stay clean for a year and he or she is fine. Sure, that's exactly what we have here: dilated pupils, stretching across one blue iris and one brown; grinding teeth; impaired speech; jerky movements. No question, Skinny Dom likes his ice. Judging from his complexion and sunken cheeks, I'd say he's been on the quartz for quite some time.

A momentary pause to catch his breath, then Dom's on the dog track again, chasing the rabbit. "So, just leave the Jeep keys with Justell and make sure you grab any and all personal possessions, since we're not responsible for those, then head over to our friends across the street, fill out a little more paperwork, and they'll give you the keys to a nice, new rental, whatever you like, for example another Wrangler or they've got Mustang convertibles, nicey nice, Hummers and other SUVs—who doesn't like a Hummer, right?—or you can go with something a little less conventional like a Mini Cooper or a Miata—then again, you're not a chick, right?—or maybe something that might be fun to drive around the island, like say a dune buggy or a Harley or a hovercraft, am I right?"

As I hand the keys to the Jeep to Justell, Skinny Dom's still behind me talking in my ear. He keeps going even as I thank him, as I give him the shaka so not to shake hands, even as I escort the kid by his nose-picking paw across the parking lot in the direction of the rental car agency.

Skinny Dom finally stops at the edge of King Kam Auto's property, as though there were an invisible barrier he can't cross. I'll have to remember that.

"What's wrong with that guy?" Josh says once we're out of the icehead's earshot.

I glance at the kid and shrug. "Too many yellow jellybeans, I guess."

CHAPTER 24

At dusk I punch the doorbell to Erin's Kaneohe home and listen to the peal. I have just a moment to glance back at my rented jet-black Maserati GranCabrio convertible parked in the driveway, before the door swings open and Erin greets me with an angry shake of the head and a shrug.

All right, so it wasn't the most prudent financial move, me renting a vehicle I couldn't afford even in the best of times. But upgrading at a rental agency is a slippery slope—you reach a point and you might as well go for it all, even if you *are* waiting out a shaky bail assignment. Besides, it's only for five or six days. A week at most.

When I step inside, I'm surprised to find Erin's parents standing in the dimly lit living room, both with their arms crossed, sneering at me.

"We were both accosted by your Mr. Ryan Flanagan today," Rebecca starts, just as the door slams shut behind me.

I continue walking toward them despite Rebecca's obvious rage. "Interviewed, you mean."

"More like *interrogated*," she says.

So much for "But whatever you do, Flan, be polite and be discreet."

"I seriously doubt that," I tell her. "I think you're misinterpreting his—"

Rebecca raises her voice another few decibels. "He actually used the words, '*Pop quiz, hotshot,*' when I asked him if I could pour myself a cup of coffee first."

"He was a big Dennis Hopper fan," I say. "Hopper's death hit him pretty hard."

"That doesn't justify his behavior," Todd says.

I hold up my hands. "Look, Mr. Flanagan's been under a lot of stress lately. His estranged teenage daughter is visiting from the mainland, and she's been quite the handful. But I assure you, whatever he did, it was because he felt it was in the best interest of your daughter's defense."

It's the perfect segue back into the case and I don't waste it. "Please," I tell them, motioning to the dining room table, "everyone have a seat. There's a lot of new information, and there are plenty of issues we have to discuss."

Once everyone is seated and relatively calm, I begin with Trevor's autopsy report.

"Stabbed?" Todd says as though he's just had the wind knocked out of him. His eyes flutter to Rebecca, who escapes them by closing her own. A lone tear sneaks past her left eyelid and slaloms down the side of her nose.

Squeezing her fingers into a fist and placing it over her face, Rebecca asks, "What was he stabbed with?"

"The ME concludes Trevor was stabbed in the abdomen with a knife," I say, "most likely something small like a switch with a three- to four-inch blade. It appears from the medical examiner's analysis that Trevor had time enough to bleed to death before being consumed by the fire."

Rebecca gazes at Todd, both eyes moist.

Todd puts an arm around her but doesn't say anything.

Leaning forward I study all three of them, waiting for an explanation. But the entire table has suddenly fallen as still and silent as Stephen Colbert in a bear cave.

"Did they find the knife?" Todd finally says.

I shake my head, then I push my chair back and stand, an uneasiness growing in my stomach. I'd assumed during my first few visits to Erin's house that she'd left the lights off, the candles aglow, to create a certain atmosphere. But with Erin's parents sitting here, I'm no longer so sure. So I lift two lit candles off the mantel and walk them slowly back to the table, setting one in front of Rebecca Downey, the other in front of her daughter.

Before my eyes adjust, I flash on my initial meeting with Erin on Hidden Beach, how she immediately flinched from my touch in the sunlight. Now, in the subdued radiance of the candle, I scan Erin's bare arms, from the tops of her shoulders to the tip of each finger. The scars are tough to make out now that her body's tanned and she's bathed in such scant light—but, make no mistake, they are there.

I look from Erin to her mother, because that's how this often works. Rebecca's scars are far more faded and buried some under the wrinkles of age. But they, too, are there.

"You're a cutter," I say quietly to Erin.

Tears in her eyes, she bows her head.

I ask, "Have you cut since you've come to Hawaii?"

"Yes," she whispers.

"What did you use?"

"A Pteroco Legend."

"A what?"

"It's an automatic switchblade with a serrated edge."

Todd leans his head back and stares into the vaulted ceiling, a helpless look creeping over his features. I follow his gaze to a lizard, who darts down a wooden rafter before vanishing into a crack at the base of the wall.

The whir of the ceiling fan mixes with the myriad of thoughts pinballing through my mind, such that I can barely focus.

I turn to Erin's parents. "I take it from your reaction to Trevor's autopsy report that you both knew about this."

Rebecca nods her head.

"Anyone else?" I ask Erin. "Does anyone else know about your cutting?"

"Tara knows," she says softly. "Mia knows. Isaac knows. And, worst of all, Lauren knows."

Rebecca's eyes light up. "You told Lauren?"

"Lauren's known that I cut for a long time. I mean, you'd have to be blind. But she's also caught me with the knife since I've been in Hawaii."

"The switchblade?" I say.

Erin nods. "I didn't dare risk bringing a knife on a plane these days. So the day after we arrived, we drove down to Waikiki and I bought one at a store on Kuhio Ave."

"It's illegal to sell or possess switchblades here in Hawaii," I say.

"It was a backroom deal," she says. "Just like you can buy weed in the back of any head shop in L.A."

A part of me trembles but it passes as I speak. "Lauren caught you with the knife before or after you learned that Trevor had cheated on you with Mia back in San Francisco?"

Erin doesn't answer. Doesn't need to.

Her haunting stare is answer enough.

CHAPTER 25

When I arrive at the district court in Honolulu, my client Turi Ahina is already on the courthouse steps waiting for me. As usual, Turi is all smiles, his round fleshy cheeks rising like the sun on either side of his lips. "Aloha, Mistah C!"

I stick my hand out for a shake but he grabs me by the forearm and pulls me in for one of his patented bear hugs. When he finally releases me it takes me a long moment to catch my breath, and another ten minutes for me to smooth out my suit.

Inside the courthouse, Turi is subject to a security search, while I flash my bar card and walk right past. We meet at the elevator bank at the end of the hall.

"Same t'ing as usual?" Turi says.

"You bet."

The prosecutor on Turi's case is a young attorney named Heather Raffa. In fact, Raffa has prosecuted nearly every drug case I've defended over the past year-plus, beginning with a buy-and-bust involving Turi Ahina himself. That case—and every case against Turi since—has been dismissed for want of prosecution, in accordance with Hawaii's speedy trial statute, Rule 48.

Beat the Speedy Trial Clock is a game I played in New York City with some regularity. Here in Honolulu, Raffa caught on quick. She began driving out to police officers' houses personally on the day of court to ensure they would appear on every case in which I went up against her. That was no good for business at Harper & Corvelli. So I did what any good lawyer would do under the circumstances: I asked her out.

Heather Raffa demurred, tried to convince me that she was seeing someone, that the relationship was going somewhere, and I relented. Whether she was flattered or felt sorry for me, I don't know. But ever since I extended my invitation Raffa and I seem to have an unspoken understanding. I cop to reasonable pleas in most drug cases I'm involved in, mostly small-time stuff, charges of possession, occasionally with intent to distribute. Raffa's conviction rate goes up in exchange for one precious exception. She lays off my friend Turi Ahina.

Since our first case together, Turi has been arrested four times. All minor drug offenses. Each case thus far has been dismissed, thanks to our unwritten contract. Raffa doesn't know that Turi saved my life—and she doesn't need to. All she needs to know is that he's important to me, and that so long as she plays ball with me on Turi, I'll continue to make her professional life a hell of a lot easier.

"Listen, Turi," I say in the hallway outside the courtroom after a silent ascent in the crowded elevator, "I'd like you to do me a favor. It has to do with the Kupulupulu Beach Resort arson case."

"Anyt'ing you need, brah."

"Keep your eyes and ears open on the street. I'm looking for an empty seat."

Turi purses his ample lips in thought. "An empty seat, yeah?"

"Someone I can point the finger at, someone who won't be in the courtroom to defend himself. Ideally a fire buff. Someone who likes to watch things burn."

"You mean, besides the end of a glass pipe, eh?"

"Yeah, besides that."

When I step into the courtroom I have Turi take a seat in the gallery, while I head up to the rail to have a brief discussion with Heather Raffa. The judge has not yet taken the bench, but Raffa is already standing at the prosecution table, arranging files and gabbing with her assistant.

"Pssst."

Raffa turns, her big bright blue eyes bearing into me like a laser. She says something in the ear of her assistant then takes her time approaching the rail.

"What is it?" she says.

In the courthouse hallways, she's as flirtatious as a Hooters waitress working the tip. But in the courtroom, Raffa's all business. As anal as any obsessive-compulsive I've ever met. And she always dresses the part. Today she's in a smart navy suit, her light brown hair falling perfectly at the top of her collar.

"We have Turi Ahina on today," I tell her.

"I know."

"So you'll ask for a month?"

"No. The State's ready," she says. "The officers are downstairs, waiting to be called up."

Half my mouth lifts in a smile, thinking she has to be fucking with me. This has to be some sort of joke.

"The State's ready," she repeats. "If you need a two-week adjournment, we'll consent. But that's all."

"And in two weeks?"

"The officers will appear again."

I take a step back from the rail and draw a deep breath. "Did I do something?" I ask.

She shakes her head no, then turns and heads back toward the prosecution table. I reach over the rail to snatch the back of her suit jacket but she's too quick.

Barbara Davenport and now Heather Raffa.

I officially have another catastrophe to deal with.

CHAPTER 26

We are seated in a dark corner of Chip's Steakhouse, an elegant open-air restaurant abutting the Kupulupulu Beach Resort. From here, Kerry Naikelekele and I are in full view of the quiet lagoon and ocean beyond. A full moon illuminates the goings-on at a private party by the pool, and I think briefly of Erin's wedding reception, of how she must have felt, watching Trevor from the corner of her eye, wondering how she could be subject to such a vicious betrayal.

"You've hardly touched your filet," Kerry says quietly as I brood. "Isn't it cooked right?"

It's cooked perfectly—charred on either side with a warm pink center—and I tell her that. I tell her, too, that I have the Simms case on my mind. That's not entirely true. I'm distant, but not because I'm pondering the evidence, the possible witnesses, my opening statement. My appetite is buried fully under thoughts of Erin Simms herself.

"How is the case going?" she asks.

I push aside the plate and lift my Glenlivet, postponing an

answer. Dragonflies skip across the surface of the koi pond like pebbles on a lake. It's the stuff of dreams, yet I'm unable to escape the maze of land mines I've set for myself. All in a mere two weeks.

"Let's not discuss the case," I tell Kerry.

"All right. Then let's finish the conversation we started the other night."

This is our second date, not counting the evening I got my ass kicked in the Kanaloa's men's room. The conversation we began—well, *she* began—on our first date involves yet another territory of the psyche I have no desire to explore. My law partner Jake Harper has been asking me such questions for the better part of a year, and he's still no closer to learning about the pre-lawyer Kevin Corvelli than Kerry is.

"Which conversation?" I ask, attempting to steer the ship into another harbor. "Our talk about the humpback whales?"

"Your parents," she says. "Come on, Kevin. I told you all about mine the very first night we met."

True enough. "I don't mean to sound aloof, Kerry, but—"

My eyes inadvertently fall upon a woman sitting three tables to my left. She looks back at me with a mischievous grin across her face. Then a bulbous bald head abruptly eclipses my view.

Sherry the cougar. And her husband Bruce Beagan.

Sometimes an island can feel so small.

"But what?" Kerry asks.

Truth is, I'm not even comfortable saying that I'm uncomfortable speaking about my childhood because I worry it places too much weight on the topic. Neither can I lie, because then I must admit to myself that there are things I want to hide. But the past, for me, doesn't need to be hidden; the past, for me, must simply step aside.

"I'm sorry," I tell her. "I just have something else on my mind."

We finish our drinks in silence and pass on dessert. Kerry's beauty is beyond words, but just like the scenery that surrounds us, it cannot pull me back to earth. A few weeks ago I'd be inviting Miss Hawaii back to my villa to meet Grey Skies, but tonight all I can do is tell her I had a great time and ask her to forgive my remoteness.

My decision to cut the date short has nothing to do with Sherry or Bruce Beagan. Nothing to do with Kerry or her persistence in asking questions about my parents. Nothing even to do with the fact that I have a brand-new jet-black Maserati sitting in the resort's garage and I'm dying to ride it into the night.

No, my decision to cut the date short rests on a desire much more sinister.

I suddenly need like nothing else in the world to be on the other side of paradise, to unclothe myself in candlelight, to meld my body with that of my client's.

To burn away this long, hot summer night with Erin Simms.

CHAPTER 27

Sitting with three strangers in the waiting room, I browse the headlines of today's *New York Times* on my Kindle, because I refuse to touch any magazine left hanging around a doctor's office. Even a psychiatrist's.

I check my watch. I arrived a half hour early for my appointment, but forty-nine minutes later I've yet to see a single patient exit the office. My initial thought is that Dr. Damien Opono is fucking with my head.

It came to me last night, as I was flooring the Maserati through the dreamlike tunnel punched into the side of the mountain on H-3 on my way to see Erin Simms in Kaneohe, that I am about to break.

Get thee to a doctor of psychiatry, I told myself. So with my hands-free—yes, it's finally a law here in Hawaii—I dialed Hoshi's home number and asked her to set up an emergency appointment with the first psychiatrist on the island she could get in touch with at such a late hour. Thirty minutes later, Hoshi left a message on my cell saying that I had a ten o'clock appointment with Dr. Damien Opono in downtown Honolulu.

By the time Hoshi left said message, I was already in Kaneohe, melting inside Erin in the hot tub on her lanai, the jets like a third set of hands massaging us in the warm, dark night. When my lips moved from hers down to the nape of her long smooth neck, Erin's soft moans soared like gulls over the bay and I knew that every thrust was putting us further at risk. But I didn't care. I had dropped Miss Hawaii at her Ewa Beach home and raced across the island to make love to an accused mass murderer. *Something*, I realized as my heart thumped hard in my chest, *is not quite right.*

When my cell phone buzzes, I put both my thoughts and Kindle to sleep, then reach into my front pants pocket. The Caller ID reads RESTRICTED but I answer the call anyway. Just another occupational hazard.

"Mr. Corvelli, this is Isaac Cassel. Erin tells me we need to meet."

"Where?"

"Waikiki?"

"All right. The Bleu Sharq on Kalakaua across from the beach. When?"

"Right now?"

"I'm on my way."

Just as I stand, a woman with a bunch of balled-up, wet tissues steps out of Dr. Opono's office.

"Mr. Corvelli," the receptionist says from behind her desk, "Dr. Opono will see you now."

"Sorry," I say, returning the phone to my pocket. "Please tell Dr. Opono that I'm flattered but I'm afraid he'll have to wait."

CHAPTER 28

"Tough man to get ahold of," I say as I sidle next to Isaac Cassel at the Bleu Sharq. Together we lean on the wooden ledge, he with his bottle of Mike's Hard Lemonade, me with a pint of Blue Moon.

"Well, I'm here, aren't I?"

He is. And that's to his credit. Getting charged with homicide is perhaps the easiest way in this world to lose friends. With the exception of Tara Holland, all initial calls to witnesses in this case have, until today, gone unanswered.

"I was told to stay away from you," he says. "Prosecutor says you're a shark."

From our open-air spot on the second floor we have an unobstructed view of Waikiki Beach. As the Pacific laps against the white sand and the Blue Moon works its magic, it's easy to forget why we're here. Yet not quite easy enough.

"Erin finally convinced me to call you," Isaac says. "But that prosecutor, Maddox, he'd have a shit if he knew we were talking."

I shrug, speak slower and softer than usual. "The prosecution doesn't own you, Isaac, whether you intend to testify against Erin or not. We have every right in the world to be speaking to one another. So don't let Luke Maddox push you around."

Isaac reaches into his pocket, pulls out a crushed box of Marlboro Reds, and sets them on the ledge, along with a mustard-colored Bic lighter.

"So Maddox called me a shark, huh?" One of Cashman's Ten Commandments is *Thou shalt not call the prosecutor a cocksucker to his face.* But this guy Maddox, he's getting into my head like no prosecutor has before. I've already broken two of Milt's Commandments in this case, so I'd better watch my tongue, lest I break a third.

Isaac bows his head then says, "So, what do you want to know, Counselor?"

"Why don't you start by telling me about your relationship with Erin Simms."

It's Isaac's turn to shrug. "Not much to tell," he says, scratching the back of his neck.

Small talk, tics—it's all currency in my field. A witness trying to buy himself some time. I try not to aid a witness by keeping silent; the less I talk, the more he has to. In this case, the longer the pause, I figure, the longer Isaac will likely gabble following it. Compensation for the time wasted.

"Erin and I were together a few months," he says. "Three, I'd say. Two years ago. Then, well . . ." He fiddles with his crushed cigarette pack, his eyes never leaving the ocean. "Then I introduced her to my best friend Trevor."

"If Trevor was your best friend, why did it take you three months to introduce him to your girlfriend?"

"Trevor had been away, out on his boat when I met her. Traveling the California coastline with his father."

Isaac has a couple days' worth of stubble but he's got the kind of face that wears it well. I'm picturing him with Erin, can't help but see him lying with her, that stubble moving up and down her long, lean body, leaving light scratches along her flesh. I clench my teeth and push the image away. This is why you don't fall for a client.

"Trevor and Erin hit it off right away," he says, finally looking me in the eye. "And that was that."

"And you?"

"I moved on."

"Just like that?"

"Just like that."

"No strain on your friendship with Trevor?"

"None," he says a little too quickly. "We were best friends. We stayed that way. Neither of us was willing to let a girl come between us."

"How about things between you and Erin?" I say. "Awkward?"

"Sure, at first. But time took care of it."

Isaac drains his bottle of Mike's Hard Lemonade, sets the empty down hard on the ledge, and resumes his glare at the calm ocean. "So what does she need?" he asks finally. "An alibi?"

"Doesn't work that way, Isaac. I read your witness statement. You were nowhere near her at the time the fire started."

"Earlier I was."

"Earlier doesn't help."

"I could retract my statement, say I misspoke."

I shake my head. "Maddox would have you for lunch."

"So what can I do?"

"You can tell me why you're flitting the bill for Erin's luxurious digs over in Kaneohe."

Isaac stares down at the swimsuited passersby crossing Kalakaua Avenue, silent. "She told you that?"

"She didn't have to."

"I care for her still," he says softly. "I admit it. I just told you, I'll do anything I can to help her."

"Like commit perjury."

He doesn't answer. Doesn't need to.

"You think she did it?" I ask him.

"Do you?"

"Doesn't matter what I think, Isaac. My job is to create reasonable doubt."

"And how do you do that?"

"Well," I say, scoping out the crowd, making sure no one can hear us, "when the circumstantial evidence is stacked up against a client as it is in Erin's case, I look for other suspects I can feed to the jury. Try to show those twelve people in the box that it's reasonable to believe someone else could have committed this crime."

He bows his head but doesn't look at me.

"Know anyone like that?" I ask.

"Like what? Someone that could've killed Trevor?"

"Someone with a motive to, yes. Someone I can place at the Kupulupulu Beach Resort at around two A.M. on the night of the fire."

"You can point at me. I can take the Fifth."

"That's chivalrous. Only I've got a credit card receipt with your name and signature on it, along with a date and time stamp that says you were drinking at the Ali'i Bar at the Meridian until twenty after two."

Isaac steps away without a word and I watch him move slowly toward the bar. When he returns, he's got another bottle of Mike's and a pint. He slides the Blue Moon over to me as I finish the last of the first.

"It was Erin's lighter?" he says. "Erin's knife?"

"I can't discuss the physical evidence with you, Isaac. You're still a witness for the prosecution."

"I know. My point is, it wasn't her lighter fluid. Trevor bought that himself for a barbeque we were supposed to have the day after the wedding."

"But Erin had access to it."

"So would anyone else who stepped into that room."

"That's right," I tell him. "But who?"

"There's someone," he says as his eyes drop to his feet. "Someone I didn't mention to Maddox or the cops because I didn't realize it was relevant until now."

I take a pull from my pint. "Who's that?"

"The night before the wedding," he says. "Trevor, Gabe, and I came down here to Waikiki for a bit of a bachelor party."

"And?"

"And Trevor got into a fight outside the Angry Rooster."

The Angry Rooster is a dive bar a few blocks away from the Bleu Sharq.

"What kind of altercation was it?" I ask him calmly. "Verbal? Physical? Something else?"

"It was verbal but it came real close to becoming physical. Thing is, Trevor was really bombed that night and he did something stupid."

"How stupid?"

"He pissed on some guy's leg."

I suppose it says something about me that I've seen it happen before, New Year's Eve 1999 in an abandoned cathedral-turned-nightclub in midtown Manhattan. "Can you describe the pissee?" I ask.

"Big guy. Dark skin but he didn't look like he was from the islands. Maybe Latino. Lots of tats. Saw him throwing back tequila shots earlier in the night."

Not much. But at least I know at which bar I'm drinking next.

"Did this big guy make any threats?"

Isaac nods. "Guy said something about cutting the head off Trevor's cock."

I tear a bite out of my orange wedge and wash it down with a slug of Blue Moon. *Ironic*, I think as I swallow. *Cutting off the head of a cock would make for one angry rooster indeed.*

Isaac and I stand there a while, like two old friends who found they have nothing in common anymore. We finish our drinks but don't say another word to each other until I'm ready to leave.

"So Maddox called me a shark, huh?"

"Yeah," he says.

I can't help but sigh. "Well, next time you see Luke Maddox, you tell him Kevin Corvelli called him a cocksucker."

Thou shalt not call the prosecutor a cocksucker to his face.

Nothing in Cashman's Commandments about having a witness do it for you.

CHAPTER 29

"Kevin, line one." Hoshi's voice over the intercom disrupts the perfect silence of the conference room. "New case."

Jake looks up from the crime scene photo he'd been squinting at. "Thank the Flying Spaghetti Monster. I was beginning to think I'd never hear those two words again."

I drop the folder I just opened onto the table. "What's he charged with?" I say, running a hand through my hair, trying to conceal my frustration.

"It's a she," Hoshi says. "And she's charged with Hawaii Penal Code chapter 711, section 1108.5."

"What the hell's that?" Jake says. "Abuse of a corpse?"

"No," Hoshi says. "Cruelty to animals."

Jake frowns. "All right. Schedule an appointment for this afternoon at—"

"Wait a minute," I say. "Hoshi, what are the facts of the case?"

Hoshi hesitates as Jake and I stare each other down across the table. Finally she says, "Defendant in Makaha killed a peacock, Kevin. With a baseball bat."

"A peacock?" I say. "Why in the hell would anyone do that?"

"She said it was constantly squawking. It drove her crazy, so she took a bat and smashed its head."

I take a deep breath. "Tell her to find another lawyer."

"What?" Jake shouts.

"We can't defend someone who did that," I say. "It's sick."

"Sick?" Jake stands and throws his arms up in the air as though the ref just blew a call in a Texans game. "We're representing a young woman accused of setting fire to a resort and killing eleven innocent people, including two children. Hell, that blaze was a hair away from killing *you*."

"*This* woman took a *baseball bat* to the head of a defenseless *peacock*, Jake."

He stands there, mystified. "And?"

"And we've got to draw the line somewhere," I say.

A solid twenty seconds of silence is interrupted again by a tentative Hoshi. "So, gentlemen, yes or no?"

"No," I tell her. "Refer her to either Russ Dracano or Mickey Fallon. Their numbers are listed in the phonebook."

Ten minutes after Jake storms out of the conference room, I'm in my office on the phone with our investigator Ryan Flanagan.

"Flan, I've got a name for you to check out. Javier Vargas."

I tell Flan all about my visit last night to the Angry Rooster, about my chat with the bartender who served a heavily tattooed Hispanic man the Monday of Trevor Simms's bachelor party. The bartender Ken Walls was kind enough to sift through that evening's receipts to identify the target of Trevor's impromptu pissing match. Walls then introduced me to a bouncer named Brent, who remembered ID'ing the guy at the door. Brent remembered that Javier Vargas and his two pals each flashed California drivers licenses. Two of the three had addresses in Los Angeles.

"Flan, I also need you to find Lauren Simms and—"

"No," he says.

"What?"

"*No.*"

"No?"

"Not you, Kev. Sorry. *Casey, I said no.*"

When Flan returns to the line he tells me how Casey has been borrowing money from him every day for the past week. "And with nothing coming in . . ." he says.

"What do you mean 'nothing coming in'?"

"Money. You know, to the firm."

"How the hell does that affect you? I pay you a salary."

"Yeah, but Jake says that the coffers are going to dry up sooner rather than later, and—"

"Listen to me, Flan. Your job is secure, I promise. Jake's had a cattle prod up his ass ever since he dumped Alison, and he thinks he's pissed at me for taking on the Erin Simms case. Pay no attention. Hopefully, we'll have the old Harper back before the start of trial."

"If you say so, Kev."

"I say so. Now let me run. I have a meeting set up with Tara Holland back in Ko Olina, and I don't want to be late."

I hang up the phone and consider knocking on Jake's office door, offering up an apology. I consider telling him to have Hoshi call that new client back to set up an appointment.

But no. There have been plenty of days in my life when I wouldn't have cared if someone set the whole world on fire just to watch it burn. But I can't recall a single moment in thirty-two years when I would've sat back and abided some so-called human being purposefully taking a baseball bat to the head of an innocent bird.

CHAPTER 30

The photographs I've seen of Tara Holland don't do her justice. She's a ravishing young woman with light chocolate skin and smoldering eyes. We're seated now in her hotel room at the Meridian in Ko Olina, each on a plush chair in a well-appointed room, the curtains open, allowing in the worst of the midday sun. But if Erin has told Tara everything that has transpired between the two of us—and I'm willing to bet she has—then I can't do something as simple as close the drapes or remove my suit jacket, or else Tara may think I'm putting on the moves. And under just about any other circumstances, she'd be right.

"Tell me how you met Trevor," I say.

"I didn't," she says. "Well, at least not in the beginning. In the beginning Erin and I met Isaac and Gabe."

"Where was that?"

"At some nightclub—I think it was called Sorbet—in San Francisco."

"Like the dessert?"

She nods. "It's shut down now. I mean, you know how long

nightclubs last in the city. This was about, say, two and a half years ago."

"So the four of you hooked up?"

"Nah, it wasn't like that. Isaac, he came up to Erin, started dancing with her. Then when Erin and I sat down—you know, Sorbet was kind of a nightclub-slash-lounge, pretty exclusive. Anyway, Isaac came over with his friend Gabe and they brought drinks. Isaac was driving hard to the hoop for Erin, but Gabe, even then he was engaged. So Gabe just played wingman and we let Erin and Isaac get a bit cozy."

"And after that?"

"They went on a few dates. Gabe and I joined them on the first one or two, until they felt comfortable with each other. Then they started flying solo—baby got wings—and that was that."

"Until Trevor came along."

Tara bows her head once. "Until Trevor came along."

"Let me ask you something a little strange," I say, leaning forward as though the walls have ears. "Isaac, I met him in Waikiki yesterday. He's a good-looking guy."

Tara smiles. "I'm sure he'd be happy to hear you say that."

I grin, nod my head slightly. "Well, let's you and me keep that between the two of us." I shift in my seat as I change direction. "I also saw plenty of pictures of Trevor." I don't mention that I saw him in the flesh at Kanaloa's on the night of the fire. "So, my question is . . ."

I'm hoping she'll finish the question for me, just come out with an answer so that I can escape this verbal dance. But she just looks at me. Don't women see it? Or is it just us men? Is there not an aesthetic hierarchy? Some sort of unwritten law that prevents women from trading down in the looks department, same as men?

"So my question is, what did Erin see in Trevor that she didn't see in Isaac?"

This time Tara doesn't hesitate. "Money." She smiles. "I realize that sounds harsh. I mean, Isaac, he's loaded. But Trevor was on another level. He was being groomed by his father to take on the family business."

"Which is?"

"SimmsWare. You probably heard of it; it's a big software company in Silicon Valley."

"Sims like the computer game? The role-playing game?"

Tara shakes her head and laughs. "No, it's nothing like that. But SimmsWare does play a large role in the gaming industry."

"So, money?" I say, lightheartedly. "That's how you ladies choose your men?"

"Not me," she says defensively. "But, yeah, I suppose lots of girls are attracted to that."

"And Erin's one of them?"

"Sure. What do you think we were doing at a club like Sorbet to begin with?"

Tara's beginning to get comfortable. She's speaking to me naturally as she would to a friend. This is how she'll need to speak to me when she's on the witness stand. Though we clearly have a *lot* to work on in the way of substance.

"Okay," I say. "So Isaac is rich, but Trevor is filthy rich, so Trevor gets the girl."

"Was," she says.

"Was what?"

"*Was* filthy rich. I mean, in the past tense."

"Well, of course," I say, "now that he's dead—"

"No," Tara says, crossing her legs. "I mean, even before he died he was no longer filthy rich. His father cut him off."

"Cut him off?"

"That's the irony, see? Isaac picks up Erin, Erin dumps him for Trevor because Trevor's father is Daddy Warbucks, but then Trevor's father cuts him off for—guess what?—*proposing to Erin.*"

I follow, but I don't want to disrupt the flow, so I tell her, "I don't follow."

Tara frowns. "Well, as you probably know by now, Erin isn't exactly what you'd call . . ." She searches the room for the right word. "Well, sane."

"Sane," I say.

"Again," she says, "I realize that sounds harsh, but you know, the girl's got troubles. It's not her fault."

"It's her mother's," I say, almost to myself.

Tara places an index finger on her nose but keeps silent.

"So that," Tara says, "coupled with the fact that Erin doesn't exactly come from money, made her a *poor* choice—no pun intended—for marriage into the Simms family."

"All right. So Trevor's father cuts him off as soon as Trevor proposes to Erin. But she sticks with him?"

"She stuck," Tara says. "But she didn't realize what she was sticking to for about the next ten months."

"Trevor went from filthy rich to dirt poor and Erin didn't realize it?"

"Trevor hid it pretty damn well," she says. "I mean, from what I heard, he liquidated everything in his name and then started his own business. Never lost a step."

"Then how did Erin eventually find out?"

She slides a silver charm up and down the silver chain around her neck. "Yours truly," she finally says.

"And how did you find out?"

"Who else? Isaac."

"Isaac blabbed to you."

"Yup."

"Knowing it would get back to Erin."

"Isaac knows there are no secrets between me and Erin."

I flush a little from the look she gives me following that state-ment. "And Mia?" I say. "How does Mia fit into all of this?"

"Mia just likes to sleep around."

I give her a doubtful look and she backpedals. "I mean, sure Mia had a thing for Trevor, probably all along. But she played it cool—you know, went out with all of us, fucked other guys. But there was always something there. Both ways, I think."

"And then one of them finally acted upon it," I say.

"That would be Mia. She was the one who asked Trevor to take her out on his boat on a day she knew Erin couldn't be there."

"Who told you that?"

Tara stalls. "Mia."

"Here in Hawaii, on the day of the wedding?" I ask.

Tara shakes her head and all of a sudden her eyes are wet. "No. Mia told me a few days after it happened."

"But you didn't tell Erin."

"No." She reaches for a tissue in the box on the table and dabs her eyes.

"Thought there were no secrets between you and Erin," I say.

She shrugs. "I figured it could only hurt her, you know. Nothing good could come of it. She wanted to marry Trevor and that was it. And I knew it was Mia who initiated shit with Trevor; she told me so. So I figured Trevor wouldn't do it again. I mean, Mia seduced him. What's that called in the law? You know, it was like entrapment."

Not exactly, but okay, close enough that I can see her logic. "And then here in Ko Olina on the wedding day, it all came to a head," I say. "Why?"

"Why do you think?"

"Why do I think Mia finally told Erin that she slept with Trevor?" I shrug. "How should I know?"

"Someone suggested Mia tell Erin," she says, "and I can assure you it wasn't me. So who do you think it was, Mr. Corvelli?"

"Kevin," I say. "Call me Kevin."

"All right. Who do you think it was convinced Mia to tell Erin she'd fucked Trevor when Erin was already done up in her wedding dress?"

Someone in the wedding party who didn't want the marriage to move forward. "Isaac," I say.

"Now you're the Batman."

CHAPTER 31

Even with a pair of retro, oversize Jackie O sunglasses hiding the top half of her head, I recognize Mia Landow the moment she steps out of the taxi. I tip the brim of my Panama Jack hat low over my eyes and raise a copy of yesterday's *Honolulu Star-Advertiser* to hide my face. It's nearing eight o'clock at night, and the number of travelers loitering outside the Honolulu Airport in Aiea is few. Enough to fill a red-eye or two, but not nearly as bustling as I usually find it.

Mia is alone, just as I anticipated. She's got a 9:45 flight to San Francisco and she checks two large pieces of luggage curbside, carrying with her only a small purse and a light blue duffel bag. Mia has been on the island for a full two weeks, and this is the first shot I'm getting to speak to her. Maddox has been hiding her well.

She'd checked out of the Kupulupulu Beach Resort the day after the fire and we had been unable to locate her since. Yesterday, Flan's connection at Continental Airlines informed him that she'd canceled her flight back to the mainland scheduled for Monday. It took some more phone calls, a few hundred dollars, and some false promises, but Flan eventually learned she'd be catching the red-eye tonight.

I follow her through the automatic doors. She stops at a machine and performs an electronic check-in. Then she starts toward her gate with her boarding pass.

"Excuse me, miss," I say from behind her. "You dropped something."

Mia turns on her heels and looks down at the floor. As her eyes come up, I lift the brim of my Panama Jack, exposing my face. No question about it—Mia Landow instantly recognizes me as well.

Her thin frame shudders and her wide mouth falls agape. Her short chestnut hair accentuates a small cutie-pie face and a neck as long and sexy as a great pair of legs.

"Don't be frightened," I tell her. "You've done nothing wrong. All I want to do is have a brief talk."

"I'm not allowed to speak with you," she says, emphatically shaking her head.

"That's not even slightly true."

She looks at her watch without reading it and tells me she has a plane to catch.

"You'll make your flight," I say. "I just want ten minutes of your time. If you'd like, we can talk on your way to the gate."

Mia removes her Jackie O sunglasses, turns, and starts walking. I take that as an invitation, remove my hat, and move right alongside her.

"In the interest of saving time," I say, "I'll tell you what I *do* know and then I'll ask you to fill in the blanks. One, you confessed to sleeping with Trevor just prior to the wedding at the

behest of Isaac Cassel, who presumably wanted to put a stop to
the nuptials. Two, by the time you made said confession, your
friend Tara had already known about you and Trevor, yet didn't
share the news with Erin. Three, after the wedding reception,
you paid a visit to Trevor when he was alone in his honeymoon
suite to apologize and ask for his forgiveness for upsetting the
ceremony."

Mia comes to a dead stop. "Wait. *What?*"

At least she was listening.

"I did *not* see Trevor at any point after the wedding reception. Certainly not in his hotel room!"

"When you slept with him on his boat, did you know Trevor
was going to go forward with the wedding?"

"To be honest, I didn't think much about it."

"Not exactly an ideal friend, are you?"

"No. I'm not. Are you, Mr. Corvelli?"

"Not at all."

"Sometimes we think just about ourselves, don't we?"

"Yes."

"Well, there you have it, Counselor. That's precisely what I
did when I slept with Trevor."

"And when you told Erin about it when she was already in
her wedding dress? Who were you thinking about then?"

"I don't know *what* I was thinking. I'd confided in Tara and
Isaac and they each gave me contradictory advice. Finally, once
we were here in Hawaii, Isaac threatened that if I didn't tell Erin
about my escapade with Trevor, then he would."

"Not exactly an ideal best man, was he?"

"No. He wasn't. But then, neither of us thought that my telling Erin about what happened on Trevor's boat would get him
and ten other people killed."

"You think Erin killed Trevor, then set the fire to cover it up?"

Mia shrugs her shoulders theatrically. "Isn't it obvious? Trevor was stabbed in the gut with a knife, Erin's knife, the knife she used to cut herself just after she heard the news that I'd slept with her groom."

Mia's making Luke Maddox's opening statement. And doing a damn good job of it.

"And the fire?" she says. "I mean, come on. Erin's lighter? She's set fires before, you know. Maybe not intentionally, but definitely accidentally while she was practicing her little self-mutilation act." She turns, her voice cracking. "I've got to go or else I'm going to miss my flight."

"But you'll be back to testify," I say.

She spins around to face me. "I don't have a choice."

The clock's ticking. I at least need to see her reaction when I ask her for her alibi. "Where were you when the fire started, Mia?"

Her shoulders slump such that her light blue duffel falls to the floor. "I was at the Meridian," she says. "After the reception, I went over to the luau there and I met some guy. When the luau was over, we went back to his room."

"And?"

"And we fucked." Mia takes a few steps toward me, looks me in the eye. "Look, I know what you're going to do to me at trial, Mr. Corvelli. I know you're going to make me out to be this heartless slut. And I realize it'll be all over the news and that it'll be in every paper from here to New York. But you know what? I don't care. People have been crucified in the press before and gone on with their lives."

"But it's no picnic," I say.

"I'm sure it's not. But what are you going to do, Counselor?

Sometimes the press gets it wrong. And sometimes they get it dead right." She turns, picks up her duffel, and quickly resumes her gallop to the gate. But long before she's out of sight, she twists that long, sexy neck around and calls back to me. "But you already know that, Kevin Corvelli, don't you?"

CHAPTER 32

"Ouch," Koa says later that night after I tell him about my meeting with Mia Landow at the airport. "You sure you don't want something stronger than that ginger ale, Kevin?"

"No," I tell him. "I've got to meet the kid tomorrow morning. We're going up North Shore to Shark's Cove. I promised I'd teach him how to snorkel."

"So how are things going with Miss Hawaii?" he says.

I shrug. "I've been preoccupied, so it hasn't gone quite as I'd expected."

"Shame, brah. That is one hot lady."

A couple next to me orders a round of mai tais and Koa steps away to mix their drinks. When he comes back he asks me if I'm hungry.

"I am."

"What you want?" he says. "Plate of them Buffalo wings?"

Thoughts of my last Buffalo wing fiasco steer me clear. "Nah," I say, getting up from my barstool. "I think I'm going to head over to Chip's, maybe get myself some of those teri sticks."

"Awright, brah," he says, reaching over the counter to shake my hand. "Be good."

What exactly does that mean?

Chip's has a packed house tonight, so I sit at the bar. Not that I mind a table for one; in fact, sometimes I prefer it. But for teri sticks and a glass of ginger ale, the bar will do just fine. Besides, tonight I'm anxious to get home, crank up the A/C, and get some badly needed sleep.

Mia is right. Sometimes it takes a non-lawyer to see through the smoke. The jury will hear witness after witness testify about how Erin was hurt, how she was fragile to begin with, how she cut herself, even burned herself at times. They will see her Zippo lighter up close, get to hold it in their hands. They may or may not see the knife, depending on whether it's found, but they will hear testimony from Lauren Simms about how she saw Erin with it—a switch with a three- to four-inch blade with a serrated edge. The same type that killed Trevor Simms.

Hotel security will testify. They'll say they were called up to Trevor and Erin's room not once but twice. That she reacted furiously to their visit, cussing them out and ultimately slamming the door in their face each time.

If someone did indeed steal Erin's little leather Fendi, the jury will want to know who. I don't have an answer. And if I don't have one come the time of trial—if I can't place someone with motive at Trevor's door—then Erin Simms is in peril. She will spend the rest of her life in a goddamn cage.

And it may be that justice is served.

Once I close out my tab I step away from the barstool and halfheartedly wink good night to a hostess I've had my eye on for months. Then I do a double take. At a table in the rear of the restaurant I see Kerry Naikelekele seated with a man with his back to me. I sigh; no question I blew it.

As I walk along the koi pond, I notice the man stand. From the corner of my eye, I watch him move casually toward the men's room.

Can't be, I think.

But it is. He sees me, too, staring at me as he winds his way through the occupied tables, not smiling, not frowning, not offering so much as a nod of the head, the prick.

Once he enters the men's room I move a little faster, wanting to put as much distance between us as possible.

I'll see him in a few days when he argues his motion to have me removed from the Simms case. But tonight I need not spend another moment looking at or thinking about prosecuting attorney Luke Maddox.

Or his date.

CHAPTER 33

After an hour of snorkeling at Shark's Cove, Josh and I are famished, so we head to Kua 'Aina Sandwich in Haleiwa for some burgers. We take a table outside and let the heat continue to have its way with us.

"Wanna see where I used to live?" the kid says after the meal. His face looks like an abstract painting, brush strokes of ketchup, mustard, and mayo beginning at his chin and working their way up past his nose.

"Sure," I say, handing him a stack of napkins. "You know how to get there?"

He nods, wiping the one spot on his face that had remained flesh-colored.

"You missed a little," I say, snatching the napkins from him and wiping his face myself. "Chicks don't dig messy eaters."

"I don't care."

"Maybe not. But I'm not letting you back in the Maserati looking like Heath Ledger's Joker, so you'd better clean up."

"WHY SO SERIOUS?" he says in his best homicidal clown voice.

It's a moment before I catch myself laughing.

Josh's empty house is a rather ramshackle two-story A-frame located between Waimea Bay and the Bonzai Pipeline on Ke Iki Beach. On either side sit bungalows hidden away by tall trees. We're practically invisible from the road, so when Josh asks if we can look inside, I shrug my shoulders and look for a way in.

And so, using my Bank of Hawaii debit card on the warped front door, I commit my first act of breaking and entering since that night I was nearly killed by gunfire in Kailua last year.

"Mommy kept our house real clean, but it's all dusty now," Josh says when we first step inside.

I sneeze. Kid's right. A quick tour and then I've got to get out of here, back into the stifling but clean Oahu air.

After a brief viewing of the kitchen and dining/living area, Josh takes me up the creaky wooden stairs. We peek into his mother's bedroom, then head over to his.

"It doesn't look the same," he says, disappointed.

"It's just a structure," I tell him, staring out the room's lone window. "In three decades I've never once lived in a place I thought of as home."

Josh silently crosses the room and stops at the window overlooking the ocean. There are a pair of surfers paddling out past the breakers. "Over there," he says, pointing to some rocks jutting out of the water. "That's where they say my mommy died."

As I stare at the spot where Katie Leffler met her end, Josh steps over to his closet and lifts up the rug inside. "What are you doing, kid?"

He lifts a loose floorboard and pulls out a pair of binoculars.

"I forgot these here," he says. "Mommy bought them for me. She was teaching me about the birds. We used to watch them together. I know, like, twenty different kinds. Every time we saw a new one, we wrote it down in a notebook."

He hands me the binoculars. I dust them off with the tail of my T-shirt and hold them to my eyes. "What a horizon," I say softly.

"What's horizon?"

I hand Josh the binoculars and point into the distance. "See that line where sea meets sky?"

He nods but says nothing.

"There's your horizon, kid." So beautiful you could cry.

I take back the binoculars for one last look before we leave.

After a moment my gaze shifts from the horizon to one of the surfers in a wet suit and Wayfarers riding a large wave back in.

Son of a bitch. If it isn't my good friend Luke Maddox.

CHAPTER 34

"This island is becoming too small."

Kerry turns and smiles at me as we walk down the beach toward the Kupulupulu Beach Resort lagoon, snorkel gear on our heads. "Kevin, I never told you we were exclusive."

I shake my head. "It's not that. Well, it *is* that, but only because of *who* you're seeing."

"Oh, so I can see other people, but not Luke?"

"You don't understand," I tell her. "The guy's everywhere. In the papers, on the news. In the ear of once-friendly prosecutors. He's turned his entire office against me."

"Aren't you adversaries?"

"Of course. But it was different here, my relationship with the prosecutor's office. It wasn't nearly as contentious as it was in New York. And it was a nice change of pace."

Our feet touch the water and Kerry wiggles her toes, splashing up a bit of ocean and sand. "Forget about him today. It's Sunday. Forget about the case."

"I can't forget about him. Even on weekends I have to see him."

"I told you I'm sorry I let him take me to Chip's. That was wrong; I know Ko Olina is where you live, where you hang out all the time. It's just that I love it here. But I promise, it won't happen again."

"I didn't just see him with you on Friday night," I say, stepping deeper into the water. I'm not wearing fins but I lower my snorkel mask. "I saw him yesterday, too, when I was hanging out with my friend Josh."

"The kid?"

"Yeah, the kid. We went snorkeling at Shark's Cove, then we stopped by Ke Iki Beach, which was deserted—except for, guess who? Luke Maddox."

"Ke Iki Beach," she says, lowering her snorkel mask, too. "Yeah, Luke told me he goes surfing there sometimes. He used to date a woman who lived over there."

"Well, I guess he sure gets around the island, doesn't he?"

Before she can respond to my juvenile—not to mention utterly hypocritical—remark, I'm underwater, kicking my legs toward the center of the warm lagoon. Visibility's good. Fish glide right by me as though we were all simply passengers heading for the Fulton Street subway station. No noise below the surface save for my breaths, amplified by the mask so that I sound like Darth Vader. As my breathing regulates a familiar calm washes over me.

For some reason I never feel freer than when I'm in the Pacific, when my entire body is underwater, weightless and untethered to anything tangible or intangible back on land. It's almost as though when I'm out in the ocean, Kevin Corvelli ceases to exist. Step into the blue and, like magic, he's gone. And with him go all of his worries, his appointments and calendar calls, his dissatisfied business partners and pissed-off members of the opposite sex. The whole lot of them. Gone.

In the ocean I'm not Kevin Corvelli. Nor am I anyone else. Just a thought. A force.

In the deepest part of the lagoon, where the Pacific dumps its excess every few seconds, I remove the mouthpiece from my snorkel gear and set it on a rock. Then I hold my breath and dive back under, my eyes wide behind my prescription mask. Below me are more rocks. I stretch my body toward them, reaching with my arm, fighting the current coming in from the ocean.

Almost there. Just a touch and then up for air.

Jammed between the rocks is something black and small like a hairbrush or a pair of sunglasses. With my right arm I reach for it, touch it, lift it gingerly with my hand, examining it like a child on his first visit to the bottom of a pool. Light hits it just right and its silver side glimmers, nearly blinding me. I shut my eyes tight, then open them again. I open and close the object I have in my hand, study it against the backdrop of the rocks.

Then out of the rocks strikes an arm, reaching for my own. I drop the object but still the arm grabs hold. Not an arm, I see now, as panic floods within me. An eel. An ugly fucking moray eel, and it is sinking its teeth into my flesh, drawing blood, coloring the lagoon a gruesome red.

I straighten my body, place my feet against the rocks, and push up with all my strength, struggling to free my arm from the eel's grip as I launch myself toward the surface. But the eel simply grips me tighter, sinks its tiny pointed teeth deeper into my punctured flesh.

When my head hits air, I fight for breath, kicking my legs so that I don't get swept back under. I raise my right arm, eel and all, above the surface. Here, exposed to the air, the eel can't breathe, so it lets go, falls back into the water like a stone.

I remove my snorkel mask and throw it somewhere, unconcerned right now about whether I'll ever find it again.

The skin on my forearm is torn, but I'll live.

The eel dove back to its home in the rocks.

But I now have another dilemma.

Kevin Corvelli is no longer underwater, so again he exists, court cases and all.

There is a murder weapon at the bottom of this lagoon. And, like it or not, whether the weapon surfaces is now exclusively my call.

CHAPTER 35

"It's not an ethical dilemma," I say. "It's a strategic dilemma."

I shift in Jake's ratty old client chair, as he rolls a chewed-up pencil back and forth across his desk. Tomorrow it will be two full weeks since the fire at the Kupulupulu Beach Resort and this case is already choking the life out of me.

"The murder weapon," Jake says quietly. "I think this one's a no-brainer, son."

Jake and I have called a temporary truce to whatever has been transpiring between us these last two weeks. Looks as though Alison Kelly is out of his life for good and he's finally coming to accept that. It also appears—surprise, surprise—that representing a defendant in a high-profile murder case is good for business. Over the weekend we received calls from three prospective clients, each asking us to take on their respective cases, each having been charged with at least one class-A felony. Hoshi returned the calls early this morning. And what do you know? Two of the three prospects actually have money. Harper & Corvelli is effectively back in business.

Knowing this—and feeling alone and desperate—I stepped into Jake's office earlier and asked for his advice.

"There's a lot to consider," I say.

I haven't spoken to Milt Cashman, and I don't dare trust the phones on something like this. If I do call him it'll be from a pay phone, and I'll ask him to find a safe landline, too. Paranoid? Maybe. But in criminal law it's always best to err on the side of caution.

"You're pretty sure it's her knife?" Jake says.

"Pretty damn sure. Erin described it to me and I downloaded a few photos of the specific model from the Internet. I was underwater but I'd bet the house on it." I down a slug of Red Bull. I didn't sleep very well again last night. "Besides, how many switchblades do you think we'd find at the bottom of the lagoon abutting the Kupulupulu Beach Resort two weeks after the fire?"

"That *would* be one hell of a coincidence," he says.

"My first thought was, of course, you don't hand over the murder weapon to the prosecution. Then I thought, what if it actually helps to exonerate her?"

"How in damnation would it do that?"

"Prints," I say.

"After the knife's been underwater for two full weeks?"

I nod. "I spoke to Baron Lee, who I'm retaining as our forensics expert. He said, theoretically, there could still be prints on the knife."

"Say again?"

"It's a long shot, but Baron tells me he's used the procedure in the past and a few times he's gotten results."

"Lifted prints off an item that's been submerged in water?"

"Using Small Particle Reagent," I tell him. "If there's a latent fingerprint on the knife, the oily components of the fingerprint residue may have been held in place by the surface tension of the water."

"Then once the weapon is exposed to air . . ."

"Exactly," I say. "The oily residue that's retaining the shape and details of the fingerprint will spread out or run, and we'll have nothing but a smudged print. But," I add, "if the Small Particle Reagent is applied immediately after the knife is retrieved from the water, it might work."

"You mean right at the scene? Right there at the lagoon?"

"In front of all those people, yeah. That's the problem," I say. "Even if we retrieve the knife at night, someone's going to see us. If not a set of eyes, then certainly the resort's video surveillance."

"Doesn't sound like a thirty-second operation either."

"The knife will need to be sprayed with this reagent immediately after it surfaces. Then the knife has to be rinsed off with clean water before it begins to dry."

"What then?"

"All that should remain on the knife after rinsing should be the reagent which has adhered to the latent print."

"Powder particles."

"Right," I tell him. "Gray prints should appear. We'd have to photograph them, then wait until the knife is dry. Once it's dry, we can lift the prints from the surface with tape, just as we would if the weapon were never submerged."

"Assuming the knife is the same one that the defendant used to cut herself, her prints are going to be on it, son."

"Even so, there may be another set of prints on the knife," I say. "What if Erin *didn't* stab Trevor? What if someone else did, and then she set the fire to conceal it?"

Jake holds a finger to his lips as he thinks about this. "Then the killer's prints might be on the knife."

I nod. "And that might be all we need. Maddox is going to accuse Erin of putting a knife in her husband's gut. If we can show otherwise, his whole case falls apart. We tell the jury if Maddox is wrong about this, then he's wrong about the fire. It's all or nothing. Absent evidence to the contrary, the State can't have it both ways."

Jake half smiles at this revelation. "*If* someone else's prints are on that knife . . ."

"Then, Jake, we have reasonable doubt."

CHAPTER 36

"But what if the knife doesn't contain someone else's prints?" Flan asks as the two of us make our way up Kalakaua Avenue toward the Grand Polynesian resort.

"Therein lies the dilemma," I say, absently rubbing the bandage on my arm.

"So you've got a decision to make."

"And fast. The longer we wait, Baron tells me, the less likely we are to find a valid print."

"And if someone else finds the knife?"

"Then all prints are likely lost, because no one is going to have the foresight to leave it where it is." I lift my Panama Jack and sweep my hand through my drenched hair, briefly wishing weatherman Parker Canton suffers a heat stroke today. "But it's a good ten to twelve feet to the bottom and the area's well-protected by eels, so chances are, the knife stays there unless we pull it up."

We drop in an ABC Store and purchase two ice cold bottles of Fiji water. At the counter Flan says, "So, I caught Casey smoking weed in my apartment the other day."

"Really?"

"Yeah, some shit called Maui Wowie."

"Ah, heavy-duty Valley Isle smokes."

"What?"

"Nothing. You were saying?"

I pay the clerk and we step back into the deadly sunshine, cracking the caps on our bottles of water.

"So, anyway," Flan says, "I now know why half my Vicodin are missing. I caught Casey popping two in her mouth before she went to Ala Moana Mall with her new friend, some giant Samoan guy, and *my* money."

"Have any of those on you?" I say.

"Those what?"

"Vicodin."

"No."

"Okay, so you were saying . . . ?"

Flan allows some of the Fiji to flow down his chin, to soak the neck of his shirt. "Casey constantly eats my food, drinks my beer, tosses her tampons in the bathroom wastebasket—I can't fucking take it anymore. It's like being married to Lucifer all over again!"

"Where's Lucifer living now, by the way?"

"Hell."

"Jersey?"

"No, the other one," he says. "Anyway, Casey stays out all night, then comes home just when I'm waking up, and what does she do? She jumps in the shower. And she doesn't just take a quickie. No, we're talking fifty-sixty minutes in there. I can't even piss!"

"Oh."

"I have to piss into a sponge."

"Why not just piss in the kitchen sink?"

"That's disgusting."

"Well, where are you pissing into the sponge?"

"Over the goddamn kitchen sink."

"I've made my case."

Meanwhile, we've made it to the lobby entrance of the Grand Polynesian, a sprawling resort resting at the edge of Waikiki. Just stepping inside stirs memories of the Gianforte case and a certain law school professor I counted among the many suspects.

"Wanna get some drinks at Duke's tonight?" Flan says.

"Nah, I can't. I have to have a nice long talk tonight with Erin Simms."

We step past the front desk and take the elevator to the nineteenth floor.

"So, what are you gonna do, knock on the door and say 'room service'?" Flan says as we step into the hall.

"No," I tell him. "You are."

"What? What do I do when they open up?"

That I don't know. But it doesn't matter. Because the door to room 1909 is open, and there's a maid standing in it, pulling the sheets off the king-size bed. I poke my head inside and there's not a shirt, not a hairbrush, not a used Q-tip to be found.

Flan and I hurry back downstairs and get the attention of a young woman standing behind the front desk.

"I had an appointment to see Mr. Gabe Guidry this afternoon," I tell her. "He was staying in room 1909, but now he isn't there."

She taps away at her computer, her eyes set on the monitor. "Oh yes," she says. "The young couple. They checked out."

"When?"

"Just this morning. They were supposed to be here for a few more days, but they just packed up and left very suddenly."

"Suddenly?"

"Yeah, it was weird. This blond gentleman came by, paid their bill for them, and drove them away."

"A blond guy, huh?"

"Yeah. A *cute* guy. All dressed up, but he still had this whole surfer-dude look going on."

"Anyone say where they were going?"

"No," she says, shrugging her shoulders. "Just the airport."

CHAPTER 37

"So what seems to be the trouble, Mr. Corvelli?"

Dr. Damien Opono is a native Hawaiian with a casual demeanor I immediately admire. He's fairly young as far as psychiatrists go, but I don't necessarily need advice from a sage these days; I need someone to talk to. And, yes, I need drugs. Something to pull me out of this funk. I feel as though I'm on the brink. It's the way I felt after Brandon Glenn was murdered at Rikers Island. How I felt nearly every day until I graduated law school and my time became my own.

"It's a woman," I say.

It wasn't what I meant to say. But the good psychiatrists, they seem to draw it out of you just by looking at you. I've got to be careful around this guy.

"A girlfriend?" he says.

"I suppose you can say that." If Dr. Opono reads the local papers, he already knows who I am, and despite the doctor-patient privilege, I have no intention of letting Opono or anyone else—not even Jake, not even Flan—know that I'm currently sleeping with a client accused of mass murder.

"And what about her is troubling you?" he says.

"She's addictive," I tell him. "She's bad for me and I know she's bad for me, and yet I can't seem to stay away."

"That's not terribly uncommon."

"No, particularly not for me."

"Oh? Why do you say that?"

"Let's just say I'm beginning to see a pattern."

"A pattern in the type of woman you become involved with?"

Nikki. Erin. "Yeah, you can say that."

Dr. Opono crosses his legs, a gesture that tells me he's not going to simply write me a prescription and send me on my merry way. "Tell me about the woman you're currently involved with."

"Intense. Unstable. Incredibly manipulative."

"Impulsive?"

"Hard to tell," I say. "Since I've met her she's stayed home a lot."

"A temper?"

"Like Tony Soprano suffering from 'roid rage."

Dr. Opono arches his eyebrows. "Wow. I'm assuming, though, she doesn't look like James Gandolfini?"

I smile. "Maybe a slight resemblance." Leaning forward on the couch, I say, "Thing is, the temper's not always raging. Sometimes she seems as delicate as a rose petal and all I want to do is save her."

"So, you're suggesting that her mood swings?"

"Like a pendulum."

"Hmm."

"And she cuts."

"Sorry?"

"Self-mutilates. She cuts herself. Sometimes even burns her own flesh."

"I see," he says, steepling his fingers. "Sounds like she could be a borderline."

"A borderline what?"

"She may suffer from Borderline Personality Disorder. It's marked by many of the symptoms you've just described."

"It's a mental illness," I say.

"Very much so. Borderlines typically possess a shaky sense of identity. They're prone to severe mood shifts and frequent displays of anger, often inappropriate, sometimes violent. Self-destructive tendencies such as self-mutilation are very common. Many of their relationships are just as you described—very intense yet very unstable. They may suffer chronic feelings of emptiness and boredom, and they may make frantic efforts to avoid abandonment, real or imagined."

"Interesting. So, when she goes from kissing me to trying to bite my ear off . . ."

"She's likely employing a defense mechanism called 'splitting.' Like a child, she sees the world as split into heroes and villains. There are no gray areas. No gray people, so to speak. At any particular moment, an individual is either 'good' or 'evil.' "

"In other words," I say, leaning back on the couch, "she can't reconcile that one person can possess both good and bad traits."

"That's right. Borderlines essentially cannot tolerate human inconsistencies."

"So, if someone she saw as all good—such as a lover—suddenly betrayed her . . ."

"She would experience that betrayal far more intensely and react far more dramatically than, say, you or I."

"It would seem to her as though someone she trusted were sticking a knife in her gut," I say.

Dr. Opono frowns, shrugs his left shoulder. "Something like that."

CHAPTER 38

"Please state your name for the record."

Ironic, because now that I know it, I'm unlikely to ever forget it.

"Sherry Beagan. B-E-A-G-A-N."

"Thank you, Miss Beagan." I take a sip of water from the defense table, then spin back around to face the witness. "I'm sorry. It's Missus, isn't it?"

"Yes."

"You're married."

"Yes."

Flan served the subpoena on her two days ago and nearly got his head knocked off by her husband. Fortunately, big ol' Bruce isn't in the courtroom today for this, the hearing on Luke Maddox's motion to have me disqualified as counsel for Erin Simms.

"Mrs. Beagan, allow me to direct your attention to Tuesday, July thirteenth of this year. Do you recall that day?"

Sherry's cheeks turn cherry. She's not nearly as sweat-free as she was the day she questioned me outside police headquarters. "I do."

I hurriedly walk Sherry through the events of that morning, establishing that she was here in Hawaii gathering information for a feature article she was assigned by a medium-size travel magazine called *The Modern Globetrotter*. Eventually, I place her at Kanaloa's Bar and Grill at the Kupulupulu Beach Resort in Ko Olina.

"Do you recall what time you arrived at Kanaloa's Bar and Grill on that day?"

"It was in the afternoon. Sometime between three and four o'clock."

"Do you recall seeing me at the bar when you arrived?"

"Yes, I do."

"Do you recall what I was wearing that afternoon?"

"A beige linen suit with a red silk tie."

"Thank you." I open an orange folder at the podium and thumb through some unrelated photocopies, as though I'm ready to pounce on her if she begins lying. "Mrs. Beagan, did you consume alcohol at Kanaloa's on that day?"

"I did."

"Do you recall what you were drinking?"

"Something called a Tropical Itch."

"An alcoholic beverage?"

"Yes."

"And do you remember approximately how many of these alcoholic beverages you consumed at Kanaloa's?"

"Several."

"More than four?"

"Yes."

"More than six?"

"Probably."

"During that time you were at Kanaloa's, did you and I engage in any conversation?"

"Yes, we talked for several hours."

"Several hours?" I say as though surprised. "I see. Do you recall whether I was also consuming alcoholic beverages during that time?"

"You were."

"Do you recall what was I drinking?"

"Mostly mai tais, but I saw you throw back a few shots of Patrón for good measure."

"Interesting." It *is* interesting, since I have no recollection of doing shots that afternoon, but what the hell; it only helps bolster my argument. "During the first hour or so of our conversation, do you recall what topics we discussed?"

"You told me you were a lawyer." She pauses. "Well, actually, the bartender told me, and you took it from there. I told you I was a freelance writer here on assignment for *The Modern Globetrotter.* I talked about my family, my mother, my father, my brother. You refused to talk about yours."

"At any point in that first hour of our conversation, did you tell me your name?"

"I did."

"As the evening progressed, from all outward appearances, how would you describe my state of intoxication?"

"You went from being slightly inebriated to repulsively drunk."

Ouch. "And upon what specifically do you base this determination?"

"Well, for one, you asked me my name at least a half dozen times over the hours we were together, yet you were never once able to use it. You kept calling me 'baby,' despite my requests that you call me Sherry. Toward the end of the evening, you were slurring your words a great deal, but you seemed utterly oblivious to it. Once or twice you said, 'I'm your huckleberry,' the meaning of which continues to elude me."

"Anything else?"

"You were also rather unsteady on your feet, though you didn't seem to realize it at the time."

"All right. Did there come a time when you and I left Kanaloa's together?"

"Yes, it was around a quarter after eleven P.M."

"Did one or both of us pay a bar tab?"

"You did. You told the bartender within a few minutes of meeting me to put my drinks on your tab."

"Your Honor, at this time, I'd like show the witness what has previously been marked as Defendant's Exhibit A."

Judge Maxa motions me forward. I hand Sherry the bar tab and ask whether she recalls seeing it. Once she authenticates the receipt, I ask her to read the date and times, the list of drinks purchased and their prices, the subtotal and total.

I then enter it into evidence. My alcoholism is now officially part of the court record.

After taking Sherry Beagan through the night, from fornication to the fire, I tender the witness to Luke Maddox, who asks a series of innocuous questions, attempting apparently to prove that I remained alert and coherent throughout the night.

Finally Judge Maxa releases the witness from the stand.

"All right," the judge says. "That was very unusual, to say the least."

Maddox stands. "Your Honor, I'd now like to put Mr. Corvelli on the stand to determine whether, in fact, he has personal knowledge and recollection of any material facts in this case."

"No, Mr. Maddox," she replies. "I think we've wasted enough of the Court's time with this matter already."

"But, Your Honor . . ." Maddox isn't giving up. He's already around the podium and approaching the bench. "Mr. Corvelli has merely established that he was drinking heavily on the night in question. He has *not* established that he was, as Mr. Harper states in his papers, 'blacked out.' In fact, I think it's a very clever ruse on Mr. Corvelli's part that he had his partner Jake Harper sign the supporting affidavit in his response papers. This way, Mr. Corvelli never admits he was blacked out, never denies under oath that he has personal knowledge and recollection relating to the facts in this case. Effectively, this strategy allows Mr. Corvelli to lie to this Court with impunity."

Judge Maxa looks at me. "Your response, Mr. Corvelli?"

I stand in front of the defense table, my body slouched as though I've been punched in the gut. "Your Honor, I'm appalled at Mr. Maddox's accusations. Frankly, the actions taken by Mr. Maddox in this case, coupled with the statements he just now made to Your Honor, cause me to wonder whether Mr. Maddox suffers from some paranoid delusion."

Maddox spins, an ugly smirk on his face. "Oh, you son of a—"

"Mr. Maddox!" the judge shouts. "You'll address your arguments to me, not to one another. Now, do you have any other witnesses or evidence you'd like to present?"

"Your Honor," Maddox says, "included in my papers are copies of notes taken by a fire investigator named Darren Watts at the scene. Those notes *expressly* show that Mr. Corvelli has a clear memory of the events of that evening—"

"*Had* a clear memory of that evening," I interrupt. "Your Honor, as Mr. Harper notes in his response papers, a potential witness may *not* testify if he lacks personal knowledge. And 'personal knowledge,' for purposes of this rule, means not only

that the witness perceived the events about which he is to testify, but that he has a *present* recollection of that perception." I
sweep my hand like a magician. "Clearly, based on the evidence
introduced today, I do not."

"Your Honor," Maddox barks, "I am certain that I can *refresh*
Mr. Corvelli's present recollection using the notes Mr. Watts
took at the scene."

Judge Sonya Maxa shrugs. "What do you say, Mr. Corvelli?
Want to give it a shot?"

"No skin off my teeth, Your Honor. *But* allow me to remind
the Court what is really at stake here. The Sixth Amendment
of the Constitution guarantees every criminal defendant the
right to effective assistance of counsel. That guarantee includes
the right to representation by counsel of one's choice. If the Court
makes the wrong determination on an attorney disqualification
motion, erroneously depriving a criminal defendant of her right
to counsel of choice, reversal of any conviction is mandated."

I point to Maddox and glance over to see the steam rising
from his ears. "That may be fine for this prosecutor, Your Honor,
because Mr. Maddox may very well be the chief prosecutor or
maybe even governor by the time this appeal reaches the high
court, but it is wholeheartedly unfair to my client."

*Not to mention to Your Honor, who certainly does not wish her
rulings to be overturned or her convictions to be reversed.*

"Your Honor—" Maddox starts. But that's as far as he's getting today.

"Enough, Mr. Maddox," the judge says, raising her right hand.
"Perhaps you're right. Perhaps Mr. Corvelli is playing a bit fast
and loose with the rules of the Court. But let me tell you what
Mr. Corvelli has also succeeded in doing. Mr. Corvelli has, by
putting Mrs. Beagan on the stand and being so thorough as to
walk her through the entire afternoon and evening, established

something else, besides his own morbid drunkenness—namely, that he and Mrs. Beagan were together the entire time, and therefore, witnessed the same events. Therefore, if the State wants a witness to testify as to what Mr. Corvelli personally observed, the State has one in Miss Sherry Beagan."

"*Missus*," I correct Her Honor.

"Your Honor," Maddox tries again.

"A lack of personal knowledge," the judge states for the record, "is an exception to the competency rule as it pertains to witnesses. 'Personal knowledge,' for the purposes of this rule, means that the witness perceived the event about which he is to testify and that he has a present recollection of that perception. There is insufficient evidence before this Court that Mr. Corvelli has a present recollection of the night in question. I, therefore, see no reason to deny the defendant the attorney of her choice, and I am accordingly denying the prosecution's motion to have Mr. Corvelli disqualified as counsel in this case."

A single rap of the gavel and Erin and I are in this together.

For better or for worse.

CHAPTER 39

"All right," I say to Jake and Flan when I enter the conference room. "We've got a few big decisions to make." I toss the Simms file on the table and take a seat. "Tomorrow is Erin's arraignment on the felony charges. I think we have to consider changing her plea."

"I don't like it," Jake says. "Too risky."

True. Approximately one percent of defendants who are charged with a felony plead not guilty by reason of insanity, and of those defendants, only fifteen to twenty-five percent succeed.

"Even if we request a bench trial?" I say.

Juries are significantly less likely to render a verdict of not guilty by reason of insanity than are judges. And after I witnessed the Honorable Sonya Maxa toss Luke Maddox around the courtroom like a rag doll yesterday, I'm inclined to take my chances with her.

"Judge Maxa is one of the smartest judges I've ever been before, son, either here or in Texas. You're not going to fool her with the usual smoke and mirrors."

"I've no intention to try. Look, we have a defendant here who has a history of mental illness and at least one psychiatric hospitalization."

"When she was seventeen," Jake says.

"Doesn't matter."

"And according to those medical records we received," he adds, "she was never even diagnosed."

"Very common," I say. "Borderline Personality Disorder is exceedingly difficult to diagnose. But Erin Simms exhibits all the symptoms."

"What *are* the symptoms?" Flan asks.

I read off the list I've already committed to memory: Unstable and intense interpersonal relationships. Impulsiveness in potentially self-damaging behaviors, such as substance abuse, sex, shoplifting, reckless driving, binge eating. Severe mood shifts. Frequent and inappropriate displays of anger. Recurrent suicidal threats or gestures, or self-mutilating behaviors. Lack of a clear sense of identity. Chronic feelings of emptiness or boredom. Frantic efforts to avoid real or imagined abandonment.

"There's no precedent," Jake says, annoyed.

"Then we *make* precedent," I say.

That's the other great thing about practicing law. Even though every argument has already been made, every issue decided, there's always the possibility of breaking new ground, blazing new trails. You just have to take what's there, the precedents—the victories *and* the defeats—and convince one jurist at a time.

"How does someone get off by pleading insanity?" Flan asks.

I open the Hawaii Penal Code to the relevant statute, already flagged with a bright red Post-it. "We need to show that at the time of the conduct, as a result of her mental disorder, the defendant lacked the substantial capacity to appreciate the wrongfulness of her conduct *or* to conform her conduct to the requirements of law."

"In other words," Flan says, "the borderline thing prevented her from *not* killing her husband and setting the resort on fire."

I sigh and look at Jake. "See, this is why we don't put this defense on in front of a jury." I turn to our investigator. "No offense, Flan."

Jake shakes his head. "I think if we go with insanity, we should go with temporary insanity."

"No," I say. "Maybe if she killed him as soon as she got the news. Maybe even if she didn't go forward with the wedding. But too much time passed. Too many events transpired in the interim. A plea of temporary insanity is as good as a plea of guilty, in my opinion."

"Well," Jake says with a tired shrug, "the point is moot unless she agrees to it. You steer her in any direction you feel comfortable. It's your case. You're the lead."

"Her key card. Her lighter. Her knife," I say, counting the three items off on my fingers. "That doesn't leave us much choice."

"What have you decided to do about the knife?" Flan asks.

"Depends on what she says to me tonight," I tell him. "But I've spoken to this guy Larry, who owns a waterproof digital camera rental service. He's agreed to go for a swim with me this weekend to document the knife's whereabouts, for posterity."

"During the day?"

"At night."

"But you're not going to retrieve it," Jake asks.

"I'm not going to answer that question, Jake."

"Why not?"

"Because, Jake, I don't know the answer to that question."

CHAPTER 40

She opens the door with a lit cigarette in hand and strikes a pose fit for a Bond poster.

"Aloha," she says.

I reach for her, grab her gently by the arm, take her inside, and shut the door behind us.

"I know where the knife is," I tell her quietly, even though I know no one else is in the house.

The color drains from her face. In the twilight I stare out at Chinaman's Hat and the surrounding bay until she's ready to speak again.

"Where?" she finally asks.

"In the lagoon."

"So what happens now?"

"That all depends on what you tell me tonight." I fold my arms, take a tentative step toward her. "It's been almost three weeks since the fire, but there may still be prints on the handle and there may still be blood on the blade."

"That's good, isn't it?"

"Not if you were the only person to touch it."

She considers this. "What if that's true? What if the person who killed Trevor wore gloves or something?"

"What makes you think that?"

"The water main," she says. "You told me they dusted it for prints and found nothing."

"That's going to be a hard sell, gloves in the middle of July here in Hawaii. That would mean this was planned, that it wasn't a crime of passion. That eliminates a lot of possible suspects we could otherwise point to."

She holds the cigarette to her lips and inhales, blows out three perfect rings of smoke. "Like who?"

"Mia, for one. Tara. Your parents. Lauren and her fiancé." I wait two beats, then add, "Isaac."

"*Isaac* had nothing to do with this," she insists.

"Well then, let me leave it at this: gloves eliminate *everyone* with *any* reasonable motive to kill Trevor, besides yourself."

"What if it was someone else? An outsider?"

"Everything that was used was yours, Erin. Your key card, your knife, your lighter."

"My handbag was stolen. It didn't have to be stolen by someone in the wedding party."

"There's no evidence of it being stolen, Erin. And there's no motive. You said yourself, there was nothing valuable in the room, nothing taken. Why would an outsider steal your handbag and pay Trevor a visit, only to kill him and set the room on fire?"

"I don't know," she says, flustered.

"And if this was planned, how did this perpetrator know there was charcoal starter fluid in the room? The entire scenario defies belief."

She swings around, stalks over to the sliding glass door, and steps out onto the lanai.

I take a deep breath and follow.

"So what are you telling me, Kevin? That I'm fucked? That I stand no chance at trial? That I'm going to spend the rest of my life in prison?" She shakes her head emphatically. "I couldn't, you know. I mean, I can't. I'd kill myself first."

"There's another option we have to consider."

She releases the bay with her eyes and trains them on me. "What's that?"

"Tomorrow is your arraignment on the felony charges. We can change your plea, prepare an insanity defense."

"I'm not *insane*."

"Insane is only a legal term. We can have you evaluated, have you diagnosed with a personality disorder, argue that the personality disorder prevented you from conforming your conduct to the requirements of law. We can argue that killing Trevor was an irresistible impulse, starting the fire a natural consequence of that impulse. In other words, your personality disorder—your *mental illness*—left you no choice."

"Then what? If I'm found not guilty by reason of insanity? I'm off to a nuthouse?"

"You'll be sent to a facility," I say gently. "You'll get some help. When it's adjudged you're no longer a threat to yourself or others, you'll be released. In a couple years, a couple *months* maybe, you'll be able to put this behind you and go on with your life."

She sighs deeply, breaks into a cry. "This is what you're recommending to me? This is your advice?"

I don't allow myself to hesitate. "Yes. I don't see any other way out. There's too much evidence, too much at stake."

On the lanai she falls into my arms, and I hold her, attempt to soothe her with my body.

Ten minutes later we step back inside her house, through the living room, past the original oils in the hallway.

We end where we end most of our meetings of late. In her bedroom.

We don't discuss the case the rest of the night.

CHAPTER 41

I lift my head off her pillow and immediately breathe in her scent. It's a little after four A.M. and it's one of those nights when I'm not sure whether I slept. Erin's arraignment is this morning; it's something neither of us can escape. So I lift my uncooperative body out of bed. Quietly I snatch my watch from her nightstand and place it on my wrist. I need to go home to Ko Olina to shower and change into my suit. Then it's back down to Honolulu to enter Erin's plea.

Finding my clothes is like a scavenger hunt and I feel her watching me from the bed. As I slip into my pants, she lifts the remote and powers on the small Samsung flat screen TV on the dresser.

". . . and it's gonna be a *hot* Aloha Friday, folks," Parker Canton yips. "An expected record high of ninety-five, a UV Index of nine. I'll tell you, I don't know where those trade winds went to, folks, maybe they're on vacation on the mainland or Japan . . ."

"Please shut that fucker the hell up," I say quietly.

Erin powers down the television and tosses the remote back on her nightstand.

"Wish you didn't have to go," she says, stretching so that the white cotton sheet falls, exposing her breasts.

"Makes two of us," I say with a soft smile. "But as they say in the movies, I'll see you in court."

Outside in the driveway I step into the Maserati. The Jeep, I'm told, has been successively repainted and I intend to pick it up this afternoon. But it will not be easy to bid aloha to this machine.

I fondle the steering wheel, exploring its grooves. Inhale the indescribable scent. I adjust the rearview though it needs no adjusting. I crack my knuckles and press my foot against the break. I slide the key into the ignition and turn.

I listen to the engine purr.

Finally, I lower the top and turn on my headlights. I place the transmission in reverse, back out, and set off for the Likelike Highway.

I see the night road without actually looking at it. In my head images play out more vividly than anything I've ever seen with my eyes. Courtrooms and crime scenes, clients and cartoon villains all vie for my attention as I increase my speed and try to steady the machine between the white lines rushing toward me.

I picture the switchblade, protected as it is by me and a moray eel.

I consider the engraved Zippo lighter, damning and wholly out of our reach.

A missing little leather Fendi and a key card that cannot be found.

A fragile woman betrayed by the man whose money she loved most.

Arguments and death threats followed by so much death.

This is our case. These are the brutal facts I'll have to contend with.

I exit the ramp onto H-3, the faint smell of oil tickling my nose.

There is no one to point to, no ghost occupying my empty seat. Hundreds of photos and hours of video surveillance tapes and I can't place anyone but Erin near the honeymoon suite. Not Erin's mother, not her maid of honor. Not Mia Landow, not Isaac Cassel. Each possesses motive yet no concrete alibi. Each is a potential suspect, but not a shred of evidence points in any direction other than Erin Simms.

I enter the tunnel punched through the mountain and listen to the Maserati pick up speed.

I'll try again tomorrow to connect Josh with his father. After the arraignment this morning, I'll meet with Jake at the office to discuss our two new cases, then maybe head to a bar and meet up with Flan. Listen to Flan go on and on and on about Casey over glasses of scotch. Next week I'll see Dr. Opono again. Get a refill on my prescription antidepressant, an SSRI I lovingly call Fukitol.

The Maserati cruises down the dark mountain.

Erin Simms won't plead insanity but maybe her lawyer can.

This is what I'm laughing about when I first press down on the brake. I glance at the speedometer. Eighty-three miles per hour and headed downhill all the way. I step down on the brake again, the pedal giving all the way to the floor. The Maserati doesn't so much as slow.

The oily smell is pungent now, the white lines flying past me like stray bullets.

Keep your hands on the wheel.

My left hand stays put, my right reaches for the emergency

brake. Lifts it up but there's no tension. The emergency brake falls back into place as though shot dead.

For a moment I'm paralyzed with fear.

Panicking, I shift gears. The transmission roars and rubber burns the second I move into second gear. The wheel tightens and I know I'm losing control.

On the side of the road I see an escape ramp for runaway trucks, but it's too late, I've already passed it.

I throw the transmission into first gear, the transmission howling like a wounded animal, the tires screeching like an eagle after its prey.

The steering wheel tries to overpower me, but with two hands I keep the Maserati steady as it coasts at sixty miles per hour downhill.

As I fast approach a tight curve, another runaway truck ramp enters my line of vision.

I pull the machine toward the ramp with all of my strength, not knowing what is waiting at the end of it. The vehicle skids in the direction of the ramp, and I can no longer look.

Keep your eyes closed, Kevin. You're in the ocean. You don't exist.

The Maserati ascends a short incline, then strikes something that gives. Then strikes something that doesn't. Last sound I hear is the air bag deploying.

Then nothing.

PART III

WAITING FOR THE SUN

CHAPTER 42

Naomi Leffler is dead.

Josh's great-aunt lost her battle with lung cancer earlier this week and now the kid sits in a client chair in front of my desk waiting for Naomi's daughter Chelsea to pick him up. Chelsea Leffler—the sole beneficiary to Naomi's will, which I drew up months ago after recovering from my accident—is young and single and living in Lahaina on Maui and she's made it abundantly clear that her custody of Josh will be temporary. I glance at my watch. I've come to enjoy spending time with the kid over the past six months but playtime for me is over. It's January 5 and tomorrow begins opening statements in the case of *State versus Erin Simms.*

"Why are you wearing a suit today?" Josh asks me as I write out a check for this past November's office rent. Since my accident, cash has been pouring from our accounts like rain from the sky, with very little of it being replenished.

"I finished selecting a jury today," I tell him.

"For that lady who started the fire?"

I take a deep breath and answer without looking at him. "That hasn't been proven yet."

"That fire killed my grandma, you know."

"I know."

"Then you must think this lady didn't do it," he says.

I speak so softly I barely recognize my own voice. "That's not something I get to decide, remember?"

"The jury does?"

"That's right."

"How do they know who's wrong and who's right?"

I lift my head and peer into the boy's big brown eyes, wondering how they've managed to remain so innocent these past six months. "Well, as I told you, the jury listens to the arguments of the lawyers for each side and hears the testimony of whichever witnesses each lawyer calls."

"What's test-money?"

"Testimony. We've talked about this. Remember, Josh?"

"Tell me again."

I scribble my name at the bottom of the check, then toss the dry blue pen into the wastebasket. "Testimony is the substance of what each witness says."

"Like I'm a witness, right?"

"Technically, yes." Josh was with me when I was preparing the witness list for the defense, and although he'll never testify I added his name to the witness list to hear him giggle. Fact is, I put half the population of Oahu on the witness list in an effort to divert Maddox's attention from the witnesses I actually intend to call.

"What is the witness s'posed to say?"

"Each witness is sworn to tell the truth, the whole truth, and nothing but the truth."

"But what if a witness lies?"

I tear the check from the Harper & Corvelli operating account and stuff it into a cheap self-sealing envelope. "Then the judge gives the witness the spanking of his or her life."

Josh's eyes go wide just as the intercom buzzes and Hoshi's voice fills my office.

"Chelsea Leffler to see you, Kevin."

"Thanks, Hoshi. Seat her in the conference room. I'll be right there."

I stand, wincing in pain. Considering the extensive damage done to the Maserati, my injuries from the accident weren't all that severe. A concussion, of course. A fractured finger on my left hand. And a dislocated knee cap on my right leg. I had been mending rather swiftly through the fall, through my thirty-third birthday in December, right through Christmas, in fact.

And then it started to rain.

And rain.

And rain.

And rain.

Typically, the island of Oahu doesn't receive all that much precipitation, at least not on the leeward side. When it does rain, areas like Waikiki and Ko Olina are spared. The mountains and windward side of the island are frequently hit with brief torrential downpours, but the only effect the precipitation has on town is the appearance of thick bright rainbows that seem to stretch from Kahuku to Koko Head. The past week proved one hell of an exception. Normally, you can escape a downpour simply by driving from one part of the island to another. But inexplicably, dark gray storm clouds now seem to hover above me wherever I turn my Jeep. Needless to say, the wet weather is pure hell on my knee.

I tell Josh to wait and proceed slowly down the hall, favoring my right leg. As I pass the local oil painting of the Mokulua

Islands, I finally pause to read the signature at the bottom. "Ah, Sandy," I mumble to myself. "Of course, Sandy."

Chelsea, a hulk of a woman caked heavily in cheap makeup, wears a brightly colored muumuu and a matching smile. She stands when I enter the conference room and somehow manages to shake my hand without my offering it.

"Nice to meet you, Mr. Corvelli."

"Kevin. Call me Kevin." I amble around the conference table and pull out a chair.

"Are you injured?" she asks.

I briefly describe for the thirty-ninth time the incident of late July. Five months into the investigation there are still no suspects, no leads. Someone, we know, unscrewed the brake lines so that the brake fluid leaked slowly onto the pavement as I made my way to H-3. The emergency brake was intentionally disengaged. The Maserati was of course dusted for prints and in addition to mine, Josh's, and Kerry's, one additional set of unknowns was recovered. Everyone at the car rental agency and King Kam Auto offered samples and were excluded, so whoever owns those prints is most likely the perp, a person who would be arrested and charged with attempted murder if only he or she could be identified.

After being released from the Queen's Medical Center during the second week of August, Flan and I covertly collected prints from every suspect in the Simms case who remained on the island. We came up blank. The prints didn't match Isaac Cassel's or either of Erin's parents. Tara Holland came up clean. As did Javier Vargas, who, we've learned, happens to be a recent transplant to Hawaii and a member of California's 16th Street gang. The mystery of the Maserati thus remains unsolved.

"Will you be taking Josh to Maui?" I ask Chelsea.

"No, I rented an apartment in Waikele for the time being.

I'm going to have a talk with Josh's father and we'll take it from there."

The intercom buzzes again. Hoshi says: "Kevin, you have a call on line three."

"Take a message, please."

"Kevin, it's Turi calling from jail."

My stomach sinks. Turi's doing ninety days at Halawa on that last drug bust in July. Ninety days because Heather Raffa wouldn't extend me an inch of professional courtesy. Not an inch because everyone knows Luke Maddox is an up-and-comer, a future head prosecutor, and Luke Maddox, for some reason, wants my head on a stick.

"Give me just a second," I say to Chelsea.

I pick up the phone and punch line three. "Turi," I say, "it's a bad time right now. Can you call my cell phone around six o'clock?"

"Sure, Mistah C. But I t'ink you wanna hear dis right now."

I swivel my chair so that I'm no longer facing Chelsea. "What is it, Turi?"

"I finally found you your firebug."

I press the receiver tight against my right ear and watch the hard rain attempt to smash through the conference room windows. "Seriously?"

"Serious as shit, Mistah C. Your pyro is sitting in the cell right next to me."

CHAPTER 43

"Ladies and gentleman of the jury, my name is Luke Maddox. And I'm going to cut to the chase."

With these words an icy tremor travels north along my spine. There is nothing in this universe more dangerous than a succinct lawyer. I should know; in the courtroom, I'm as succinct as they come.

"The defendant Erin Simms is guilty of the crimes of arson and first degree murder and here's why. *Here* is what the evidence will show."

I lean back in my chair with a silenced sigh. An attorney possessed of the rare ability to state his opening concisely is like a fine storyteller. By being economical with his words, summarizing only the most basic and necessary evidence, Maddox will be able to magnify his intensity without confusing the jury with redundant or useless information. Like hammering in a nail without splintering the wood.

"The defendant Erin Simms was betrayed," Maddox exclaims as he marches in front of the jury box like Braveheart before a battle. "Betrayed by the man she loved, the man she was about to marry. And the defendant learned of this betrayal just moments before her wedding ceremony here on the island of Oahu."

As Maddox takes the jury on a journey through Motive City, my mind slips back to yesterday's telephone conversation with Turi. Prisons offer prosecutors and defense attorneys alike one of the greatest opportunities to obtain information on open cases. Snitches, opportunists, A-1 nutballs, they all like to talk, but for most, truth isn't high on the list of topics they'd care to discuss. But this inmate Turi discovered at Halawa seems to have as much information about the Kupulupulu Beach Resort fire as I do. And I suspect that only the arsonist himself knows more about this case than the lawyers who are about to try it.

"During this trial, ladies and gentlemen," Maddox continues, "you will hear testimony from members of the defendant's wedding party who will describe in great detail how furious the defendant became upon hearing the news that her fiancé, her soon-to-be husband, had been unfaithful to her, had in fact had sexual relations with one of the defendant's very best friends, one of her *bridesmaids*, Mia Landow, a mere two weeks before the wedding.

"Now, no one in this courtroom can fault the defendant for being angry, no. Who wouldn't be angry? Who wouldn't be *livid* after learning of such a betrayal—and on her wedding day, no less? But what the defendant did later that evening is criminal and inexcusable.

"What did she do? She committed murder. The defendant murdered her new husband Trevor Simms in cold blood. Stabbed him in the stomach with a four-inch switchblade and allowed him to bleed out right there on the king-size bed in their honeymoon suite.

"But, ladies and gentlemen of the jury, that's not all the defendant did. To cover up the heinous deed she had done, to conceal her horrible crime, the defendant then set fire to their honeymoon suite, a fire that rapidly spread through the entire sixteenth floor of the Liholiho Tower, taking the lives of ten other people. Ten innocent guests of the Kupulupulu Beach Resort, two of whom were children."

Maddox solemnly lists their names without notes. For the younger victims, he follows their names with their ages.

Next to me Erin shivers and I turn and whisper in her ear, remind her to mind her body language. I haven't yet told Erin about the inmate at Halawa and I don't intend to. Not until I know for certain that this inmate holds information that can be used to exonerate her.

"Now the defense is going to *contest* that it was the defendant Erin Simms who stabbed her husband. My adversary, Mr. Kevin Corvelli, is going to *contest* that it was the defendant Erin Simms who set fire to the Liholiho Tower of the Kupulupulu Beach Resort on that hot night this past July. The defense will contest these facts, because . . ." With a humorless smile, Maddox shrugs his broad shoulders and holds out the palms of his hands. "Because what else are they going to do?

"But you, ladies and gentlemen of the jury, will not be swayed, will not be fooled. Because you will hear evidence during this trial that will convince you beyond any reasonable doubt that the defendant Erin Simms stabbed her husband in the gut and watched him bleed out, then set fire to the tower to conceal her crime."

Maddox allows for a dramatic pause, a hush that undoubtedly touches each of the jurors in the belly, before moving on to the evidence he is about to present.

"You will hear testimony from the defendant's friend Mia

Landow," he says, "of death threats the defendant made earlier in the day against her then-fiancé, who had betrayed her.

"You will hear testimony from Izzy Dufu, assistant chief of resort security, who was called to the defendant's room *twice* because of heated arguments between the couple earlier that night.

"You will hear the testimony of Dr. Derek Noonan, this county's chief medical examiner, as to how each of the defendant's victims, including her husband Trevor Simms, died.

"You will hear testimony from veteran fire investigator Inez Rios, who will explain as precisely as possible how the fire started and how it spread.

"You will learn from Honolulu homicide detective John Tatupu all about the department's murder investigation and the eventful arrest of the defendant Erin Simms.

"Finally, you will hear the testimony of Trevor Simms's sister Lauren Simms, who observed a Pteroco Legend switchblade in the defendant's possession just hours before Trevor was murdered.

"And you will see physical evidence, ladies and gentlemen. You will *see* the Zippo lighter—engraved with the initials ED for Erin Downey—that the defendant used to set the fire.

"You will see remnants of the canisters that held the charcoal starter fluid that the defendant used as an accelerant so that the fire would take and quickly spread.

"You will see photographs of the suite where the defendant began this massacre, the fire's point of origin marked by a distinctive burn pattern in the shape of the letter V.

"And you will see—though I will try to spare you as much of the macabre as possible—images of the eleven dead. All that remains of the defendant's victims."

Maddox swallows hard, stares up into the courtroom's fluorescent lights until it looks as though he's properly suffering from his own words and thoughts. He turns slightly away from the jury and pokes a pinky finger into the corner of his left eye, before spinning back around, a tear surfing the curve of his cheek.

"Excuse me," he says, his words barely audible. Quickly Maddox straightens himself, stands tall and bold as an intrepid prosecutor should, and looks each of his jurors in the eye.

Then, like a practiced thespian, he tenderly strikes a clenched fist into an open palm and shakes the pair to symbolize his solidarity with the twelve men and women in the box. "You and I," Maddox tells the jury, "are here in this courtroom today for the very same, simple reason. To see that justice is done."

When Maddox finishes with his opening statement less than an hour later, I'm already drained. Every last drip of confidence I stepped into the courtroom with this morning has evaporated, and I fear that it shows on my face.

I'm an empty shell of an advocate.

No longer sanguine but fatalistic.

I am, in every respect, outgunned.

Unless Turi's man at Halawa can be placed at the Kupulupulu Beach Resort at twenty after two on the night of the fire, there's a damn good chance I'm going to lose this case.

CHAPTER 44

He has the reddest hair I've ever seen, so red that it can't be real. But then, what the hell do I know? The red jungle of tresses hasn't been cut or cleaned in some time, that much I'm sure of. His face is so white that it blends in with the institutional walls. Eyes so pale blue that the irises are nearly transparent. He's slight; still, there's danger in those skeletal hands with or without a weapon. True madness makes up for a good deal of brawn. For once I'm glad that a sheet of protective glass separates me from the prisoner. This is because Corwin Pierce is not my client. I'm simply a visitor visiting during visitors' hours on visitors' day.

Corwin Pierce stares at me. Studies me and smiles. Smiles as though he's about to let me in on the greatest secret the world's ever known.

I've already sanitized the scratched-up black phone. Still, I hesitate putting the receiver to my ear. I hold it just close enough so that I can hear him.

"Turi says you're a lawyer."

The voice is strange, doesn't remotely match the face. It's as if his words are emanating from some bizarre far-off place. There's a disconnect, an odd time delay as though the audio and video are running on separate tracks. I shake off the eeriness and lift the receiver in front of my mouth to speak.

"That's right," I say softly. "And Turi tells me—"

"You're the lawyer I seen on the TV." His is a sleepy voice. Quiet, shy, almost as soft as a young woman's. Yet, originating from that face the slightest utterance becomes intimidating.

I nod. "You watch a lot of television, Corwin?"

He giggles. "Only the news and nature programs. Sometimes, if no one's home, the naked channel."

I lean forward, keep my own voice low and steady. "Who do you live with?"

"Who do you think I live with?" More sniggering.

"I don't know."

His gaze follows something behind me but I don't turn around. "I lived with my father's mother till they put her in a home."

"So now you live alone?"

He looks at me as though I'm hurling insults at him. "I didn't say that." Suddenly, he covers his mouth with his free hand as though to control his own laughter. When he recovers, he says: "That's not what you came here to talk about, is it, though?"

"No."

"You came to hear my poetry."

Before I can respond he's reaching into his pocket. He pulls out a wrinkled piece of lined paper folded four times over. He opens it slowly as though he's about to announce the Academy Award winner for Best Picture. Finally he presses the page up against the glass. My eyes reluctantly follow the words as he recites them from memory.

if i were a god,
> *god help you all.*
>> *the world would witness why.*

i'd drown the fish,
> *fell the trees,*
>> *cut man down to size.*

i'd clip birds' wings
> *and damn all good things,*
>> *while i laughed at their demise.*

if i were a god,
> *god help you all.*
>> *the world would catch ablaze.*

i'd douse this sphere
> *in gasoline,*
>> *end this planet's days.*

i'd strike a wooden match,
> *warm my ice cold hands.*
i'd toast my bread
> *and clear my head,*
>> *while my new sun*
>>> *sung my praise.*

"You wrote that?" I say quietly.

"Well, who in Hell do you think wrote it, Corvelli?"

The voice accompanying his outburst is decidedly masculine. A guard looks over, first at Corwin, then through the looking glass at me. I bow my head as if to say it's all right, everything's under control. Madmen are a large part of my line of work.

When I look back at Corwin Pierce he is rocking back and

forth. His mouth is a straight line, his lips seemingly sealed with cement.

"You know why I'm here, don't you, Corwin?"

It's a solid minute before he says, "You want to talk about fire."

"Not just any fire, Corwin. The fire in Ko Olina this past July."

"That was a good fire," he says without emotion.

I keep my hand from trembling by pressing the receiver tighter against my ear. All concern for germs has abruptly vanished. "Was that one of yours?"

Corwin Pierce has a history of setting fires. Over the past decade he's pleaded twice to destruction of property, even served a little time. He burned a garage. An abandoned shed. A field. But never before has he taken lives or even come close. True, his fires have escalated in size. In fact, the fire he's in for now involved a pickup truck and a tree. Word is, his actions could have resulted in a brush fire so large it could have competed against a recent disaster in northern California.

"It was one of mine," he says, giggling again. "My masterpiece. My opus."

I lean forward, try not to flinch as I look him in those dead blue eyes. "Tell me what you told Turi Ahina. Tell me how you did it."

"I was bored," he starts, his feminine voice falling into a monotone. "I don't usually get so bored but I did that day, so I went outside and walked to the road and I hitched a ride with some locals from Waianae early in the afternoon. Didn't know where they were headed and I didn't care. I curled up in the bed of their pickup and fell asleep, and when I woke we were passing through the gate into Ko Olina, headed for one of the lagoons."

"What were their names?"

"The locals?" He shrugs. "Don't know. Never saw them before, never saw them again. We drove down to the fourth lagoon, parked and parted ways. I found myself a nice shade tree and sat down under it and at some point I fell asleep. I woke sometime late that afternoon, walked around a bit, found someone's unattended cooler full of sodas and sandwiches and helped myself. Then the night came around.

"Ran into some guys who were drinking beers out past the marina by Barbers Point. I was going to try to steal some but they offered and I accepted and we got to talking. I only had but one or two, but I sat there with them for hours."

"What were their names?" I say.

"I'll get to that," he snaps. It's Corwin's first break from the tone he immediately fell into when he started his story. Corwin clears his throat and scoots his chair forward. "First the fire."

I lean back on the hard plastic chair and cross my legs. "It's your show," I tell him.

He'd seen them earlier in the day, he tells me. The bride and groom, the wedding party. So he knew his target. He'd found an old Seattle Mariners cap that afternoon and placed it on his head, along with a cheap pair of sunglasses he'd found near the garbage. Probably ladies' glasses, he says.

He spied on the last leg of the reception, waited while everyone went up to their rooms, then watched the newlyweds argue at Kanaloa's from beyond the gate. Heard the bride cussing out her husband *and* the bartender.

"I didn't like the looks of her chubby hubby," he says. "Thought it would be nice to see her doughboy go up in flames."

So when the couple left Kanaloa's he followed them up to their room.

"How did you do that?" I ask.

"They got in the elevator alone, the two of them, and I waited until the door closed, then watched the lights above it. Saw that the elevator traveled up and up and up and up until it reached the sixteenth floor."

Corwin took the stairs. At this point he had no real plan, just knew he wanted to do some damage. Maybe not kill anyone, maybe just scare someone a bit. Then opportunity knocked. Or rather hotel security.

He heard a few expletives, then saw the door slam in their face.

As they walked away, he heard one security guard say to the other something about charcoal starter fluid in the room and it felt as though destiny were calling.

He hung in the stairwell, thinking, checking the floor every once in a while. His heart was pounding—it was one ginormous rush, he says, as though he'd just snorted three fat lines of crystal meth.

Then the luck. Serendipity, he calls it. The bride left the room and made for the elevator and she was alone.

He followed her. First downstairs then to the lagoon, which was beautifully pitch-black and empty.

She was drunk, no question about it, he says, so it was easy. She stood up, walked around a bit, left her handbag perfectly unattended in the sand.

In the darkness he couldn't make the bag out, but later he would see it was a little leather Fendi. He crossed over to the nearby construction site, unzipped it, and examined its contents.

He found the knife first. A switchblade, he says. And, of course, the Zippo lighter that he figured belonged to her husband Ed because of the engraved letters. Both of these finds were great but what Corwin really wanted was the key card to their room. And the key card was in there, too, zipped up in a small side compartment.

Finding the valve to the water main was easy. He knows this kind of shit, he tells me. He removed his T-shirt and used it like a glove so that he wouldn't leave any prints when he turned the valve.

He couldn't waste much time. Sooner or later, even in the dead of night, someone might notice. Some guest might call the front desk and complain. "There's no fucking water," someone might say. But then, he had to time it all just right, too. He couldn't be seen. Not by security or staff, not by the guests, and certainly not by any of the resort's video surveillance cameras.

He figures it was just past two when he made it back to their room. First he listened at the door for conversation, television, radio, anything. Then he used the key card to enter the honeymoon suite and found the man in bed and asleep.

"I was able to pour out all the charcoal starter fluid before he even stirred," Corwin says. "Then the fucker woke up so I buried the bitch's knife in his gut. Watched him bleed like a stuck fucking pig."

"Then what?"

"Well, you don't need to be Sherlock Holmes to figure the rest out, lawyer. I slapped my thumb down on the flint wheel of that bitch's lighter and tossed it onto the juice." He smiles that sick, twisted smile he smiled when I first arrived. "Then God said, 'Let there be fire.'"

I have Corwin Pierce tell me the story again and again and then once more. Barely a word of his narrative changes—certainly none of the facts—though on the fourth and final time around

Corwin Pierce lets me in on the big secret, the denouement of his tale.

"The spics I drank beers with over at Barbers Point," he says, "turns out they were gangbangers from L.A. They paid me to do this shit."

"How much?"

"A couple hundred."

"Why did they want it done?"

Corwin leans forward, presses his nose up against the glass. "One of the spics said this guy pissed down his leg the night before," he says, barely able to keep from cracking up.

"I see." I glance at the clock on the wall. "Why didn't you tell me this before?"

He sits back, blows out a breath. "Suspense, lawyer. It's not what you put into a story, it's what you leave out."

Tired, I nod and remain silent for a while. "You left something else out," I say finally.

"Did I?"

"You did."

Corwin Pierce waits. When I don't elaborate a look of pure fury creeps back onto his stark white face. "Well, what was it I left out, Corvelli, that you would like to know?"

I let his question hang in the air for another few moments. I set the receiver down on the counter and stand as though I'm ready to leave. I smooth out my suit and straighten my tie as he watches me. Finally, putting the bulk of my weight on my good left leg, I lean forward, lift the receiver and press it against my ear.

"Tell me. What did you do with the knife, Mr. Pierce?"

On this and only this, Corwin Pierce remains perfectly silent.

CHAPTER 45

Judge Sonya Maxa asks Mia Landow if she would care for a recess before looking at me and saying, "Your witness, Mr. Corvelli."

"Thank you, Your Honor."

Mia watches me hobble to the podium the way a bartender watches a loud drunk: guarded, unsure of what to expect, afraid of the next words to spew from my mouth.

"Good afternoon, Ms. Landow. We've met before, have we not?"

"We have, yes."

"Good, now tell me, Ms. Landow . . ." I can almost feel the individuals in the gallery listening, hanging on every word of my first few questions. Since I refrained from making an opening statement until after the close of the prosecution's case, no one, including Luke Maddox, is quite sure what I am about to say, what type of strategy I intend to employ, if any. "To your knowledge, what was Trevor Simms's business?"

Mia frowns with relief, clearly anticipating another line of questioning. No doubt she's been dreading for months seeing me stand at this podium from her perch on the witness stand, having me delve into her sexual proclivities. Truth is, if it would assist me in winning an acquittal I wouldn't hesitate to paint her as a backstabbing harlot with the morals of a cable news commentator. After all, in my profession, the outcome is all that matters. How I arrive there is trivial. But I don't disgrace witnesses just for kicks. At least not anymore. Unless, of course, they truly have it coming to them.

Fortunately for both me and Mia, Maddox opened the door to Trevor's business dealings on direct examination by attempting to show that Mia Landow was more to Trevor than just an object of his lust, that she received more from him than just a single roll in the hay in the harbor. The less tawdry Trevor's infidelity, Maddox no doubt figured, the less sympathy it would merit for Erin Simms. And what better way in America to establish a trusting relationship than by displaying an open line of communication about one's own finances.

Maddox calmly rises from his chair. "Objection, Your Honor. Could Mr. Corvelli please specify the time period he is inquiring about?"

"Absolutely," I say. In fact, I phrased the question to goad Maddox to his feet. "Strike the previous question and let me ask you this, Ms. Landow. In the time period that you knew Trevor Simms, did his line of business ever change?"

Maddox sits, no doubt realizing he shouldn't have pulled the trigger on this first objection. Early on, that is my strategy, to adapt to Maddox's objections so well that it seems as though I feed off them; to obliterate his confidence, make him gun-shy, make him second-guess himself each and every time he stands to object.

"Yes, it did."

"And to your knowledge, when did this change in business occur?"

"Just after he and Erin became engaged to be married."

"Do you know the reason behind Trevor Simms's change in business?"

Mia hesitates for a moment, undoubtedly calculating how much to say. She's a witness for the prosecution and Maddox would if he could dress her up in a State uniform to remind her of such. Ultimately, Mia throws caution to the wind and goes with the truth.

"Yes, I do. Prior to their engagement, Trevor had been working as an executive for his father's software company, SimmsWare. But Trevor's father didn't approve of Erin as Trevor's fiancée, so Trevor and his dad had a sort of falling out."

"I see. And did this falling out result in Trevor Simms's termination from his father's company?"

"Yes, it did."

Flan's week-long trip to San Francisco proved a worthwhile investment. In fact, in these financial times, were it not for the ten other dead, I could probably skate Erin on the charge of killing her husband simply by revealing everything Trevor did during the final year of his life.

"That must have been difficult for Trevor," I say. "Did you notice much of a change in Trevor's behavior after he lost his position with his father's company?"

"How do you mean?"

"Say, for instance, Trevor's spending habits. From what you observed, did Trevor Simms's spending habits change at all following his dismissal from SimmsWare and his loss of an executive salary?"

"No, they didn't. If anything, Trevor became even more reckless with his money."

"Why do you suppose that is?" I say, inviting Maddox's objection. I want the jury thinking about this question before I answer it myself.

"Objection," Maddox says. "Calls for speculation."

"Withdrawn," I say, before Maxa can rule. "Ms. Landow, immediately following Trevor Simms's dismissal from SimmsWare, did you know what type of business he had decided to go into?"

"Not at first, no."

"Did there come a time when you learned what type of business Trevor Simms went into following his termination at SimmsWare?"

"Yes."

"When?"

"Trevor confided in me a couple of weeks before his wedding."

"Do you recall on which particular day Trevor shared this information with you?"

"The day we spent alone on Trevor's boat in San Francisco Bay."

Thanks to her testimony on direct the jury needs no reminder as to what else transpired on that day.

"To the best of your recollection, Ms. Landow, what did Trevor Simms tell you with respect to his new business on that day?"

"Objection." Maddox is up again. "Calls for hearsay."

"Your Honor," I say, "may we approach the bench?"

Maxa motions us forward and both Maddox and I manage to make it all the way to the bench without once glancing in the other's direction.

Once we are out of earshot of the jury box, I say, "Your Honor, I verily believe the witness's answer will be fully admissible as a statement against interest."

The hearsay rule prevents a witness from repeating a statement made by someone else when that statement is being used to prove the truth of the matter asserted. One of the hearsay rule's many exceptions, however, is when the statement made would be against the declarant's—in this case Trevor's—interest. The logic behind this exception is that if one makes a statement *against* his own interest, it is far more likely to be trustworthy.

"Are we talking about criminal conduct, Mr. Corvelli?" Maxa asks.

"Of the foulest kind, Your Honor. Financial."

"In that case, let me clear the courtroom. You can ask these questions outside the presence of the jury and then I'll make my determination as to whether the statements are admissible." Maxa pauses. "Unless . . ."

"Yes, Your Honor?"

"Unless you can save me the trouble and present this evidence in some other fashion."

"I'd be delighted to, Your Honor. Anything I can do to expedite justice."

I hear Maddox mutter "fuckhead" as I amble back to the podium.

While I was up at the bench Jake placed Flan's blue folder on the podium. I open it now and remove its contents. "Your Honor, I would like to enter this set of documents marked as Defendant's Exhibit B." Jake delivers a copy to Maddox's table as I present my set to the clerk for proper labeling. "May I approach the witness, Your Honor?"

"You may."

"Ms. Landow," I say, handing her the papers, "do you recognize this set of documents?"

Mia takes her time looking them over. "Yes, I do."

"Do you recall when you first saw them?"

"On the day Trevor and I spent alone on his boat in San Francisco Bay."

"Do you know what these documents relate to?"

"Trevor's new . . . business," she says.

"And what was that business, Ms. Landow?"

"Trevor described it as something similar to a Ponzi scheme."

There's a slight rattle from the gallery at the mention of the words *Ponzi scheme*. Maxa quickly extinguishes it with a soft rap of her gavel.

Maddox is on his feet. "Objection. Hearsay, Your Honor."

Maxa shakes her head. "Overruled. If that's not a statement against interest, then I don't know what is."

"By Ponzi scheme," I continue, "you're referring to a fraudulent investment operation. Correct, Ms. Landow?"

"Correct. Trevor collected money from honest investors using the ruse that he was starting his own software company. With his background at SimmsWare, it was easy for Trevor to convince investors that anything he started was a wise investment."

"But Trevor Simms had no intention of starting his own software company, isn't that also correct?"

Mia nods on the stand. "That's right."

"Yet Trevor Simms was able to pay returns to his investors in order to convince them to continue investing with him. How did he manage that?"

"Trevor paid returns to individual investors with their own money or with money he received from subsequent investors."

"Silicon Valley's Bernie Madoff," I remark.

Maddox objects and Maxa sustains but I've made the connection I wanted to and even earned a few chuckles from the jury box to boot.

"Ms. Landow, that set of documents you now hold in your

hands, tell me, does that set contain a list of names under the heading *Investors?*"

Mia flips a page, glances at the header. "Yes, it does."

"Now, from your personal knowledge and understanding, from Trevor Simms's own admission, would you characterize the individuals on that list as people who Trevor Simms swindled?"

"Absolutely."

I turn to the jury. "Do me a favor, Ms. Landow, and read for me the names listed next to the following numbers under the heading *Investors.*" I clasp my hands behind my back. "Twenty-six."

"Tara Holland."

"Thirty-eight."

"Isaac Cassel."

"Fifty-six."

"Gabe Guidry."

"Seventy-one."

"Todd Downey."

"You know all four of these individuals, Ms. Landow, isn't that correct?"

"That's correct."

"And were any of these four individuals that Trevor Simms *swindled* present on the island of Oahu on the day of Trevor and Erin's wedding—or more pointedly, on the night of the fire?"

"Yes," Mia says, matter-of-factly. "All four of them were."

CHAPTER 46

"Where the hell is Flan?"

No sooner do I say it than a soaking wet Ryan Flanagan steps through the door and into our conference room.

"Sorry, Kev. Had to bail Casey out of jail this morning."

"Jail?" Jake says. "What the hell for?"

"She was riding around downtown Honolulu last night with some thugs in a stolen car." Flan shakes it off. "But enough about her. How did it go in court yesterday?"

"We accomplished what we set out to with Mia Landow," I tell him. "We've doubled-down on the motives of a few viable suspects. But there is still no physical evidence pointing at any of them, and our best prospect, Isaac Cassel, has a paper alibi."

"And you exposed Trevor Simms for what he was, I assume?" Flan says as he takes a seat next to Jake.

I nod. "Thing is, putting the victim on trial in this case isn't going to win it. Bottom line: there were eleven victims."

"Can't put 'em all on trial," Jake says.

"That's right. Which means, we lose unless we have someone reasonable to point to. What we need to do is pick a party and fill that empty seat."

"What happened with Turi's firebug?" Flan asks.

"Full confession from Corwin Pierce," I say. "Four times, story didn't change a bit."

"Well, that's great."

"Hell it is," Jake says.

"There are three problems with pointing at Corwin Pierce," I tell Flan as the rain pounds against our floor-to-ceiling windows. "One, his story is too perfect, down to the last detail."

"What's wrong with that?" Flan says.

"His confession sounded rehearsed," I say. "He recited it from memory like he did a poem he wrote, some crazy shit he made me listen to when I first got there."

"So?"

"So he could have picked up those details from watching two hours of Marcy Faith. She has been blathering about this case on her prime-time national cable news show for six months now, revealing every scintilla of evidence—admissible or inadmissible—to the masses and speculating on precisely how the crime was committed."

Jake shakes his head wearily. "One more thing the American system of justice has to thank brainless cowards like her and Gretchen Hurst for."

"All right," Flan says. "What else?"

"Two," I tell him, "Corwin Pierce, this notorious fire-junky, this pyromaniac, this fucking crazier-than-hell sociopath, claims he was *paid* to take out Trevor Simms."

"By who?"

"By *whom*," I say.

"Fuck you. By whom?"

"By Javier Vargas."

"The Angry Rooster?"

"The Angry Rooster."

"What's wrong with that?" Flan cries. "That's motive."

"Exactly," I say. "Firebugs and motives don't mix. Pyromaniacs like Corwin Pierce don't set fires for money. They set fires to get off, to watch shit burn."

"Instant gratification," Jake adds. "See the flames, smell the smoke, then watch as the world spins into chaos all because of something you created. Sit back and listen for the alarms and sirens, watch for the fire engines, the flashing lights. It's a rush. It would be an insult for someone like Pierce to be asked to do it for a couple hundred bucks."

"Not to mention," I add, "since when do violent-as-all-hell L.A. street gangs hire out their wet work to head cases like Corwin Pierce?"

Flan shrugs his shoulders, frustrated by the entire conversation. "Can't this Corwin Pierce and Javier Vargas be exceptions?"

"Sure," I say. "And we have no choice but to follow up on this lead. But here's the third problem." I lean back in my seat and painfully cross my right leg over my left. "Corwin Pierce knew every single detail about the fire—how it started, where it started, what happened to the lighter, all of it. *Everything* except for one thing, one crucial piece of information that even Marcy Faith can't squawk about."

"Which is?"

"He couldn't tell me what the hell he did with the knife."

CHAPTER 47

I am standing at the podium completely frozen for the moment and I can't think of a time in my career as a trial lawyer or even as a law student taking part in mock trials when I stared at a witness this long and couldn't conjure a single question to ask him.

"Mr. Corvelli," Judge Maxa prods.

I stare at Koa and he at me and neither of us can speak for entirely different reasons and I realize then that I have lost that fire in my belly. I wonder briefly if I will ever be able to participate in another trial of any kind, whether this is once and for all the last stand for Kevin Corvelli.

"I have no questions for the witness at this time," I say in a voice that is not my own. "But I would like to reserve the right to recall this witness during the defense's case-in-chief."

"Very well," Maxa says, and Koa is excused, released from the witness stand, and as he passes me he whispers something that sounds like an apology, but he has no reason to apologize because he told the truth.

Koa told the jury on direct examination about Erin and Trevor Simms and their actions at Kanaloa's on the night of the fire. He answered yes when asked whether there had been an argument between the newlyweds, whether the argument had been heated, whether the argument became physical at any point during the evening.

"Yes," Koa said. "At one point, the defendant slapped the victim hard across the face."

Koa testified about his own dispute with Erin Simms, how she refused to obey the bar's no-smoking policy, how she then attempted to take her alcoholic beverage beyond the black iron gate. He described what she was wearing at the time—the red dress already burned into my memory—and I saw her clear as I had that very night. Finally, Koa described in sufficient detail the Zippo lighter Erin used to light her cigarette at the bar.

"Silver," Koa said. "And I believe it was engraved, though with what words or letters I couldn't tell you."

Slowly I make my way back toward the defense table and my right leg sends an urgent message of pain to my brain and I hobble, glance out the window at the continuing rain, and wish that I was somewhere else.

"Please call your next witness, Mr. Maddox," says Her Honor, and he does.

Izzy Dufu is a large man but not by Samoan standards. On direct he testifies about his position as assistant security chief at the Kupulupulu Beach Resort, where he has toiled for the past seven and a half years. His obvious courtroom jitters clearly endear him to the jury but they put me on high alert. Because I have seen Izzy around the resort, I've witnessed him introduce performers in front of crowds that would overflow this courtroom. Suffice it to say, Izzy Dufu is not ordinarily what you would describe as the shy type.

"Good afternoon, Mr. Dufu," I say once the witness is proferred to me. "Or may I call you Izzy?"

I want to calm those jitters, get him comfortable speaking with me, so that when I hammer him to hell and back the jury will notice the difference in his demeanor.

"Yes, sir," he says. "Izzy's fine."

To accomplish this, I throw a few softballs to start, allow him to rehash his work history and the duties of his current job. Then I take him suddenly and without preamble to the night of the fire.

"The second time you visited Mr. and Mrs. Simms's honeymoon suite," I say, "that's when you tell us you first observed the canisters of charcoal lighter fluid, correct?"

"Yes, that's right, sir."

"That second visit, that is also when you tell us you first observed a small leather Fendi handbag, is it not?"

"That's when I first and last saw the handbag, that's correct, sir."

"Izzy, would you kindly remind the jury where the handbag was situated when you observed it during that second visit to the honeymoon suite?"

"The handbag was sitting on the nightstand next to the bed, sir. On the right-hand side."

"I see. And would you also remind the jury where the canisters of charcoal starter fluid were situated when you observed them during that second visit to the honeymoon suite?"

"The canisters were on the floor in front of the minifridge in the corner of the kitchenette."

"That would be the far right corner of the suite, correct?"

Izzy thinks about this. "Yes, that's correct, sir."

"How many canisters did you see?"

"Three."

"You're sure there were three?"

"Certain."

"And remind us, Izzy, what was the brand name of the charcoal lighter fluid you say you saw in the room?"

"Kingsford."

"Kingsford? And you're certain of that, too?"

"Yes, sir."

"You read the labels?"

"I recognized the containers. A lot of barbecuing goes down at the resort, so I've seen that brand hundreds of times."

"And you are certain, Izzy, that the handbag you observed on the nightstand was a Fendi?"

"Yes, sir."

"It couldn't have been a Gucci?"

"No, sir."

"Couldn't have been Prada?"

"No, sir."

"Could it have been Coach?"

"No, sir."

"How about a Burberry?"

"No, sir."

"Definitely a Fendi?"

"Yes, sir."

"How was the handbag positioned when you observed it?"

"Standing straight up on the nightstand."

"And this handbag was about five or six inches tall, you testified? About nine or ten inches wide?"

"Yes, sir."

"And the handbag read *Fendi* across the front of it?"

Izzy hesitates. "No, sir. I don't believe I said that."

"All right, but you did testify that you were certain this handbag was a Fendi. How did you identify the manufacturer of the handbag if the handbag didn't read F-E-N-D-I across the front of it?"

"By the markings," he says.

"The markings?"

"You know, the logo." He clicks his fingers as he searches for the right word. "The insignia."

"The insignia?"

"Yeah, the two capital F's performing sixty-nine on each other."

Even Judge Maxa smiles but she quickly puts an end to the chuckles by slapping her gavel. She was once a trial lawyer; she understands the importance of momentum.

Grinning, I say, "I won't ask you to draw us a picture, Izzy." When the new round of chuckles dies off, I add, "But I will ask you to describe for us the Burberry insignia."

Izzy shakes his head, still smiling. "That I can't do."

"Okay," I tell him. "Then please describe for us the Coach insignia."

Izzy's smile begins to fade. "Sorry," he says. "I can't."

"Prada?"

"No, sir."

"No problem, Izzy. I'll give you an easier one. Describe the Gucci insignia for us."

The smile has vanished, the nervous tics returned.

"No?" I say. "Not even Gucci? Even I can describe the Gucci insignia."

"Then you'd better go ahead and do it," Izzy says before Maddox can rise with his objection.

"Sustained," the judge says. "Strike Mr. Corvelli's last comment."

I fold my hands together at the podium and watch Izzy squirm a bit on the stand. "How is it then, Izzy, that you came to recognize the Fendi insignia?"

There are plenty of acceptable answers Izzy can provide that will help to resurrect his credibility as a witness, at least half a dozen answers I can think of off the top of my head that will stop me dead in my tracks. Izzy is reaching for one of them, I can see that. But I can also see that each of those answers remains safely out of his grasp.

"The two F's," he says, nearly mumbling now. "They just, you know, came to me as I was looking at the handbag on the nightstand."

"So right away, you recognized the bag as a Fendi?" I say.

"Not right away . . ."

"But as you were still looking at the bag?"

"Yes, sir. I took a long, hard look at it."

Gotcha. "You testified earlier, didn't you, Izzy, that on your second visit to the Simms's honeymoon suite, you stood at the door for a grand total of under a minute while Erin Simms hurled expletives at you?"

A hesitation. "Yes, sir."

"And you testified that during the entire exchange Erin Simms stood in the doorway in what you perceived as an effort to block your entrance into the suite?"

A visible swallow. "Yes, sir."

"And you testified that Erin Simms refused to open the door all the way, that in fact, Erin Simms opened the door no more than quote 'the size of my fist' at any time during the exchange?"

A slow nod. "Correct, sir."

"But in that time, in *under a minute,* with a woman blocking your view and hurling expletives at you, with the door open no more than *five or six inches,* you were able to not only observe but to *identify* three canisters of Kingsford charcoal lighter fluid *and* a small leather Fendi handbag that were situated, by your own admission, no less than *twelve to fifteen feet apart* from one another?"

Izzy stares at me with moist eyes, his lips visibly trembling. "What can I say, I have exceptional observation skills."

"That you do, Izzy. Either that or one hell of a fertile imagination."

CHAPTER 48

". . . secrets?" Josh says.

We're sitting on my lanai in Ko Olina, the kid and I, for what may very well be the last time. Sebastian Haslett, the boy's father, expressed no interest in taking custody of Josh, so the issue will be left for the courts to decide. Sometime next week, Josh will be interviewed in downtown Honolulu by a state social worker. For the time being, however, the kid is still living with Chelsea in Waikele, where I picked him up this morning, because Chelsea prefers to spend her days alone in Waikiki having a good time.

"What?" I ask him.

I'm not listening. My mind is whirling, tossing around images of Erin and Trevor and the night of the fire. I'm thinking of Brandon Glenn. Wondering how it is going to feel to lose this case, to lose Erin Simms forever. I'm trying to decide whether I can go on, whether I can remain in Hawaii, whether I can continue practicing law.

"I asked if you had any secrets," Josh says.

"A few," I tell him.

Josh is sitting in the chair beside me, stroking Grey Skies in his lap as it continues to drizzle. With all that has happened to the kid in his brief life, I wonder how he can stand it, how he can seem so unaffected. Then I realize something I've said to myself a countless number of times: Kids are resilient.

But it catches up with them in time.

Like Erin.

Like Nikki.

Like myself.

"What kinds of secrets?" Josh says.

"Well," I say without looking at him, "if I told you they wouldn't be secrets anymore, now would they?"

"So you should never tell a secret?"

I immediately call to mind Brandon Glenn's secret, that he was gay, a fact that had I known it at the time, may very well have won him an acquittal. Brandon's secret was a secret that could have saved his life. A secret that would have changed nothing between us had he told me.

Then I think of Joey Gianforte's secret, that he was engaged. That secret nearly cost Joey a lifetime stay in the pen.

"What if you have to give test-money?" Josh says.

"Testimony," I correct him for the umpteenth time.

Immediately my mind leaps back in time to yesterday, to Izzy Dufu's testimony. Why did he lie? What did Izzy Dufu have to gain by saying he identified the little leather Fendi? Was he coached by Maddox? If so, why? Would an up-and-comer like Luke Maddox suborn perjury and risk an ethics charge just to place the little leather handbag in the honeymoon suite at that particular time of night? It doesn't add up, doesn't make sense. Unless Izzy is somehow involved in the crime. Well, he or Luke Maddox.

"What about testimony?" I finally say.

"You told me that you have to say the truth, the whole truth, and nothing but the truth."

"That's right."

"And that if you lie, the judge will give you a spanking."

"That's right."

"But what if you have a *big* secret that you're not s'posed to tell?"

"Then your lawyer won't put you on the stand."

"What if your lawyer doesn't know about the secret?"

I'm about to give the kid the most vital piece of advice an attorney could share with his client—*It is imperative to tell your lawyer everything*—when my cell phone rings on the coffee table in my living room. "Excuse me," I say as I step past the sliding screen door.

I flip open the clam shell and put it to my ear. "Speak."

It's Flan returning my call. "What can I do for you, Kev?"

"Have Hoshi draw you up two subpoenas addressed to the Kupulupulu Beach Resort. One for a copy of any and all excessive noise complaints received at the front desk on the night of the fire and one for a printout of all security passkey activity, including the passkey belonging to Izzy Dufu."

"But we already received that stuff," Flan says.

"We received a copy from Maddox's office. Now I want a certified copy directly from the resort, and I want you to stand there while they print it. Then we'll see if the two match up."

"You got it," he says.

I click END and immediately put a call through to Milt Cashman's cell.

Five rings later Milt answers the call. "Speak," he hollers into the phone.

It's well after eleven at night in New York but there's plenty of background noise: loud music, the clanking of forks and knives, the sound of a champagne bottle being uncorked.

"Is this a bad time?"

"Never a bad time for you, Kevin. I'm at Tao with Rabid Dawg. We just today beat that bullshit gun charge."

"Congratulations," I say.

"Thanks, Kev. Now what the hell do you want?"

"I need some information on that former L.A. prosecutor I told you about over the summer."

"The cocksucker?"

"That's him."

"What do you need to know?"

"We have everything official on him—everything from the California State Bar, everything from L.A. County. I want some *unofficial* information. I want to know what *really* drove this bastard out of town."

"You want his Brandon Glenn," Milt says matter-of-factly. "Hold on." Milt doesn't bother covering the mouthpiece on his phone. "Hey Dawg, what's the name of your West Coast agent?" Pause. "That's right, the Korean Jew. Give him a call at home, it's only eight P.M. in L.A. Ask him if he knows anyone in the L.A. County Prosecutor's office. I'm looking for shit on a guy named . . ."

"Luke Maddox," I tell him.

". . . Luke Maddox," Milt says. "Good." Then Milt's speaking to me again. "All right, Kev. Give us a little time on this. I'll get back to you soon as I hear anything."

"Thanks, Milt."

"Hey, what are Jews for?"

I close my phone and slip back onto the lanai. "Now, what were we talking about, Josh?"

He thinks about it a moment. *"Transformers."*

CHAPTER 49

I am a zombie.

Where once stood an impetuous vampire now stands an impotent, shuffling corpse. I cross the threshold into Erin's Kaneohe home for perhaps the last time. We sit on the rattan sofa without looking at one another. My tongue feels too thick in my mouth to speak. I can't hold her, can't caress her, can't take her into the bedroom for one final escape. The Fukitol has stolen my sex drive and, truth be told, I'm not certain I want it back.

"We're going to lose, aren't we?" she says finally.

I say nothing. For the first time I want to back down from this fight. I want to fly away from these islands and pretend I was never here. I want to leave behind all courtrooms and all clients and all prosecutors, most particularly Luke Maddox. My latest professional freefall, I'm convinced, all started with him. But the fire in my mind is doused. For some reason I can't truly hate him. And I fear if I can't hate him I can't win.

"We're going to lose, aren't we?" she says again.

"No."

"No?"

"No. I promise."

"How can you promise that?"

"Because I can't allow you to be convicted," I say. "I won't be able to live with that."

"But you can't control—"

"I am in control," I insist. I still haven't once looked at her. "I've always been in control."

"What did you want to be when you grew up?" I ask her, standing in the darkness on her lanai.

"An artist," she says without hesitation. "Or a musician. I couldn't decide."

"What happened?"

"What always happens, I suppose. Reality takes over."

"Whose reality?" I ask.

Her head turns toward me but I still can't look at her, not even in the dark. "I don't understand," she says.

I think she does.

"What did *you* want to be when you grew up?" she asks.

I shrug. "I wanted to go to Hollywood, to be in some way involved in the making of movies. Maybe as an actor, maybe as a screenwriter."

"What happened?"

"The Dreamkillers," I say, before I turn away and step inside.

We don't discuss the case the rest of the night. These charges are what brought us together and these charges are in all likelihood what will tear us apart. But this story—her story, my story, our story—started well before the night of the fire. And for the first time since Erin refused to change her plea to not guilty by reason of insanity, I ask to hear her side of it.

"My mother was always the domineering type," she says while we lie atop her made bed, fully dressed, both of us staring through the darkness at the ceiling. "Pretty sure that's what drove my biological father away. Nothing he did was ever good enough for her. She'd tell him to work more hours, then complain he didn't spend enough time with his family. She constantly criticized the way he dressed, the way he looked, threw a fit if he put on a baseball cap or didn't shave."

"Did she drink?" I say.

"She drank but the alcohol actually seemed to calm her. I was always more frightened of her when she was sober. And always more afraid of what she'd say in public than in private. The tantrums, the screaming, it was scary, even when the rage wasn't directed at me. *Especially* when the rage wasn't directed at me. I always wished she'd hit me rather than embarrass me."

"Did she hit you?"

"Sometimes. But it was almost a relief when she did. That was the only time she could understand my running away from her. And I dreaded the inevitable moment a half hour later when she'd be on the other side of my locked door apologizing. Because I knew as soon as I opened that door the whole fucking thing would start all over again. The only variation was the minutia that would cause the spark."

"Why not keep the door locked?"

Erin almost laughs. "Because if I did that, a few minutes later I'd hear the drill. And over the drill more of her screaming and it was always just a matter of time. I had to always be by her side, even when she hated me. Growing up, there was nothing and nowhere in the world that was solely mine. My toys were hers; she made a constant point of telling me that, that she could take all of them away from me at anytime, even my favorite teddy Corduroy. My room was under her roof so she claimed she had complete access to it always, even when I was thirteen or fourteen and needed a little privacy. I couldn't keep a journal because it would be read. I couldn't write notes to boyfriends because they would eventually be found and destroyed."

"Sounds like a toss-down of a prison cell," I say.

"She wanted to make sure I didn't have anyone else in my life. Just her. Always her. She became afraid when I made friends, did everything she could to make sure I didn't have relationships with boys, even when I was seventeen or eighteen years old. God, I was such a social misfit. And no one understood why. I was the pretty girl who couldn't get a date to the prom."

"But then college . . ." I prod.

"My mother wouldn't pay, wouldn't cosign my student loans, unless I continued to live at home. And she held it over my head, same as my car, a cute little red Geo Storm. Reminded me all the time that she could take everything away with a couple phone calls. So college was just a repeat of high school. If anything it was worse because I knew I had the option of quitting school and getting a minimum-wage job and making a clean break, getting my own apartment and living paycheck to paycheck."

"But that was something else you feared you'd never escape."

"Yeah," she says. "In hindsight I probably would have been better off but I was so scared. I would have zero family support and no way of advancing without a higher education. I still had no friends."

"What about Tara and Mia?"

"I mean, we've known each other since forever, but we didn't become real close until after college when I finally got out of my mother's house. By then, of course, it was too late to pursue my passions. Thanks to my mother's pushing and pulling, I had a degree in fucking *food science,* something I had absolutely no interest in. It was just another way for her to remain in control."

"So after college . . ."

"After college I took on small jobs that had nothing to do with my degree. I was a bank teller at First Fidelity, an assistant manager at an In-and-Out Burger, a saleswoman in the shoe department at Sears. I was so depressed, so lonely. That's when I started throwing myself at men. All these wonderful relationships that lasted all of two or three weeks. Until I met Isaac."

"And then Trevor," I say.

"Trevor was me getting greedy. I wanted to be with somebody who could take care of me the rest of my life so that I would never once after the wedding have to set foot in my mother's house again."

"Your mother's marriage to Todd didn't help?"

"It helped a bit. Deflected some of the crazy, you could say. Todd makes a good target because he's perpetually quiet, doesn't like arguing so he hardly ever answers her back. He just takes it, and I think that pisses her off more than anything. I think she *needs* to fight."

"And the cutting?"

"Funny thing is, I started cutting long before I realized my mother did. I started when I was around twelve. At first it was just little scrapes with an opened paperclip. Then I started using a sharp pencil but I became afraid of lead poisoning. That's when I switched over to knives. My legs were always a favorite target, but eventually I moved up to my belly, my arms, my wrists. At fourteen I started smoking, and on my way home from school, I'd stop in this dog park and sit on a bench, and when I was through, I'd stub the butt out on one of my thighs."

I cringe.

"But cigarette burns are very noticeable," she continues. "So

I started using lighters and matches and the blisters weren't as conspicuous. Burning seemed to give me the most relief. I can't explain why, it just hurt better than the burning inside. I didn't feel as empty after I burned myself. I felt full, almost alive. Before I burned, I dreamt everyday of jumping off the Golden Gate Bridge."

"Then you started a fire."

"Then I started a fire," she says with a single bow of her head toward the dark ceiling. "It was in the break room at this bullshit job I had at a chain pet store. Someone walked in unexpectedly and I dropped the match I was holding under my upper arm and it fell right onto a stack of old *L.A. Times* we used to line the bird cages."

There were three similar incidents, none of which are admissible at trial, all excluded as "prior bad acts."

"That's around the time my mother found out," she says. "But I don't think we've ever spoken a word about it. Even after I spent a few days in the psych ward at St. Claire's."

"And your mother," I say, "she never tried to get help for herself?"

"That's the worst part of it, Kevin. It was so obvious to everyone else that something was terribly wrong with her. But . . ."

I slowly lower the lids of my eyes and finish her thought. "But she didn't see it," I say.

CHAPTER 50

"Dr. Noonan," Luke Maddox says from the podium, "in the case of Trevor Simms, were you able to determine the cause and manner of death?"

The chief medical examiner shifts in the witness chair so that he can direct his answer to the jury. "I was."

"And what did you discover to be the cause of death?"

"A sharp-force injury to the lower abdomen."

Noonan's words are drawn out as though dipped in molasses, tinged with a throaty German accent.

"In layman's terms, Doctor?"

"The victim was stabbed."

"Stabbed," Maddox repeats. "And what did you determine the manner of death to be?"

"Homicide."

"Homicide," Maddox says again. "Is it possible, Dr. Noonan, that you may be mistaken about this determination? Is it possible, for instance, that the manner of Trevor Simms's death may actually have been accidental?"

"No."

"Why not, Doctor?"

"Because in order for this stab wound to have been accidental, the victim Mr. Simms would have had to fall onto the sharp object. There is no evidence of that. In fact, there is much evidence to the contrary. Chiefly, that the victim Mr. Simms was discovered faceup on his bed with a sharp-force wound to the front of his torso."

"All right," says Maddox. "Well, then isn't there a possibility that the manner of Trevor Simms's death may actually have been suicidal?"

"No. If possible, that is even less likely."

"Why so?"

"Because," Dr. Noonan says directly to the jury, "if the wound were self-inflicted, there would very likely be smaller, shallower wounds associated with it. These are called hesitation wounds and they vary in both size and depth. They are caused by an individual who is working up the courage to make the fatal stab."

"Nevertheless, can a stab wound be suicidal in the absence of these hesitation wounds?"

"Unlikely, but yes."

"Are there any other reasons, then, Dr. Noonan, that cause you to believe that Trevor Simms's manner of death was not suicidal?"

"Well, for one, it is exceedingly difficult for someone to stab himself with enough force to be fatal. Secondly . . ." Noonan looks from Maddox to the jury with a slight grin on his face. ". . . it would hurt like a bitch."

Cue uncomfortable laughter from the gallery.

Judge Maxa doesn't even bother to admonish the witness. Noonan has probably used that exact line in at least a dozen homicide trials featuring death by stabbing in order to lighten the mood, to break the proverbial ice. Maybe even to awaken a dozing juror or two.

"So, Dr. Noonan," Maddox says, "just so that we're clear for the jury: Setting aside for the moment the fact we established earlier—that Trevor Simms was dead at the time the fire started—is it reasonably possible that the stab wound found on the victim's abdomen could have been self-inflicted?"

"Not reasonable at all."

"Thank you, Doctor." Maddox walks over to the prosecution table and takes a long sip of ice water. When he returns to the podium his voice is charged, his body language more lively. "Now, Dr. Noonan, tell us: Is it clear from your study of the wound on Trevor Simms's abdomen that whoever inflicted that wound intended to kill him or to cause serious bodily harm?"

The ME allows for a practiced pregnant pause before saying, "As clear as the nose on my face."

"Dr. Noonan," I say from the podium, "on direct examination you testified that your examination of the wound on Mr. Simms's body led you to the conclusion that he was likely stabbed with a knife, and that the knife likely possessed a blade between three and four inches in length. Is that correct?"

"Yes, Mr. Corvelli, that is correct."

"And you supposedly made this determination after using a probe and carefully plumbing the depth of the wound on Mr. Simms's torso, is that correct?"

"Yes, it is."

"Would you explain to the jury why the blade could not have been any shorter than three to four inches?"

Noonan looks at the jury and says, "Because the wound on the victim's abdomen was just under three inches deep."

"I see." I follow Noonan's gaze to the jury box. "Now, Dr. Noonan, would you kindly explain to the jury why the blade used could not have been any *longer* than three to four inches?"

Noonan smiles gently; this is old hat to him. "It could have been longer."

"It could have been *significantly* longer, isn't that right, Dr. Noonan?"

"I suppose—"

"You suppose? Well, tell me, Dr. Noonan, did you find on Mr. Simms any abrasion that suggested to you that the knife had been thrust into Mr. Simms's abdomen all the way to the hilt?"

"No, I found no evidence of that."

"Would you explain to the jury what a hand guard is in the context of a knife?"

"The hand guard is the piece of metal between the handle and the blade that prevents the user's hand from sliding down onto the blade."

"If this hand guard struck Mr. Simms—in other words, if the knife had been thrust into the torso all the way to the hilt— could it have left a patterned abrasion?"

"It could have if the hand guard struck the victim with enough force."

"But in this case, it didn't."

"That is correct."

"Then how is it, Dr. Noonan, that you can suggest to this jury that the measured depth of the wound reflects the actual length of the blade?"

"Well, I cannot say with certainty that the blade was between three to four inches long."

"Really?" I say, turning to the defense table, where Jake is already standing and extending to me my legal pad. "Because on direct examination, you said the exact opposite. Mr. Maddox asked you, and I quote, 'Can you say with a reasonable degree of certainty that the knife used on the victim Mr. Simms possessed a blade that was between three to four inches in length?' You, Doctor, replied, and I quote again, 'Yes, I can.'"

"Objection, Your Honor." Maddox is standing, but his voice remains calm. "Is Counsel asking a question or simply reading back testimony?"

Judge Maxa looks at me. "Well, Mr. Corvelli?"

"My question is, what is your final answer, Dr. Noonan? Was the blade necessarily between three to four inches in length or not?"

"The blade was *at least* three to four inches in length."

"At least?" I say. "Well, that's a tremendously different statement than the one you made in your direct testimony, isn't it, Dr. Noonan?"

"I don't believe so."

"You don't? Doctor, you told this jury just hours ago that you believed with *a reasonable degree of certainty* that the knife used on Mr. Simms possessed a blade three to four inches in length. Now you say that the blade was *at least* three to four inches in length. Which means, does it not, that the blade used on Mr. Simms could have been *five* inches in length?"

"It could have."

"Or *six* inches in length."

"It is possible."

"Or *seven*, maybe *eight* or even *nine* inches in length."

"Possible," Noonan says. "To clarify, the measurement I offered is only the minimum length of the blade."

"The *minimum?*" I say. "Just the minimum? So all this discussion on direct examination about the blade of the knife being three to four inches in length was incorrect?"

"Not incorrect," he says. "Perhaps not completely accurate."

"Not completely accurate. Might I remind you, Dr. Noonan, that a young woman's future hangs on the outcome of this case. Isn't accuracy the only way to ensure that my client Mrs. Erin Simms receives a fair trial?"

Noonan doesn't answer.

"So that there is no mistake, Doctor," I say, "all this talk about a knife with a three- to four-inch blade is inaccurate, a figment perhaps of Mr. Maddox's imagination?"

"Objection!"

"Sustained."

"All this talk by Mr. Maddox in his opening and in his questioning about a Pteroco Legend switchblade being used on Mr. Simms, it's all a fabrication, wouldn't you say?"

"Objection, Your Honor! Objection! Objection!"

"Sustained!" Maxa raps her gavel. "Mr. Corvelli!" she yells as I open my mouth for one final tirade.

I pause and shake my head wearily. "No more questions for this witness, Your Honor." I turn and look at Maddox. Loudly I say, "He's obviously all yours."

CHAPTER 51

Judge Maxa keeps her head down as she pecks away at the keyboard of her laptop on the bench. Absently she says, "Any questions for this witness, Mr. Corvelli?"

"No, Your Honor," I say.

Maxa looks up, as does the witness, in complete surprise.

"But I believe my partner Jake Harper does."

Honolulu PD forensics expert Alison Kelly visibly deflates on the stand and looks to Maddox for help but there is no cavalry coming. Jake gathers his notes and walks slowly to the podium, never taking his eyes off his dear ex-girlfriend, Alison Kelly.

At first I dismissed the strategy as grade-school bullshit, bush league psych-out stuff that I might have utilized to delight my fellow law students in mock trials. Then I reconsidered. After all, cable news commentators like Marcy Faith make a mockery of the American system of justice every single day. Because of voices like hers, the defense perpetually plays "away" games; thus, we, as defense attorneys, might as well exploit fully any advantage we can. In fact, I'd say it is our duty.

"Morning, Ms. Kelly."

"Good morning, Mr. Harper."

"Ms. Kelly," Jake says slowly, "on direct examination you testified that all fingerprints found in the honeymoon suite where the fire allegedly started matched either the deceased Trevor Simms or the defendant Erin Simms, is that correct?"

"Yes, that is correct."

"And on the exterior of the door to the honeymoon suite—the side facing the hallway—that was also dusted for latent fingerprints?"

"Yes, it was."

"And will you please remind the jury, Ms. Kelly, how many latent prints were found on the exterior of the door to the honeymoon suite?"

"On the side facing the hallway, three latent prints were recovered."

"And who did those prints belong to, Ms. Kelly?"

"Two belonged to the victim, Trevor Simms. One belonged to your client, Erin Simms."

"And that's all?" Jake says, shrugging his shoulders. "Those are the only latent prints the forensics team could recover from the door to the honeymoon suite?"

"Again, on the side facing the hallway, yes."

"Hm," Jake says staring down at his notes. "That's interesting. Do you know why that is interesting, Ms. Kelly?"

"I suspect you'll tell me, Mr. Harper."

Jake puts his hands out in front of him. "No need to sass me, ma'am. I'm just trying to get to the truth here."

Truth is, there are going to be some fireworks this afternoon. Thanks to something seemingly innocuous said to me by Corwin Pierce, I sent our forensics expert Baron Lee back to the crime scene yesterday. And Baron found something, well, interesting.

Jake clasps his hands behind his back and pitches forward, his eyes rising from Baron Lee's report to his ex. "To your knowledge, Ms. Kelly, did the forensics team search for any latent prints besides fingerprints on the exterior of the door to the honeymoon suite?"

Alison Kelly shifts uncomfortably on the witness stand and steals a glance at me. "Not to my knowledge, no."

Last year in the Gianforte case Dapper Don Watanabe and I dueled over the admissibility of lip prints as identification evidence in a criminal case. Alison Kelly was caught in the middle of our duel, and suffice it to say, I came up on the short end.

"Are you familiar with the term 'anthropometry,' Ms. Kelly?"

"I am."

"Very good," Jake says, smiling. "Will you kindly explain the term to the jury?"

Alison Kelly clearly swallows an urge to shout at Jake for patronizing her. "Anthropometry," she says, her face tingeing red, "is a system of body measurements used for personal identification."

"Kind of like fingerprints?"

"No, not really."

"Well then, kindly explain the difference, Ms. Kelly?"

"Fingerprint analysis is a widely-used, thoroughly-tested scientific method for positively identifying individuals. Fingerprint analysis has proven an acceptable form of identification in the forensics community and in the courts of the United States. Anthropometry, on the other hand, is a very general term relating to various measurements of parts of the human body."

"Which parts?" Jake asks.

"Well, if I recall correctly, there are eleven: height, bust, length and width of head, width of cheeks, length of the left middle finger, length of the left foot, length of the right ear—"

"Let's pause right there," Jake says, "because the right ear happens to be what I'm most interested in."

From the corner of my eye I watch Luke Maddox, who remains perfectly calm, sitting forward, his arms crossed on the prosecution table. He should be standing, shouting his objections, because we're springing this on him—but he's not. He's perfectly fine with what is happening, and I suspect Alison Kelly, despite her apparent irritation of having to deal with Jake, is, too.

Maddox thinks we're playing right into his hands.

"Are you familiar, Ms. Kelly, with the use of ear print analysis as a means of forensic identification?"

"I'm familiar with it," she concedes, "but it is much more popular in Europe than in the United States."

"So we're a bit behind in that particular area of forensic science," Jake states as fact.

"I wouldn't say that."

Jake ignores her. "Ms. Kelly, would you be surprised if I were to tell you that in addition to the fingerprints found on the exterior of the door to the honeymoon suite, there was another latent print discovered by the defense's forensics team—an ear print, to be specific?"

Maddox finally objects, feigning outrage.

I hide my smile behind my hand.

Feign your anger now, Luke, because this is just the beginning. You're not going to have to feign anything but calm come tomorrow.

"Sustained," Maxa says. "The jury will disregard Mr. Harper's last question."

"Then, *hypothetically*, Ms. Kelly," Jake continues, "were a latent ear print discovered on the exterior of the door to the honeymoon suite, what would that suggest to you?"

Maddox doesn't object to Jake's use of a hypothetical; Maddox thinks he's still steering the boat.

Alison Kelly shrugs. "That someone pressed their ear against the door, of course."

"And hypothetically speaking, Ms. Kelly, why would anyone press their ear up against the exterior of a hotel room door?"

"My guess would be to listen to whatever was going on inside."

"Again, hypothetically, Ms. Kelly, based on your knowledge and experience, who in your estimation would want to hear what was going on inside someone else's honeymoon suite?"

The witness purses her lips. "Security, maybe."

"Hypothetically, why would security want to hear the goings-on in someone's honeymoon suite?"

"If there was a complaint for excessive noise, for instance."

"An excessive noise complaint," Jake says. "Wouldn't then security be able to hear said noise from the hall without pressing their ear up against the door and invading a young couple's privacy?"

"Possibly."

"If you are correct, Ms. Kelly, then, hypothetically, that ear print should match the size and shape of the ear of Mr. Izzy Dufu or some other security employee of the resort, isn't that right?"

"I would assume so."

"Again, hypothetically, Ms. Kelly, if this ear print *didn't* match up with anyone from the resort's security team, would you say that it is likely that someone *else* other than security pressed their ear up against the door to the Simms's honeymoon suite?"

"That's a logical assumption."

"And hypothetically, who might that be?"

"Could be anyone," Alison Kelly says.

"Anyone? Is likely that one of the room's current occupants would press their ear up against their own door?"

"Anything's possible, Mr. Harper."

"But if that hypothetical ear print didn't match up with the size and shape of the ear of either of the room's current occupants—say, Trevor or Erin Simms—that would exclude them, correct?"

"I suppose."

"Hypothetically, Ms. Kelly, if that ear print didn't match anyone working security for the resort or either of the room's current occupants, then someone *else* pressed their ear up against that door, right?"

"Probably."

"Someone who wanted to listen inside, correct?"

"Yes."

Jake's voice suddenly rises in pitch, his pace quickens. "Maybe someone who wanted to know if anyone was in that room. Someone with something nefarious on his mind, someone who wanted to rob or kill that suite's occupants or set that suite on fire—"

"Objection, Your Honor."

"Sustained. Mr. Harper?"

"My apologies, Judge."

"Any more questions, Mr. Harper?"

"No, Your Honor. The witness and I are through."

CHAPTER 52

The courtroom is jam-packed with journalists today—including Sherry Beagan, who was somehow able to secure a front-row seat. Of course there's nothing unusual about a courtroom jam-packed with journalists for a murder trial, especially one of this magnitude. The unusual part is that I personally invited every single one of them. And assured each that the events of this morning would shock their audience to the core.

Jake stands at the defense table, leans across the back of Erin's chair, and whispers in my ear. "Sure you wanna do this, son?"

I answer by standing up.

"Your witness, Mr. Corvelli," Maxa calls from the bench.

"Thank you, Your Honor. And good afternoon to you, Detective Tatupu."

"Counselor," he responds with a slight nod of the head.

There are many unwelcome side effects that come with the prospect of cross-examining a genuinely good cop: abnormal dreams, anxiety, dizziness, drowsiness, dry mouth, flushing, increased sweating, increased urination, loss of appetite, nausea, nervousness, restlessness, ringing in the ears, stomach pain, stomach upset, taste changes, trouble sleeping, vomiting, and weakness, to name a few. Indeed, for defense attorneys on trial, good cops present a constant hazard—they can single-handedly steer a jury toward a conviction with the right tone of voice, the right look, the right credentials. But the one good thing about a good cop is that you can count on him to be consistent. You can always count on him to tell the truth—regardless of the consequences to the prosecution.

"Detective, let me begin by asking you, are you familiar with a man named Corwin Pierce?"

Behind me I can almost feel Maddox smiling.

"Yes, Counselor, I am."

"Can you describe Mr. Pierce's physical appearance for the jury?"

"Mr. Pierce is approximately five feet, nine inches tall. A slight build, maybe a hundred-forty pounds. Rather unique red-orange hair and light, light blue eyes. Caucasian, very pale complexion."

"In what capacity do you know Corwin Pierce, Detective?"

"In his capacity as a lawbreaker, I guess you could say. Mr. Pierce has been arrested by our department on several occasions, including once just recently."

"Mr. Pierce's most recent arrest," I say, "what was the most serious charge?"

"Arson."

Chatter spreads through the gallery like falling dominoes. No one on the other side of the rail is quite sure where I'm heading with this, but the media is no doubt texting or tweeting their speculation already. No doubt much of that speculation will end up on the air. CORVELLI JUST PUT A FIGURE IN THE EMPTY SEAT, some of these texts or tweets will undoubtedly say. HIS NAME IS CORWIN PIERCE.

"Were you involved in Corwin Pierce's most recent arrest, Detective?"

"No, I was not. Mr. Pierce was involved in an arson investigation and I am assigned to the homicide division."

"I see. Were you *ever* involved in a case in which Corwin Pierce was arrested?"

"No, I was not."

"Were you *ever* involved in a case in which Corwin Pierce was a suspect?"

"No, I don't believe so." He shakes his head. "No, I think not."

"Did you ever meet Corwin Pierce?"

Tatupu shakes his head again. "Face-to-face? No."

"Then tell me, Detective, how did you do such a fine job describing Corwin Pierce's physical appearance a few moments ago?"

"I have viewed photographs of Mr. Pierce. Booking photos."

"I see. On how many occasions did you view photos of Corwin Pierce?"

"Just once, I believe."

"Did you review any or all of the arrest file on Corwin Pierce at the time you viewed these photos?"

"Sure."

"You viewed these photographs, these booking photos, Detective, before or after Corwin Pierce's most recent arrest?"

Tatupu hesitates. "After," he finally says.

I shrug my shoulders enough so that the entire courtroom can see. Then I ask: "Why?"

Tatupu avoids looking at Maddox for as long as he can, then

finally his eyes dart over to the prosecution table. I note the look to the jury by following Tatupu's gaze myself.

"Did you view the photographs of Corwin Pierce in connection with your investigation in *this* case?" I ask helpfully.

Tatupu breathes a sigh of relief. "Yes, that's correct."

I shrug my shoulders dramatically yet again. Then I ask: "Why?"

Tatupu scratches his chin, buys some time.

"Remind me, Detective, when was Corwin Pierce's most recent arrest?"

"Five or six weeks ago."

"By that time you had your suspect—my client—in custody for months already. Certainly you weren't harnessing any doubt at that time?"

"No, Counselor, I was not."

"Then why did you view the booking photographs and arrest file of Corwin Pierce in connection with the Kupulupulu Beach Resort fire, Detective?"

"Objection, Your Honor." Maddox is on his feet. "Counsel is moving far beyond the scope of direct."

Maxa frowns deeply at the prosecutor. "Mr. Corvelli is asking the lead detective about his investigation into this very case, Mr. Maddox. Objection overruled."

"Detective," I say, "please answer the question."

"Your Honor," Maddox says, standing again, "I would like to request a fifteen-minute recess."

"Request denied."

"But Your Honor—"

"Mr. Maddox, *sit down.*"

"Detective," I say again, "please answer the question."

"Do you need the question read back to you, Detective?" Maxa says.

"No worries, Your Honor," I say. "I'll ask the detective again." I move in front of the podium where I can see the sweat budding on Tatupu's forehead. "*Why*, Detective, did you view the booking photographs and arrest file of Corwin Pierce in connection with the Kupulupulu Beach Resort fire, the subject of this very trial?"

"I was asked to," he says.

"By whom?"

Maddox renews his objection. "This is work product, Your Honor."

"Then I am a dancing chicken," the judge says to light laughter. "Overruled."

When I glance back, Maddox is still standing, this time glaring at me. His cheeks are ashen, his mouth half-open as though preparing to catch flies.

"*Who* asked you to view Corwin Pierce's file, Detective Tatupu?" I say with some urgency.

"Well, I wasn't asked to view Mr. Pierce's file specifically," the detective says.

"What specifically were you asked to do, Detective?"

Tatutpu draws a breath. He's made a decision, the right decision, to answer my questions accurately and honestly just as I knew he would.

"I was asked to do a search for arson investigations in which we currently had a suspect in jail awaiting trial."

"Again, Detective, I ask *who* assigned you this task?"

The slightest pause. "Luke Maddox."

I point to the prosecution table. "The same Luke Maddox who is prosecuting this case?"

"Yes, Counselor."

"Did Mr. Maddox tell you *why* he was making such an unusual request?"

"Objection to the characterization of the request as 'unusual,'" Maddox says.

"Fine. Strike the last question," I say. "Detective, at the time Mr. Maddox made the request, did you find the request to be unusual?"

"I did," he concedes.

"Then I ask again, did Mr. Maddox tell you *why* he was making such an *unusual* request?"

"Mr. Maddox didn't tell me and I didn't ask."

"Was Corwin Pierce the only arson suspect in jail awaiting trial at that time?"

"That I could find, yes."

"And what did you do when you discovered Corwin Pierce was in jail awaiting trial?"

"I did what I was asked to do. I reviewed the file and passed it on to Mr. Maddox."

Maddox rises again. "Objection, Your Honor. I fail to see any relevance whatso—"

"Overruled. Have a seat, Mr. Maddox. And please do everything humanly possible to remain *in* it during the rest of Mr. Corvelli's cross-examination of Detective Tatupu."

"Do you know what Mr. Maddox did with Corwin Pierce's file after you gave it to him?" I say.

Tatupu shakes his head. "You would have to ask him."

I turn and face both Maddox and the jury. "Oh, I'm quite sure Mr. Maddox will be asked that very question at some point under oath." I spin back to Tatupu. "But tell me, Detective, did *you* become curious about what Mr. Maddox intended to do with Corwin Pierce's file after you gave it to him?"

"Of course."

"You wanted to find out?"

"Sure."

"To that end, Detective, what, if any, steps did you take?"

Maddox is up again. "Objection. Is the detective the one suddenly on trial here?"

Maxa looks up. "I believe *you* are, Mr. Maddox."

The gallery erupts with talk and movement.

Maxa lifts her gavel and threatens to clear the courtroom. "The objection is overruled. Please answer the question, Detective."

"I followed up by checking with the Hawaii Department of Corrections."

"And what, if anything, did you discover, Detective?"

"That Corwin Pierce was subsequently transferred from the OCCC to the Halawa Correctional Center."

"On whose authority, Detective?"

"On the authority of Deputy Prosecutor Luke Maddox."

As the gallery again alights with hushed conversation, Judge Maxa stands. "I think maybe it's time for me to see both lawyers in chambers."

I hold up my right hand. "Just one last question, Your Honor." I don't give her time to refuse the request. "Detective Tatupu, are you familiar with a man named Turi Ahina?"

"I am."

"How so?"

"I believe Mr. Ahina is a client of yours."

"More than a client," I say, stepping away from the podium toward Judge Maxa's chambers. "It should be noted for the record that Turi Ahina is more than just a client of my firm. And that Deputy Prosecutor Luke Maddox knows it."

CHAPTER 53

"You know who the fuck I am?" Maddox shouts the moment we step back into the hallway outside Judge Maxa's chambers.

"A prosecutor," I say calmly. "At least for the time being."

We're close enough to each other that I can smell the coffee on Maddox's breath, the breasts of our suit jackets magnetized by ire, the two of us squaring off and brushing against one another like manager and umpire following a blown call on a play at the plate. Then he grasps my lapels, and I his, and through sheer rage I overpower him, slamming him into the blah yellow wall with all the force I can muster.

I don't know who throws the first punch. All I know is that our bodies collide with violent force and before I can consider the consequences we are both on the floor outside Judge Maxa's chambers tearing at each other like sharks.

Maxa's clerk, a number of court officers, a few lawyers all rush to intervene, to attempt to separate us, but punches are already landing, many to Maddox's pretty face and a few to my own and there's blood, lots of blood, more blood than you would ever expect as a result of a brawl between two lawyers at a courthouse.

It's then, as Jake and Court Officer Perry pin me up against the far wall, blood spilling down my chin onto my starched white shirt and blue silk tie, that I realize the fire has returned to my gut.

Minutes ago in Judge Maxa's chambers, Luke Maddox looked as though he might soil his pants. The way things were left in the courtroom, much of the media and all of the jury undoubtedly had dozens of questions they would have liked to ask. Maxa cut things off before things went too far—before, as Jake said, she couldn't put the shit back in the horse.

"These are very serious accusations, Mr. Corvelli," Maxa said to me.

All of us, Jake included, were standing in her chambers, the tension so thick it seemed to suck up the air. Maxa remained standing in her long flowing black robe, her jaw set so tight it couldn't have been broken with a hammer.

"I'm well aware, Your Honor," I told her.

Maddox began to speak but Maxa immediately cut him off. "I don't think you should say a word right now, Mr. Maddox. You can only get yourself in deeper. Regardless of the truth of Mr. Corvelli's allegations of prosecutorial misconduct, I suggest you speak to counsel before addressing these issues in any manner in any forum whatsoever."

Maddox remained quiet after that.

"As for the trial . . ." Maxa said. "Mr. Corvelli, I'm inclined to grant you a mistrial. Until these allegations can be proved or disproved, I don't see a reason why you or your client should have to proceed."

Of course, I cannot prove the allegations without the cooperation of Corwin Pierce, and there is little to no chance of obtaining that. There are records—Flan searched for them at my request—of Maddox visiting Pierce on multiple occasions at Halawa, but there is no way to prove what was said, no way to establish with reasonable certainty that Maddox fed the details of the crime to Corwin Pierce and directed Pierce to confess to the crime to Turi Ahina, knowing damn well it would get back to me and lead the defense down a dark one-way road toward a conviction.

Of course Judge Sonya Maxa is suspicious enough, as she well should be, to grant the defense a mistrial.

"I don't want a mistrial, Judge," I hear myself saying. "I intend to win an acquittal."

A mistrial was precisely what I had wanted when I rose to question Tatupu about Corwin Pierce, it was what I meant when I told Erin that I wouldn't allow her to be convicted, that I was in complete control. But at some point during my cross-examination of John Tatupu, something in me snapped. I grew angry, angrier perhaps than I've ever been in my eights years as a lawyer. I was finally able to hate Luke Maddox, *truly* hate him, headful of Fukitol or not.

Now Jake Harper and Court Officer Perry stand in front of me, continuing to hold me back. Maxa is staring down at the spill of blood on the floor as it spreads like fire toward her chamber door.

"Go, get yourselves to a hospital," Maxa says, arms folded across her chest. "Get stitched or stapled or whatever you need to do, because I will see both of you in my courtroom tomorrow morning at nine o'clock sharp, prepared to question the State's next witness. And, so help me, you both better look presentable."

CHAPTER 54

Inez Rios's direct testimony takes almost an entire day. Luke Maddox, standing tall at the podium with a stitched-up split upper lip and two shiners, deliberately parades the investigator through the history of fire, from its discovery by early man through present day. By four in the afternoon I'm more afraid of fire and its destructive properties than the scarecrow from the *Wizard of Oz*. When Maddox finally tenders the witness I know I should suggest to Judge Maxa that we adjourn and call it a week. If I only had a brain.

Instead I limp to the podium, my right knee protesting loudly and violently over yesterday's hallway brawl. "Good afternoon, Ms. Rios. It's late in the day and I realize everyone wants to go home, so I'll just ask you a few questions and perhaps we can resume on Monday—or Tuesday rather, since Monday's a holiday."

I glance at the jury to see whether they're still paying attention, then I get right to the heart of my cross-examination.

"Ms. Rios, you testified earlier today that given Dr. Noonan's findings as to the cause and manner of death of Mr. Simms, you thought it very likely that this fire was started in order to conceal the crime of homicide, correct?"

"Correct, Counselor."

"Aside from Dr. Noonan's determination as to the cause and manner of Mr. Simms's death, is there any physical evidence to support this claim?"

"Of course," she says. "The fire was clearly started in the honeymoon suite where the murder of Mr. Simms took place."

"Location," I say. "I'm glad you mentioned that, Ms. Rios, because you testified on direct that the point of origin, identified by a prominent V-shaped burn pattern, was discovered on the lower part of the wall across from the bed on which Mr. Simms's body was found. Isn't that right?"

"That's right."

"And that location is where the bulk—or say, the lion's share—of the charcoal lighter fluid was also discovered, isn't that correct?"

"Yes, with trailers heading in the direction of the bed."

"Trailers, plural?"

"No, I apologize. Trailer, singular. There was one trailer of lighter fluid found heading from the point of origin in the direction of the bed."

I stand back from the podium and look up at the ceiling as though trying to formulate my next question. "If, right at this moment, Ms. Rios, you wanted to set me on fire, would you attempt to do so by dousing the jury box with lighter fluid?"

Maddox is up. "Objection, Your Honor! What kind of question is that?"

"Withdrawn," I say quickly, bowing my head. "I apologize, Your Honor. That question was poorly phrased." But the jury will sure as hell remember it.

I step up to the podium again. "Let me take you briefly down another road, Ms. Rios. In your report, you state that there were three potential exits in the Simms's honeymoon suite, correct?"

"Correct, Counselor."

I count them off on my fingers, inadvertently exposing my bruised knuckles to the jury. "The front door. The door that led to the neighboring suite. And the sliding glass door that led out to the lanai. Isn't that right?"

"Yes, it is."

"From your investigation you determined that at the time the fire started the sliding glass door to the lanai was closed, correct?"

"Yes."

"And, unless the front door was somehow propped open, that door was in all likelihood closed as well, right?"

"Right. The front door is designed in such a way that it closes itself."

"But this third door, this door to the neighboring suite. That door, you determined, was *open* at the time the fire started?"

"That's correct."

"How do you account for that, Ms. Rios?"

"Objection."

"Your Honor, I'm simply asking Ms. Rios to formulate an expert opinion based on her many years of experience investigating fires."

"Overruled. Ms. Rios, you may answer the question."

"In my opinion," Rios says, "before setting the fire, the arsonist was checking for potential avenues of escape."

"But that door to the neighboring suite was not, in fact, a potential avenue of escape for the arsonist, was it?"

"No, it was not."

"Why not, Ms. Rios?"

"Because the second door, the interior door, into the adjoining suite was locked."

"So, Ms. Rios, are you suggesting that the arsonist discovered that this second door was locked and therefore dismissed that exit as a possible avenue of escape?"

"I think that's very likely."

"And yet, Ms. Rios, not a single fingerprint was discovered on the knob of the interior door to the neighboring suite, correct?"

"That's correct, Counselor."

"Nor, Ms. Rios, was a single fingerprint discovered on the knob of the exterior door to the neighboring suite, isn't that right?"

"That's right, Counselor."

"And how do you account for that?"

"Well, unfortunately, Mr. Corvelli, we don't always find fingerprints where we might expect to find fingerprints."

"Fair enough. But why do you suppose, Ms. Rios, that the first door to the neighboring suite was left open?"

Rios shrugs. "Carelessness?"

"Carelessness," I repeat. "But on direct examination you detailed all of the quote-unquote *'painstaking efforts'* the arsonist apparently made to use this fire to conceal the crime of homicide, didn't you, Ms. Rios?"

"I did."

"Then what advantage, Ms. Rios, does leaving that door open give the arsonist, if the arsonist set this fire in order to conceal the murder of Trevor Simms?"

Rios shrugs again. "None that I can think of."

Judge Maxa follows Rios's answer by asking me if this is a good time to break until next week.

"Just one final line of questioning, Your Honor." I flip the page on Rios's report. "Let's talk briefly about the accelerant, Ms. Rios. The charcoal lighter fluid. In addition to finding the accelerant in massive amounts at the point of origin, and in addition to the trailer leading to the bed, a fair amount of lighter fluid was also discovered in the neighboring suite, correct?"

"I'm not sure I would characterize it as a 'fair amount.'"

"How *would* you characterize it, Ms. Rios?"

"I believe in my report I call it a 'puddle.'"

"And how do you account for that 'puddle' of accelerant discovered in the neighboring suite, Ms. Rios?"

"Spillage."

"Spillage?" I repeat. "More carelessness, Ms. Rios?"

"I suppose so."

"On direct this morning, Ms. Rios, you characterized the arsonist as 'meticulous,' did you not?"

"I did."

"Tell me, Ms. Rios, in your twelve-plus years as a fire investigator here in the state of Hawaii, would you say that the individual who set this fire in the Simms's honeymoon suite is the most careless, meticulous arsonist you've ever come across?"

CHAPTER 55

"The question now is, do we put on a defense at all or rest and go straight to closing arguments?"

Leaning against the conference room window, Jake says, "That's like asking me if I want a drink when you're standing there with an empty bottle in your hand."

I sigh heavily. Jake's right. I'm convinced we did as much damage as we could to Maddox's case-in-chief, but staging our own defense is another matter entirely. Maddox was leading us down a blind alley with Corwin Pierce and Javier Vargas and we called him on it, raised serious questions about the prosecution's integrity, just as Johnnie Cochran & Company did to Marcia Clark and Christopher Darden in the O. J. Simpson trial. Bottom line is, though, unless we have another suspect to point to, our only argument to the jury is that the government didn't meet its burden of proof.

Maddox rested his case earlier today after putting Trevor's sister Lauren Simms on the stand. Lauren was an effective witness: articulate, sympathetic, memorable. In addition to putting a switchblade in Erin's hand on the afternoon preceding the fire, Lauren provided that third dimension of a victim that is sometimes so difficult to achieve. Lauren was so good, in fact, that I decided not to cross, not to question her about Trevor's business dealings with her fiancé Gabe Guidry. If, ultimately, we go in that direction, I'd much rather call Guidry himself during our case-in-chief.

"Who are you thinking about putting on?" Jake asks.

I lean back in my seat, watching Jake watch the rain. "Tara Holland and Isaac Cassel are useless because neither can offer Erin an alibi. And Maddox will kill Tara on cross because she witnessed the death threats. She'll have to corroborate everything Mia said on direct and we don't want her doing that."

"How about Isaac?"

"The best man is another story. My fear is that Isaac will jump at the bit to protect Erin on direct and then bury us on cross. Besides, what can we get from Isaac that we couldn't get from Mia Landow?"

"That leaves who? Baron Lee?"

"To testify to the points we already got Alison, Noonan, and Inez Rios to concede to."

"Maybe we should pull up the knife," Jake suggests.

"Too late for that," I say. "Even if the knife has a known arsonist's prints all over it now it'll look staged. Besides, if there are no unknown prints on the door knobs or anywhere else in the honeymoon suite, then the true arsonist—assuming there even is one—used gloves. Introducing Erin's knife as Erin's knife is just one more reason to convict. We can't hand Maddox the murder weapon this late in the game."

Jake finally turns from the window and sits across from me. "Son, I know we've had our differences these past six months. Partly because of Alison, yes, but partly because you made a business decision without consulting me. You wouldn't even hear me out. And that, son, is how you do a lot of things. You're an alpha dog, I can accept that. But I'm still your partner and I deserve to be heard."

"Look, I'm sorry, Jake . . ."

"No need for apologies. What I'm getting at is this: If you want to reverse yourself and ask Maxa for that mistrial, I'd understand. We can't afford to try this case again, but at least Erin will get another shot. Who knows? Maybe something will turn up between now and then."

I don't tell Jake that my refusal of Maxa's offer to grant a mistrial had nothing to do with our six hundred grand. Instead, I dump a manila folder full of photographs onto the conference room table. Each of us have studied thousands of these ordinary tourist photos of the day and night of the fire for the past six months. I'm certain we didn't miss anything. But I need a prop to say what I have to say to Jake.

"There's something I need to tell you," I start. I still haven't let Jake in on my relationship with Erin, but I suppose now is better than never.

"What's that, son?"

As I flip through the pictures, I say, "Mind you, this didn't start until a few weeks after we agreed to take on the case . . ."

Jake leans forward and crosses his arms on the conference room table.

I set aside a few of the photos. "Let's get the original digital images of these," I say, stalling for time. "These are garbage. This guy in the Boston Red Sox cap has red-eye in every shot."

"The computer will help with that?" Jake asks.

"With the touch of a button," I tell him. "It's called red-eye reduction."

"I'll get Flan on it. He should be here any minute now. So you were saying, son?"

Just as I'm about to finally let Jake in on my romantic relationship with Erin these past six months, the conference room door swings open with that insufferable squeak like nails on a chalkboard. Flan steps in, shaking himself off like a wet dog.

"Don't you own an umbrella?" I say.

"Funny, Paris Hilton," Flan says in a huff. "But you guys are going to want to come downstairs with me to Sand Bar right away."

"What for?" Jake asks.

"CNN is looping the latest celebrity sex tape. And you're not going to believe who has the starring role."

CHAPTER 56

"Can you *believe* this sleazeball?" Marcy Faith shouts into the camera.

"She's talking about you," Flan says to me.

"I'm aware."

We're standing at the bar downstairs, Seamus now more than willing to raise the volume for this, news of the Kevin Corvelli-Erin Simms sex tape that has apparently been making the rounds on the Internet the past three hours.

"Beautiful setting," Jake says of Erin's lanai overlooking Kaneohe Bay. "I like the way they were able to capture China-man's Hat in the background."

"Quality's good, too," Flan says. "Even the stills. Have you seen the stills yet, Seamus?"

"Yeah," Seamus replies, "one of my favorite porn site's got them. Uncensored, too!"

"Nice."

"There's your mistrial, right there, son," Jake says to me. "Or your suspension."

"Or disbarment," Flan throws in.

Jake shrugs. "Is doing your client even prohibited in the Hawaii Ethics Code?"

"I don't know," I tell him. "I never bothered reading it."

"You don't say."

"It *is* one of Milt Cashman's Ten Commandments, however," I tell him as I pull out a barstool. "Double Glenlivet on the rocks, Seamus."

"On the house," he says.

Well, that's something at least.

Two hours later Flan and I are still sitting at a booth in Sand Bar, Jake having taken off for home.

"I'm not putting on a defense," I tell Flan. "I've just decided."

"You sure that's a decision you wanna make after throwing back a fifth of Glenlivet?" he says.

I set my glass down. "Seems to be the only time I'm me."

Flan rests a hand atop the manila folder full of photos I had Hoshi bring down from the conference room a half hour ago. "Then do you still need digital copies of these photos, or should I forget it?"

"Might as well get them," I say, trying to get the rim of the rocks glass to my lips again. "Won't cost much. Besides, Harper and Corvelli's about to pull in six hundred grand on a bail assignment."

On the table Flan's cell phone starts dancing around.

"Go ahead," I say, as though he needed permission. "Tell Casey I said hi."

Flan stares at the Caller ID. "It's Baron Lee," he says. He puts the phone to his ear and has a conversation that I don't bother listening to. I'm thinking that over the weekend I'll have to pre-pare my closing statement.

If only I had someone to point to.

Flan sets down the phone, takes a pull off his Bushmills, then looks up at me. "Not going to believe this," he tells me.

"What, is FOX News showing pictures of me on the can?"

"Maybe, but that's small news compared to this, Kev."

"Let's hear it, Flan."

"That unknown print on your Maserati," he says, "Baron Lee's found a match."

"And?"

"And I think this bit of news better wait until you sober up a bit. Because now the shit's *really* about to hit the fan."

CHAPTER 57

"Please call your first witness, Mr. Corvelli."

"The defense calls Josh Leffler."

"Objection!"

"Your Honor," I say, "Mr. Leffler has been on our witness list now for months."

"Your Honor," Maddox says, *"Mister* Leffler is four years old."

I turn to Maddox. "How do you know how old he is?"

Maddox looks at me. "What?"

"Counselors," Maxa says, "for the last time, you *will* direct any and all comments to the Court. And I'll see you both in my chambers *now*." She raps her gavel and stands. "I believe both of you know the way."

"What's going on here?" Maxa says to Maddox once we are safely inside her chambers.

"Mr. Corvelli just called a four-year-old to the stand, Your Honor. That's what's going on."

"How about it, Mr. Corvelli?"

"Your Honor, Mr. Leffler—"

"Stop calling him 'mister,' Counselor. It's not going to affect my ruling."

Maddox steps in. "Your Honor, it is well-established that minors of Josh Leffler's age are disqualified from testifying under the Hawaii Rules of Evidence."

"Mr. Maddox couldn't be more wrong if he tried, Judge. In fact, the Court in *Republic versus Ah Wong* determined that, quote, 'There is no precise age within which children are ex cluded from testifying. Their competency is to be determined, not by their age, but by their degree of knowledge and understanding.'"

Maxa says, "*Republic*? When was that case decided, Mr. Corvelli?"

"Eighteen ninety-six, Your Honor. And it is still good law."

"This is absurd," Maddox says. "Mr. Corvelli is making a mockery of this Court."

"Your Honor," I say, "under Rule 603.1 of the Hawaii Rules of Evidence, a person is disqualified to be a witness *only* if the person is incapable of expressing himself so as to be understood, or incapable of understanding the duty to tell the truth."

Maxa holds up a hand. "Let me get this straight, Mr. Corvelli. Months ago you argued that *you,* an officer of this court, were unfit to serve as a witness in this case. Yet today, you are arguing that a *four-year-old* is perfectly fit to serve as a witness?"

"Precisely, Your Honor. A witness must possess the capacity to perceive and to recollect. Due to my overindulgence on the evening of the fire, I lacked the true capacity for either."

Maddox barks out a mad laugh. "I feel like I just stepped into another dimension, Your Honor!"

"Judge," I say, "when Mr. Maddox rejoins us in *this* dimension, I suggest he refer to the case of *Territory versus Titcomb*, in which the Court announced that, quote, 'The proper test must always be, does the lunatic understand what he is saying, and does he understand the obligation of an oath?' If so, it is up to the jury to determine the weight of his testimony."

Maxa frowns. "Are you now telling me the boy is a lunatic, Counselor?"

"No, Your Honor. But the lunatic test does apply here."

"And you said *Territory versus Titcomb*, did you not?"

"*Titcomb*, yes, Your Honor. I thought the name was funny, too."

"No, I'm not referring to *Titcomb*, Mr. Corvelli. I'm referring to *Territory*. What year was that case decided?"

"Nineteen thirty-eight, Your Honor."

"And do you have any case law, Mr. Corvelli, that is dated in the last sixty years or so, since Hawaii became a state?"

"The cases I'm citing are still good law, Your Honor. They have not been overturned. Whether Hawaii was a state, a territory, a republic, a kingdom, or anything else is wholly irrelevant."

"Your Honor," Maddox weighs in, "I'd like some time to research this issue . . ."

"Denied. You've had months since you received Mr. Corvelli's witness list. You should have done your research during that time, as Mr. Corvelli clearly did."

"Well," Maddox tries, "surely Your Honor would like to take the time to research this issue before making a decision of this magnitude."

"May I?" I say, pointing to the judge's bookcase. I step past Maddox and remove the Hawaii Rules of Evidence. I open the tome on Maxa's desk and flip to Rule 603.1. "Here, Your Honor. Each of the cases I cited are right here in the commentary to Rule 603.1. Your research shouldn't take more than ninety seconds. Mr. Maddox and I can wait in the hall if you'd li—"

"*No,*" Maxa shouts. "You and Mr. Maddox will wait right here where I can see you. Mr. Curnow from Maintenance adamantly informed me that he's *finished* with cleaning up lawyers' blood outside my chambers."

CHAPTER 58

"Josh," I say softly, leaning casually against the witness stand, "do you know the difference between telling the truth and telling a lie?"

The courtroom is empty except for Maddox, Judge Maxa, Erin, Josh and myself, for this, a hearing to determine the competency of Josh Leffler as a witness in the case of *State versus Erin Simms.*

Josh peeks behind me at Maddox, who stands with his arms folded, trying no doubt to intimidate the little guy.

"Yes," Josh says tentatively.

"What is truth?" I say.

Again the kid hesitates. I assure him everything is all right.

"That's when you give test-money and tell what really happened."

"And what is a lie, Josh?"

"That's when you make stuff up. Like the police do sometimes."

I try not to flinch even though that last sentence could lose me my one and only witness. Maddox is already pointing at Josh as if to say, *See? The kid's an idiot.* But Maxa nods her head, takes down a note, and tells me to continue.

"If you give testimony in this case, Josh," I say, "will you tell the truth about what really happened the night of the fire, and about anything else Mr. Maddox, the judge, and I might ask you?"

"I have to," Josh says, a solemn expression spreading across his face. "I have to and I will."

With the jury seated but the gallery cleared, I ask the judge once again if I may approach the witness and she agrees.

"Now, Josh," I say gently, "do you remember the night of the fire?"

"Of course," he says. "That's when my grandma died."

Slowly, cautiously, I take Josh back to the sixteenth floor of the Liholiho Tower. I have him describe the location of his room, ask him if he remembers a light blue band on the door knob to his neighbor's suite. He does. He also remembers Grandma going to sleep after taking her Am-beans and how thirsty he was but there was nothing in the room to drink.

"The sink didn't work," he says. "And Grandma's soda tasted all oogie."

So he grabbed a dollar bill and stepped out into the hall in search of the vending machine he'd spotted earlier. He wanted a Dr Pepper. "Because it's delicious," he says.

"What happened when you found the vending machine?" I ask him.

"The red light was lit. That meant no more Dr Pepper."

"So what did you do?"

He twists a lock of brown hair around his finger. "Nothing."

I swallow and remind myself to be patient; he's just a kid. "Well, then, what happened next?"

"You showed up," he says. "Naked."

"Well," I say, my face flushing, "not *naked*, right?"

"No, you had Underoos on."

I don't press the issue. Since the video and stills of Erin and me in the hot tub on her lanai surfaced, I have very little dignity left to protect.

"What happened next?" I say.

"We went downstairs."

"To another vending machine?"

"Yeah. That one had Dr Pepper in it."

"So you bought one?"

"You bought half for me."

"What do you mean by that, Josh?"

"I only had one dollar and Dr Pepper is two dollars where people speak English."

"You had no change?"

"No."

"Why not?"

"Because Grandma gave me all her coins downstairs so that I could make wishes."

"Every coin she had?"

"Yeah. When I asked for more, she showed me her empty purse."

"And you threw these coins your grandmother gave you into the fountain downstairs in the resort's lobby?"

"Yeah, and I made wishes."

"One wish over and over? Or many wishes?" I ask.

"Many wishes."

"And what was your most important wish, Josh?"

"I can't tell you or it won't come true."

"Fair enough," I say, smiling over at the jury.

I take Josh through the rest of the night, from the trip back upstairs to being locked out of his room, to the alarm shrieking while he sat alone in the stairwell, peeing his pants. He tells the jury about how I found him surrounded by murderous black smoke, how I lifted him onto my shoulder and carried him down "thousands" of flights of stairs, how I saved him from the fire.

"But no one saved Grandma," he says.

In the back of the courtroom one of the double doors opens and Hoshi pokes her head in.

"I'm sorry, young lady," Maxa says. "But this is presently a closed trial."

"Your Honor, if I may have a moment," I say, "that young lady is my assistant."

"Very well, Mr. Corvelli. But please make it brief."

I head to the rear of the courtroom, where Hoshi is holding a small manila envelope. She hands it to me. I open it, take a glimpse at the photograph inside, and nod my head.

"One more thing," I whisper to Hoshi. "Head back to Ms. Raffa's office and tell her I said, 'Mahalo.' And tell her . . . Tell her that I'm glad we're friends again."

Hoshi nods and then she's swiftly out the door again.

"Josh," I say when I return to the witness stand after placing the envelope inside my suit jacket, "will you please tell us what you were doing at the Kupulupulu Beach Resort on the night of the fire? What was your purpose for being there with your grandmother?"

"Grandma was going to take me away from the island," he says.

"To the mainland?"

He nods. I remind him he has to speak up for the court reporter. "Yes," he says way too loudly into the microphone. A court officer steps over to adjust the mike and to demonstrate to Josh how he should use it.

"Why was Grandma taking you to the mainland?" I ask once the court officer steps away again.

"To live with her."

"Why were you going to live with your grandmother?"

In a small voice, he says, "Because my mommy died."

"I'm sorry," I tell him. "When did your mommy die?"

"The night before the fourth of July."

"Where? Where did your mommy die, Josh?"

"In the ocean."

"In the ocean, where?"

Fighting tears, he says softly, "Behind my house."

"Up North Shore?"

"Yeah."

"By Ke Iki Beach?"

"Yeah."

"How? How did your mommy die, Josh?"

Maddox leaps to his feet. "Objection, Your Honor. Relevance?"

"Can we not talk about this?" Josh asks me.

"I'm sorry, Josh," I tell him, "but we have to. Just for a little while." I turn to the judge. "Your Honor, if you'll allow me just some leeway, I'll establish the relevancy within the next few questions."

"Overruled," Maxa says. "But don't stray too far, Mr. Corvelli."

Josh sets his gaze on Maddox and his lower lip begins to tremble. I take a deliberate step to my right blocking Josh's view of the prosecutor.

"How did your mommy die?" I say again.

"She drownded," Josh says, eyes tearing up.

"Drowned?"

"Yeah."

I picture the kid as we stood alone in his room, gazing out his window. I see him holding his binoculars to his eyes, watching for the horizon.

"Did you see your mommy die?" I say.

"Objection!"

Josh heads into a full-on cry.

"Counselor?" Maxa says to me. "Is this really necessary?"

"It is, Your Honor." I say again to Josh, this time a little firmer: "Did you see your mommy die, Josh?"

Josh is shaking his head, wiping tears as they come.

"Remember what we talked about, Josh," I say. "Remember what happens if you don't tell the truth."

He looks up at me from between his tiny fingers.

When he does, I motion with my eyes to Judge Maxa and grimace theatrically.

"Did you see your mommy die?" I repeat.

The kid breaks, holds his head in his hands.

Maddox says: "This is awful, Your Honor. At the very minimum, I suggest we take a recess."

"No, Your Honor," I say. "We're almost done here. Did you *see* your mommy die, Josh?" I say again. "The *truth*. Did you *see* your mommy die?"

"Yes!" he finally cries out.

"With your binoculars?"

"Yes!"

"From your bedroom window, Josh?"

"Yes!"

"And did she die from an accident like the police told you?"

"No!"

"Objection, Your Honor! This is getting—"

"Shut up!" I scream back at him.

Maxa is rapping her gavel, yelling at both of us.

"Was she alone when she died, Josh?" I say urgently.

More hysterics, crying, shaking of the body, shaking of the head. I want to reach out and grab the kid, lift him in my arms, and carry him out of here, just as I did on the night of the fire. But someone else in this courtroom needs saving today and someone else needs to get burned.

"Was she *alone* when she died?" I repeat.

"No!" Josh cries out. "She wasn't alone!"

"Who was with your mommy when she died, Josh? A man or a woman?"

"A man! A man! A man!"

"A man was with your mommy?"

"Yes! Yes!"

"And what did you see that man do, Josh?"

Sobbing so hard, Josh nearly falls off his chair on the witness stand. Maxa rises to her feet but I hold up a hand.

I lean in to the witness stand. "We need to hear your secrets," I tell the kid softly. "You have to tell us your secrets."

Josh shakes his head, says something inaudible before crying out, "Then they wouldn't be secrets anymore, would they, Kevin?"

Using my own words against me. I lean in again, whisper, "Tell me your secrets, Josh, and I'll tell you mine. We'll trade."

"No," he shouts. "No, no, no, no, no!"

"Your Honor," Maddox says, "*please!*"

"Okay. Mr. Corvelli, I have no choice . . ."

I lean into the witness stand one last time, take Josh's head in my hands, and whisper in his ear. "Please, Josh. If you don't want to do this for me, then do it for your mommy."

"*Okay,*" Josh cries, turning to the judge. "I saw him hit her. He pushed her into the ocean!"

I take a step back, raise my voice again. "So it wasn't an accident? Your mother was murdered, wasn't she, Josh?"

"Y-yes! Yes! He killed her! Drownded her right in front of me!"

I step to my left so that I'm no longer obstructing Josh's view of the prosecutor. "Do you know this man?" I say, pointing at Luke.

Josh nods, tears flying off his face. "Yes!"

"How do you know him, Josh?"

"Objection!"

"He was dating my mommy when she died."

You're a defense lawyer, Kevin, I remind myself. *All you have to do is place someone—anyone—in that empty chair just long enough to win an acquittal.*

"And he was there, wasn't he?" I say urgently. "Luke Maddox was at your house on the night your mommy was murdered, wasn't he, Josh?"

"Yes!" Josh shrieks. "But—"

"It's all right, Josh," I shout as Maddox jumps out of his seat again. "Not another word! You've told us everything we need to know."

"OBJECTION!" Maddox shouts as he moves past the podium in the direction of the bench.

I stand, my back to the witness, taking deep breaths, clenching my fists, prepared to take on Maddox if he comes at the kid.

Standing, slapping the gavel with all her might, Maxa howls, "Both lawyers! In my chambers! Right *NOW!*" She turns to her court officer. "And call security to my chambers. One of these lawyers—and I'm not yet sure which—is spending the night in *jail.*"

CHAPTER 59

"What in the *hell* is going on here?" Judge Maxa wants to know as soon as we enter her chambers. Guards stand at the ready just outside her door. "Mr. Corvelli, you know better than to attempt an ambush in my courtroom. If this is nothing but an attempt to give the jury a show, I'll have you in lockup tonight. This is *not* New York, Counselor, and you sure as hell are *not* on Broadway."

"Your Honor," I say, "several things have come to light during the course of this trial, and only today has everything added up."

"You have five minutes to do the math, Counselor! Or else I intend to issue you a contempt citation and to revoke your client's bail!"

I slip my hand inside my suit jacket, remove the envelope, pull out a photograph, and drop it onto Maxa's desk.

"What is this?" she wants to know before looking at it.

"It's a photograph of Mr. Maddox and Katie Leffler, Your Honor, taken at a staff picnic for the prosecuting attorney's office two days before Katie Leffler was murdered."

"This is the boy Josh's mother?" she says, lifting the photo off her desk.

"Correct, Your Honor."

"And you and the boy are accusing Mr. Maddox here of *murdering* her?"

"Your Honor—" I say.

"No, Mr. Corvelli. Before you continue, I want to know how the hell this relates in any way to the case against your client."

"Your Honor, the police were operating on a faulty assumption," I say, "specifically that Trevor Simms was the target of the arson at the resort."

Still standing behind her desk, Maxa says, "You're saying that he wasn't?"

"No, Your Honor. Trevor Simms's death was incidental. The target of the arson was Josh Leffler."

"The boy? *Why?*"

"Because Josh was a witness to his mother's murder, Your Honor."

For the first time I glance at Maddox, who is standing slightly behind me, hands clasped behind his back. He looks back at me from behind two mounds of puffy black-and-blue flesh but remains silent.

"Not a word, Mr. Maddox," Maxa says as though he needed to be reminded. Her eyes dart back to me. "I assume you have evidence of this, Mr. Corvelli."

"Of course, Your Honor. There was plenty of physical evidence left at the scene." Again I count off on aching, gnarled fingers. "One, the exterior door to the adjoining room—Josh Leffler's room—was left wide open. Two, the point of origin was just outside that door rather than on or near the bed. Three, the accelerant trailed under that door—that locked interior door that led to Josh Leffler's room—for no other discernable reason.

Four, the pennies outside Josh Leffler's room—the boy testified neither he nor his grandmother had any coins; the pennies were used to trap Josh and his grandmother in their own room during the blaze."

"What?" Maxa says. "How so?"

"It's done in college dormitories all the time, Your Honor. Students penny other students in their own rooms, stuff coins between the door and the door jamb so that whoever is inside the room cannot get out. I've done it myself on occasion."

"Assuming all this is true, Counselor," Maxa says, "what evidence points to Mr. Maddox as the perpetrator?"

"Your Honor," I say, "it should have been clear to me at my client's initial arraignment. Mr. Maddox requested bail in an amount exactly equal to my retainer, which was in an amount exactly equal to everything my client's parents had on hand. Mr. Maddox did this to have me taken off the case, figuring I wouldn't continue if I didn't get paid. It caused plenty of contention between me and my law partner, but we agreed to take on the bail assignment, and it's crushed us financially. Mr. Maddox's backup plan was to have me removed by motion, by pretending he intended to call me as a material witness at trial."

Maxa looks at Maddox but says nothing. She turns back to me. In a low angry voice, she says, "I hope to hell for your sake, Mr. Corvelli, that that is not all you have."

"It's not, Your Honor. Mr. Maddox attempted to block my investigation at every turn. He warned every one of his witnesses not to speak to me. He went as far as to hide Mia Landow and to help Lauren Simms and Gabe Guidry get off the island before my investigator and I could interview them. He turned the entire prosecutor's office against me. He made certain that the deputy prosecutors assigned to my other cases stuck tough and fought for convictions, mainly against my client Turi Ahina, knowing damn well Turi would wind up in Halawa."

"Sounds to me as though Mr. Maddox was doing his *job*, Counselor." Maxa is growing impatient.

"Let's fast-forward to the trial, Your Honor. The testimony of Dr. Noonan—the ME playing fast and loose with his words in a murder trial, suggesting the exact size of the blade used on Trevor Simms. Izzy Dufu, assistant chief of resort security, clearly lying about what he observed when he went to the Simms's honeymoon suite. They were coached, Your Honor, fed everything they needed for Maddox to obtain a conviction, so that he could walk away clean."

Maxa continues to cut holes through me with her eyes.

"Then, of course, there is Detective Tatupu's testimony," I say. "Mr. Maddox tried to feed the defense Corwin Pierce as a suspect. Maddox had Pierce transferred from the OCCC to Halawa so that Pierce could get in my client Turi Ahina's ear. Then Maddox fed all the information he could about the crime to Corwin Pierce in order to convince me to point to Pierce at trial. Only Mr. Pierce was nowhere near Ko Olina that night and Mr. Maddox knows it. If I went for the bait, I would have assured that Erin Simms was convicted on all counts."

Maxa shakes her head emphatically. "Mr. Corvelli, you are making a case for a mistrial, something I offered to you days ago. You are insinuating that Mr. Maddox used trickery to obtain this conviction, but you have *not* provided me one iota of evidence that Mr. Maddox in fact committed this crime!"

"Your Honor, Mr. Maddox's reasons for leaving California are officially buried, but my investigators have discovered why he's no longer a prosecutor in the Golden State. He's had a previous arrest for domestic violence in L.A. County, and it was suggested that he obstructed justice in several cases in which he was involved as a prosecutor."

"*Once again,* Mr. Corvelli, I am hearing *nothing* relating to the Kupulupulu Beach Resort fire. What makes you so damn sure Mr. Maddox here committed this crime?"

"Because, Your Honor," I say, finally allowing myself a few slow deep breaths, "this past July, three weeks into this case, three weeks into my friendship with Josh Leffler, Mr. Maddox tried to have me killed."

CHAPTER 60

"Maddox has already lawyered up," Jake says as I enter the conference room.

I step over to the windows and gaze out at the night sky.

"Can't say I blame him," I tell Jake. "He's facing a dozen counts of murder and one count of attempted murder, not to mention obstruction of justice."

"According to the news reports, Maddox is at the station on South Beretania now, refusing to talk."

"Who's his lawyer?" I ask.

"Russ Dracano. He's all Maddox could afford."

"That's what you get for working for the State."

Jake laughs. "Guess so." Then he turns serious. "Where's the kid?"

"Chelsea picked Josh up and took him home after court. I've already told Tatupu that no cop will be allowed to question him until after Erin's formally acquitted. And, even then, not without me present."

Suddenly the door to the conference room swings open, squeaking and scaring the hell out of me.

"Congratulations," Flan shouts, slapping his palms together.

Following him is a girl of about seventeen, slender with curves in all the right places, a smile that hits you hard in the chest.

I nod to both of them. "Couldn't have done it without you, Flan."

"Gentlemen, I'd like you both to meet my daughter Casey."

She sets her purse down on one of the plush conference room chairs and shakes Jake's hand, then holds it out for me. I think of the used condoms, the footprints on the ceiling of Flan's jalopy, and say, "Sorry, I think I'm coming down with something."

"Maybe swine flu," Jake says.

Casey covers her mouth with her hand. "Is that still going around?"

We all look at her.

"I've had a sore throat and fever," she says. "And it burns like hell when I pee."

Flan's shoulders slump. He puts an arm around her and says, "We'll pay a visit to the doctor in the morning, honey."

"Two murder cases, two acquittals," Jake says to me to break the silence. "Son, you're on fire."

"Poor choice of words, old man," I tell him. "Damn poor choice of words."

"Well . . ." he says, standing from his chair. "What do you say we all head over to Whiskey Bar to celebrate?"

"You guys go on ahead," I tell him. "I'll meet you there."

As soon as they leave I'm on the conference room phone dialing Erin's number. Although we've had no opportunity to discuss it at length, I know she's upset over the hot tub footage. Not because she's embarrassed by it, but because of how it might affect our future together. Along the same lines, she is fiercely concerned that the end of the trial will mean the end of our relationship, something I have never once hinted at.

I wait five or six rings, then hang up without an answer. Technically, her trial is not over and at least for the time being, Erin remains out on bail. Still restricted to her home. I wonder briefly whether she's sleeping. Whether she's sleeping alone.

I remove my suit jacket and set it down on the conference room table, then head to my office to shoot Erin an e-mail.

"Sandy," I say softly as I pass my favorite oil painting. "Of course, Sandy."

I sit behind my desk and pop the top on a Red Bull. Then I open my e-mail account. Six new e-mails appear in bold, one from Ryan Flanagan. The subject line reads DIGITAL COPIES—STATE VS. SIMMS. I immediately open the e-mail and download the attachments.

There are just a few photos, a half dozen in all, those in which the subjects' eyes had looked like the devil's. But their eyes are all clear now.

What the fuck is this?

I zoom in on the first photo. The guy with the Boston Red Sox hat suddenly seems familiar. Thin as a rail and without the red eyes I can see that one iris is blue, the other brown. A condition known as heterochromia. I looked it up on the Internet a while back, but now for the life of me I can't remember why.

I pull my cell phone from my pants pocket. I open the clam shell and speed-dial the number to Flan's cell. He doesn't answer; I leave him a voice mail and tell him to call me back right away at the office. Then I toss the cell on my desk and head back to the conference room.

As soon as I enter the conference room I notice Casey's purse sitting on one of the chairs. I hesitate to touch it, but it's drawing me in like a magnet, covered as it is with capital F's performing 69 on one another.

Just as I pick it up, the office phone rings. I lift the receiver, still studying the handbag, and flatly mumble the words, "Kevin Corvelli."

It's Flan. "Hey, Kev, you called?"

"Yeah," I say, sounding as though I'm in a trance. "Casey left her handbag here."

"Just leave it on Hoshi's desk. I'll pick it up in the morning. Unless you want to carry it with you to Whiskey."

I shoulder the receiver and turn the purse over in my hands. "You buy this bag for her, Flan?"

"No," he says. "It was a gift from one of her two dozen boy-friends."

The little leather Fendi is a bit worn but not all that old. I hold the handbag to my nose. It smells harshly of soap.

"Which boyfriend?" I say.

I hear Flan call over to Casey. "Hey, sweetheart, which one of your boyfriends gave you that handbag?"

I can't hear her answer. Then Flan is back on the line. He says, "Kev, you still there?"

"I'm here," I tell him as I snatch my suit jacket off the confer-ence room table.

"The handbag was a gift from some grease monkey named Dominic."

CHAPTER 61

The headlamps of my Jeep burn a trail through the night as I head west on H-1 toward Waikele. The black sky remains open, thick droplets of rain carrying out their kamikaze missions, targeting my windshield and roof. My right foot presses against the accelerator as I fish around in my pants pocket for my cell phone, but nothing. I left the fucking thing on my desk.

I'm on my own.

The Ho'Omalu Village, a middle-income apartment complex off Lumiauau Street in Waikele, is where I picked up Josh for our last playdate. When I fly past the abutting park I realize I've gone too far. I throw the Jeep in reverse and tear backward down the dark, empty street.

Killing the lights, I pull into the complex and park the Wrangler in the first spot I find. I then step out into the downpour and sprint in the direction of Building H.

When I spot it, I bolt around back. It's pitch-black in the back lot, not a single light brightening the lined blacktop. Mercifully, Chelsea's apartment is on the first floor. I pinpoint her lanai in the darkness by recognizing the cheap plastic outdoor furniture dripping with rainwater. The vertical blinds remain closed. No lights are visible inside.

Slowly, I approach the lanai, then quietly push a plastic chair aside to get by. Holding my breath, I try the sliding glass door and to my incredulity, it slides.

I push aside the blinds and step inside.

My entire body tingles with a feeling I barely recognize. It isn't fear. Not the fear that ran through me last year in Kailua when I was being chased by Alika Kapua and a loaded Smith & Wesson. This is something more like anger, like hatred, like rage. *And it's about damn time,* I tell myself.

My suit is soaked to the skin, my hair plastered to my skull. I push away the rain from my eyes and hurry forward quietly through the living room, the carpeted floor squeaking ever so slightly under my feet.

Then someone rounds the corner.

In the bleak moonlight entering through a curtained kitchen window, I can barely make him out. Just a thin man with a ball cap and gloves, but it's enough. Before a second thought flashes through my mind I'm darting at him, leading with my clenched right fist.

I hear the crack as my knuckles connect with his temple, knocking the cap off his head. His body slumps to the shag carpet and then I'm on top of him, nailing him again and again in the face.

He's screaming something but I can't make it out, so I stop punching and grab him by the throat instead.

I stare into his bloodied face.

"Where's the boy, Dominic?" I say through clenched teeth.

All he does is choke.

"Where's the fucking boy?" I say again.

Something like "gone" emanates from his broken throat.

I loosen my grip, smack him hard on the side of the head, and spit in his face.

That's when I feel the pinch in my stomach.

As I lift my torso, Dominic pushes the blade in farther, twists it, turns it, searches for a vital organ in the right upper abdomen. With my left, I strike him in the face again and try to stand up, simultaneously pulling the stiletto from my gut with my right.

Hurts a hell of a lot more coming out than it did going in.

I back away, my vision blurry. I'm already dizzy, cold, feeling faint. Stumbling, I drop to one knee just as Dominic begins to get to his feet.

Summoning every scrap of strength, every shred of rage, I launch myself off my bad right knee and charge forward, swinging at the prick with my right. The awkward, off-balance hook I deliver connects squarely with the left side of his throat.

Time seems to freeze.

In the dimness an inky liquid flows like a faucet from between Dominic's lips.

That's when I realize I still have the knife in my fist.

Gazing into his mismatched eyes I'm frozen like a block of ice. But I need to find the kid.

I release the knife, manage a few slow, painful steps forward as Dominic's body brushes against the wall, then slumps to the floor.

As I pass him, my eyes lock on the stiletto still lodged in his throat.

The sensation that washes over me isn't at all what I expected. In fact, although I know I never have, it distinctly feels as though I've done this before.

CHAPTER 62

The body of Chelsea Leffler lies spread-eagle on the floor of her bedroom, the white cordless phone clutched in her hand. Cautiously, I kneel beside her, peel each thick finger off the bloodied receiver, then put phone to my ear.

Nothing. The line is as dead as Dillinger and I'm on my own again.

As I press the palm of my hand against the hole in my gut, a gurgling noise suddenly sounds from Chelsea's throat, startling me.

I lean over her and lift the lids of her eyes—dilated, even with the lamplight spraying us from the corner. I check her thick neck for a pulse, feel a beat, but it's feeble.

"Where's Josh?" I say softly.

"P-p-p-p . . ." she tries, crimson bubbles rising from blue lips, popping, spilling scarlet down her triple-chin.

With my free hand I reach for a dresser drawer handle and fish around for a piece of fabric. I dig out an empty white pillowcase and press it to my stomach, futilely trying to ebb the bleeding. I feel weak and woozy, light-headed as though at any moment I might white-out.

I again attempt to lift myself up but fall forward onto the floor next to Chelsea. Immediately I'm smacked in the face with the blended stench of shit and piss and blood and perfume and death.

With images of the fire blazing through my mind, finally I roll myself over, try again to rise, and rasp, "I'm going for help."

A few seconds later I'm actually on my feet, lurching in the direction of the door. Pressing the now-crimson pillowcase against my stomach, I squint away my double vision and teeter forward.

Fortunately, as I stagger through the frame, I hear a drifting Chelsea Leffler mutter her last word.

CHAPTER 63

"Park," she'd said.

From the road the park appears to be one wide open field but as I charge through the long blades of grass and thick mud I realize that the rear portion of the park is pure forest. The rain continues to drop from the sky like nails. Tree branches take swipes at my cheeks but I barely feel them. I lower my head and hasten through the muck like a crazed Doberman, searching the pitch for the kid.

I resist calling out for fear that I may expose Josh's location, just as I exposed Erin Simms on Hidden Beach with my electric-orange Jeep.

The blow to the dead center of my back feels as though it were delivered by sledgehammer. I'm paralyzed, facedown in the mud before I even see my attacker.

Then a body lands on top of me, straddles my lower back, a rigid hand holding my face down in the pungent, putrid earth.

"I'll fucking kill him, Josh," Sebastian shouts from a few inches above me.

Mud flooding my open mouth, I can't speak, can't warn Josh to run like hell, never mind me.

"I'll fucking kill him, Josh," Sebastian shouts again. *"Come out now or your lawyer friend is dead!"*

No sound but the teeming rain as it slices through trees and angrily pounds the earth's surface. Even though I know I'm about to go, a wave of perfect relief washes over me.

But suddenly the silence is broken by a child's scream—"Please, no!"—coming from behind the broad trunk of a nearby tree.

The grip on the back of my head loosens and I lift my eyes enough to see the kid step through the downpour like a dream.

"Leave him alone," the kid cries.

"Get over here, Josh," Sebastion demands as he continues to straddle me. "Get over here and I'll let him go."

The kid takes two quick steps before I'm able to shout, *"No!"*

I get a swift punch to the back of my head for my troubles.

And the kid's still coming.

"I have to, Kevin," Josh says, resignation washing over his face. "I have to and I will. You saved my life. Now I have to save yours."

"Run, kid," I shout. "Run, goddamnit! He's gonna kill me anyway."

Then my face is buried in the mud again and I can't breathe, the weight of the bastard on top of me sinking me deeper and deeper into my wet grassy grave.

"Come *here,*" Sebastian shouts at the kid.

With all the strength I can muster, I force my head up. "You fucking coward," I spit out, choking on soil as I try again to scream.

"Coward?" Sebastian says in my ear as I drown. "You're calling me a coward? Let me tell you something, Corvelli. It's easy dying to protect someone else. It's fucking hard to kill to protect yourself. Especially your own boy."

I can almost feel the blood spilling out of my gut, mixing with the rain and mud. I twist my head to the side. "You killed the kid's mother," I say with quiet rage.

"That's right, Corvelli. Know why? 'Cause Katie and I were trying to set things right, trying to make things work. Then the filthy cunt started fucking that goddamn pussy-boy prosecutor."

Josh is stepping this way, his footfalls coming closer.

"And the kid saw you," I say softly with a faceful of pain.

"Right again, Counselor. I saw him up in that window with his goddamn bird binoculars. I would've done him right then and there but some fuck neighbor turned his lights on."

"The kid didn't say anything, ya know," I mutter through clenched teeth.

"I know." A hint of sorrow permeates his voice for the first time. "He's been a good boy. But, with all your fucking digging, that secret was only gonna stay inside of him for so long, Corvelli, and you know it." Sebastian presses my face into the mud again. "That's it, Josh. Come here and I'll let your friend go."

The kid cries, harder even than he did on the stand.

This is how I'm going to die, I finally realize. *Drowned facedown in the mud.*

Everything glows as I fall deeper and deeper into the abyss.

And then instantly it is as though Kevin Corvelli doesn't exist, as though I'm ten feet below the surface of the Pacific, eyes open, pushing water past me like the fins of a big fish, detached wholly from every worldly thought, every worry, every other human being who has ever lived. I'm underwater yet filled with fire, drowning in blue-hot flames. I'm reaching with my outstretched arm for the rocks, straining my body toward the bottom, extended fingers grazing it just barely, just briefly, and then I am determined to rise, rise, rise again, using a reserve of strength I never knew I possessed, launching myself to the surface so that I can breathe in that tropical air again, steal one long last look at that horizon.

Without thought my fingers clench into fists, scraping up two handfuls of mud, then I am pushing myself up on my knuckles, my entire body rising on the strength of two tired, rarely-used biceps, and I can feel my rider cling tighter to the torn jacket of my suit.

I've got one shot at this, I think. *One chance to throw this fuck off me like a mad bull.*

Just as the kid pauses about five feet away from us, I heave myself and Sebastian's 180 pounds up with all my might. It's not enough to buck the killer off me, but it's enough for me to angle my body and ultimately twist around so that I'm facing him. He immediately presses his weight against my bleeding gut and before I can scream his hands close tight around my throat.

He's choking the life out of me. Instead of drowning I'll be strangled—if I don't bleed out first.

Dr. Noonan's going to have his work cut out for him, I must.

Suddenly the kid runs at him, head down, screaming like a rock star in the throes of his final set.

Sebastian glances up and it's all the help I need. I shove one of my two fistfuls of mud in his face and say, *"Choke on this, you psychotic fuck."*

I follow with a second fistful of mud to his mouth, then I reach for his eyes, press my muddy thumbs in on the lids as he screams, something black oozing from the corners of each eye.

Finally I'm able to throw him off me, his body rolling a few yards before coming to a halt at the base of a tree.

Painfully I push myself to my feet and hobble toward him.

I hover over Sebastian Haslett as he lies on his back fumbling for his eyes with his hands. Then I'm straddling him as he straddled me, striking his face with my closed right fist again and again and again and again.

"Stop!" Josh screams.

I ignore the kid.

"Kevin, please! You're gonna kill him!"

"He has it coming," I shout as my fist comes down on the raw flesh of Sebastian's face again.

It's then I realize I intend to murder the kid's father with my bare hands.

PART IV

END OF THE NIGHT

CHAPTER 64

When I arrive at the lagoon at dawn most of the area is already cordoned off with blaring yellow police tape. The water in front of the Kupulupulu Beach Resort itself looks as though it's readying itself for a *Jaws* shoot. What once was a picturesque blue is now a grisly violet.

The body floats faceup, naked, arms spread as though crucified to the surface of the water. Even now her face is beautiful, a visage burned into the mind, a smoking, stinging memory that will remain with me until my very last moment of life.

I lower the Panama Jack hat until it pushes against the rims of my prescription sunglasses. The sky is clear, the sun is rising, and the photographers are vying for optimum space.

"Slit both wrists with a switchblade," John Tatupu says from behind me.

I already know. The blade lived at the bottom where I left it, waited for her for six whole months, guarded by nothing more than a moray eel with a sharp set of teeth.

"We can't be sure yet," Tatupu says, "but we think it may have been the knife that killed Trevor Simms."

"What makes you think that?" I ask.

"Got a full confession from Sebastian Haslett overnight at the Queen's Medical Center. Told us everything, including where he dumped the knife."

"That's good." I finally turn to face him. "Catch him without a lawyer?"

"No, actually. Mickey Fallon sat there reading a newspaper the entire time."

"Figures." I turn back to the lagoon.

"You did a number on Haslett, Corvelli. He's lucky to be alive. His buddy Dominic, though, didn't fare so well."

"You looking for a statement, John?"

"No, there's plenty of time for that later. I just wanted to express my condolences to you for your client."

I feel photographs being taken of me, the lenses violating me in ways most could never comprehend. Me in my soaked-through suit, covered in scarlet from head to toe.

"You been to the hospital yet?" Tatupu says.

I nod my head. "It's not so bad. Just lost some blood."

"They released you pretty quick, Corvelli. You still look very pale."

"HMO," I tell him, but that's not the truth. I'm a fugitive from Wahiawa General, pulled off a brazen escape just before they could transport me to Honolulu, to the Queen's Medical Center. I think I'm due a blood transfusion, but when I heard about Erin, I figured it could wait. At least Wahiawa stopped the bleeding.

"Here come your friends," Tatupu says, looking over my shoulder.

I turn and see an entourage heading this way: Dapper Don Watanabe, Luke Maddox, even old man Frank DiSimone.

"Do me a favor, John," I say. "Keep Maddox away from me."

"He wasn't the one who tried to kill you, you know."

"I know," I tell him. "I just don't fucking like him."

And I'll forever blame him for Erin's suicide, regardless of what her suicide note says.

I turn and start walking painfully away in the direction of the resort.

"One thing that bothers me," Tatupu says from behind me.

I stop but remain with my back to him. "Yeah, John?"

He comes up behind me so that I can feel his warm breath on the back of my neck. "Yeah," he says. "I can't for the life of me figure how Erin Simms knew the knife was at the bottom of the lagoon."

"Come to say 'I told you so'?"

"Hell, no, son. You know me better than that."

I suppose I do.

We stand on a hill under a palm tree a few hundred yards from the lagoon, away from the photographers and cops, away from the gawkers and closet fans of raw violence.

"So what happens with the kid now that Chelsea's passed on?"

I shrug. "Foster home, I guess."

Jake nods but says nothing more on the subject. There's nothing more to say.

After a few minutes of silence, Jake leans against the trunk of the palm and clears his throat. "Tatupu tells me that Sebastian Haslett had some help aside from his boy Dominic."

"I know," I tell him, my voice little more than a rasp. "I had Flan subpoena the passkey records for hotel security. Erin said she might have opened the door voluntarily the first time Izzy

Dufu visited. The time of the first noise complaint and Izzy's first use of the passkey to enter the honeymoon suite didn't match up. Izzy went in there while Trevor and Erin were both out of the room to case the joint."

Jake sighs. "For fifty bucks."

I shrug. "Izzy didn't know what Sebastian was going to do with the information. Probably he thought it was just going to be a simple in-and-out thieving. Happens every day at large resorts all over the world. Izzy knew he fucked up; that's why he doctored the records before sending them off to Maddox."

"What I don't get," Jake says, "is why Sebastian Haslett would enter the Simms suite knowing Trevor was in there."

"He didn't know it," I say, swallowing hard, craving a drink of cold water. "Dominic spotted Erin down near the beach sucking face with a guy. Figured it had to be her husband, which meant the suite had to be empty."

Jake shakes his head incredulously. "So Trevor caught Sebastian by surprise." After a moment he asks, "Who was the guy she was smooching with?"

"Isaac."

"The best man."

"That's right."

"If Isaac had stayed there on the beach with her she would have had her alibi."

"She and Isaac got into an argument," I tell him. "That's when Isaac took off for the Meridian, inadvertently creating his own paper alibi."

"How do you know all this, son?"

"Talked to Isaac this morning. He's the one who informed me that Erin was dead."

"How'd he get ahold of you?"

"He didn't," I say. "I got ahold of him. He picked up the

phone the last time I dialed Erin's number from the hospital. After we talked about the night of the fire Isaac told me she'd left me a letter. He'd already opened it, so he read it to me over the phone. Then he threatened to kill me."

"Jesus," Jake says. "What the hell did the letter say?"

I don't answer him and Jake knows better than to press.

"I'll let you alone now, son," he finally says, gently resting a hand on my shoulder. "We all right now?"

I nod without looking at him. "We always were."

Jake crosses his arms against his chest. "I'm sorry I allowed a little thing like money to come between us."

"You were going through a lot with Alison," I say.

"Oh, I was going through a hell of a lot more than that, son."

I remove my sunglasses and look at him.

Jake says, "I've been sober now going on six months."

My eyes narrow. *Am I so obtuse?* I think. *So self-involved that I didn't even notice that my partner had quit drinking after spending so many years in the bottle?*

"Wasn't easy," he says, "and I sure as hell didn't want to burden you with it. I'm only telling you now to explain. Maybe help you avoid the same mistakes I made in my life. You're one hell of a lawyer, son. Don't you waste your talent and piss away your prime the way I did mine."

I watch as Jake wipes the sweat from his eyes.

"No more secrets between the two of us," he says. "Can you live with that, son?"

I bow my head. "Turns out, I can live with a lot of things, Jake."

He turns to leave.

"About the secrets, Jake," I say, spinning him around. "I should tell you that last week I turned down a new case. Some prick—our prospective client—clubbed to death a pregnant monk seal."

"Well," he says, "the hell with it. Like you said, we've gotta draw the line somewhere."

He sticks out his hand and I stare at it.

"Think I'm coming down with something," I tell him. "Maybe the swine flu."

Jake nods and offers up a knowing grin. "Jeez, that Casey is something, isn't she? What a hell of a cross for Flan to bear."

"She'll be all right," I say, lifting my Panama Jack and wiping the sweat from my forehead. "Flan's a good father. He's going to let Casey make her own mistakes, and he's always going to be there to bail her out. Can't ask for more than that."

"Suppose that's true." Jake stuffs his hands in his pants pockets and his voice takes on a serious pitch. "Son, I ever tell you I have a—"

"No, you didn't, Jake. And let's keep it that way for the time being, huh?"

He nods, takes one final look at me, says, "I reckon a closed book is better than no book at all."

Then he walks on down the hill.

CHAPTER 65

Standing in the shallows of Hanauma Bay, Josh looks back at me and asks for the third time why I won't join him in the water.

"Jellyfish," I tell him.

"Jellyfish?"

"Yeah, someone lost a foot here the other day. Didn't I mention it?"

Josh scrambles to the beach and drops down at my side, breathing as hard as a beached dolphin. "Holy moly," he says.

Holy moly, indeed. Actually, there are no box jellyfish in Hanauma Bay today. They only visit the island of Oahu once a month, nine or ten days following a full moon. But I can't go into the water with my stomach freshly stapled up, and I don't want to explain that to Josh. And I sure as hell don't want to explain how I was injured or show him the wound. Safe to say, the kid's been through enough.

"Thanks for coming with me to the inner-view yesterday," the kid says.

"No worries, Josh. It was my pleasure."

"That lady is nice."

"Good people," I agree. "You run into them every once in a blue moon."

Josh digs a hole in the sand in front of him while I lie back in my Tommy Bahama trunks and T, tipping my Panama Jack over my face. The last three Percocet are kicking in and I feel content, could probably even drift off to sleep.

"Are you going to keep your promise to me?" Josh says.

I nudge my hat up just enough so that I can speak. "What promise is that, Josh?"

"When I was giving my test-money you promised that if I told my secrets, you would tell me yours."

Sighing, I say, "I did, didn't I?"

Josh doesn't say anything but I assume he's nodding his head. Hell, he's right. I owe the kid some secrets and it's time I paid up.

"When I was a kid about your age," I say, "I used to throw pennies in the fountain all the time. Pennies, nickels, dimes, quarters, fifty-cent pieces even. Anything I could get my hands on. And by my logic—even then I tried to remain logical at all times—if a penny bought you one wish, then a nickel bought you five, and a dime bought you ten, and so on. But no matter how many wishes I bought, for as long as I can remember I always wished for the same damn thing."

"That's silly," he says. "Because if just one of your wishes came true, you'd be wasting all your other wishes."

"See, Josh, I looked at wishes more like lottery tickets. The more wishes I bought, I figured, the better the chance I had of one coming true. And the one wish I wished over and over again was the most important wish in the world for me."

"What did you wish for?"

I lift the Panama Jack to the top of my head as I sit up and look at him through prescription sunglasses. My face does a hell of a job disguising the pain. "I wished I had a dad," I say.

Josh stops digging his hole and stares up at me.

"I never met my father," I tell him. "And I always thought I was missing out on this amazing . . . thing. Someone to take me to Mets games, teach me the proper way to shoot a basketball, tell me the secret to picking up women."

"But you had a mommy."

"I had a mother," I say. "A mother who screamed at me at the top of her lungs when I didn't put my toys away. A mother who held a blow dryer to my head till I cried every time I sweat, even in ninety-degree heat. A mother who hid food from me, who put me to work when I was just a kid. A mother who wouldn't let me outside to play, who wouldn't let me have friends my own age. A mother who hit me until I got too big and began hitting back. A mother who ransacked my room every time I left my house for school. A mother who spent a fortune on herself but refused to help me pay for college or my law degree."

"Your mommy sounds horrible," Josh says.

"Maybe. But there are a lot of mothers like that. A lot of fathers, too. And I didn't realize until I started practicing law and meeting some of my clients' parents that maybe I was better off having never met my father. Who you're born to is like a crapshoot. Sometimes a kid is better off when he's raised by complete strangers."

Josh nods his head. "Like I will be," he says. Then: "But, Kevin, my mommy was good."

"I know," I tell him. "My point is, kid, you'll hear a lot of bullshit over the span of your life about how important blood is."

"You need it to live."

"Sure you do," I say, grinning. *Don't I know it.* "But it doesn't matter so much whose blood runs through your veins. It doesn't matter so much who you came from, only who you become."

"I want to be a hero," he says, "like you."

"I'm the furthest thing from a hero you'll ever find," I say, shaking my head. "Fact is, there are no heroes or villains in this world, Josh. People just like to label other people that way because it fits neatly into their understanding of the world. It ties things up nicely on the ten o'clock news. There are good soldiers and bad soldiers on every side of every war. There are good cops and bad cops in every city, just as there are good lawbreakers and bad lawbreakers on every city street. But the important thing to remember is, no one is either *all* good or all bad, Josh. Everyone is gray."

"Like Skies," he says.

I take a deep breath. "Sure. Like Skies," I say.

Josh returns to digging his hole in the sand. "When I grow up," he says without looking at me, "I want to be a lawyer, Kevin."

"That may change in time," I tell him, tipping my Panama Jack back over my eyes as I lie down. "But you take your dreams, kid, and never let them out of your sight. There are these people out there, I call them the Dreamkillers, and you'll meet them at every stage of your life. They'll try to impose their own reality on you every chance they get, but you can't let them. However crazy your dreams sound to everyone else, you chase them. Let your dreams, not the Dreamkillers, guide your every decision in life. Because no matter what anyone tries to tell you, kid, as far as lives go, you only get the one."

Satisfied and slightly high, I close my eyes behind my hat and drink in the silence.

"Everything all right?" I ask Josh a few minutes later. "You've been awfully quiet."

"Everything's fine, Kevin," he says, closing his tiny hand around mine. "I'm just watching the horizon."

CHAPTER 66

"Have a minute?"

I'm standing in the hall outside Judge Narita's courtroom waiting for my client, an icehead from Nanakuli charged with breaking and entering.

"Make it quick," I say, not unkindly, to Sherry Beagan.

She points to a bench at the end of the hall and I walk with her, my right knee finally nearing a hundred percent, my upper abdomen another story.

"I've called your office a couple hundred times," she says. "Your receptionist keeps telling me you won't take my call."

"I know," I say, sighing. "For some reason, Hoshi still refuses to lie on my behalf. We may have to let her go."

"All right," Sherry says as we sit, "since we're short on time, I'll get right to it then. I'm leaving the island this weekend and I need to interview you for my book."

"You have a book contract?" I ask, crossing my right leg over my left.

"I do."

I lean back, bury my hand in my left jacket pocket and pull out a bottle of Percocet. I uncap the bottle, drop three pills in my hand, put my palm to my mouth, summon some saliva, and dry swallow them one at a time.

"All right," I say finally. "What do you want to know?"

True to her word, she doesn't hesitate. "The police report on Erin Simms's suicide states that she left a note and that it was addressed to you."

"Yeah."

That note is now part of the record with the Disciplinary Board of the Hawaii Supreme Court in the matter of *In re Kevin D. Corvelli*. The grievance was filed by Rebecca Downey, Todd Downey's name conspicuously absent from the charge. Todd Downey's name is also absent from the lawsuit filed against Harper & Corvelli by Rebecca Downey through her attorney Russ Dracano for the return of the six hundred thousand dollars in legal fees we obtained once Erin Simms's bail was finally released. There is no merit to either claim, but I'd be lying if I said all of this—the grievance, the lawsuit, the accompanying publicity—is not a major pain in the ass.

"Well? What did the suicide note say?" Sherry asks.

I hesitate—but then, what the hell do I have to hide? In a few months it will all be considered public information anyway, available to anyone by written request through the Freedom of Information Act.

"The gist?" I say. "That she feared I'd abandon her once the trial was over."

"That's why she killed herself?"

Slowly I shake my head. "It's not that simple, Sherry. Erin Simms was remarkably complex. You could write a dozen books about her and you'll still just be chipping away at the surface. But, to wrap it up neatly for the masses, yes, as a borderline, Erin possessed an irrational fear of abandonment and a complete inability to exist alone."

"So her suicide . . ."

"Was a frantic effort to avoid abandonment," I tell her without emotion.

Sherry tilts her head back to the ceiling, then looks at me. "Well?" she says, softly. "Was Erin's fear really irrational? Was the threat of abandonment real or did she imagine it? Kevin, you're the only one who can answer that."

I smirk, ever surprised at how simplistic everyone needs things to be. "Not even me, Sherry. I have no idea what would have happened after the trial had Erin not committed suicide."

She waits a few beats, then asks, "Do you blame yourself for Erin's death?"

"No," I say without the slightest pause.

There is plenty of blame to go around in the suicide of Erin Simms, and in all likelihood it should start with her mother. Erin was tethered to Rebecca Downey from the day she was born in California until the day she took her own life in a lagoon nourished by the Pacific in Ko Olina. But her mother didn't have the power to hold her daughter hostage all those years. To a certain extent, of course, Erin allowed it. And Erin is partly to blame. But I have little doubt that during her teens and twenties, Erin was fed a steady supply of the usual platitudes about unconditional love. I'm certain that if she ever complained about the torture she was put through, she was told at one time or another to "honor thy father and mother." The words "tough love" no doubt sprung from someone's lips along the way. Sadly, still today, divorcing your mother or father—walking away from a bad parent even as an adult—carries a far uglier stigma than divorcing your spouse did in the old days.

Society can be so damn stubborn in its notions of right and

wrong. For whatever reason it becomes ingrained that we have to remain loyal to those who bore us regardless of whatever else they've done to us during the course of our lives. Bullshit. That advice comes from the same people who tell you that you have to remain forever in any shit town you're from, that you should die within a fifty-mile radius of where you were born.

"Who *do* you blame for Erin's death?" Sherry asks.

I do blame Luke Maddox, though I don't tell her that. It wouldn't read well in a true crime manuscript, and my words would undoubtedly follow me around the rest of my legal career. But certainly Maddox's attitude, many of the decisions he made—Corwin Pierce among them—contributed to this case continuing far longer than it ever needed to.

As though Sherry read my mind she says, "Luke Maddox has made some very strong statements against you."

As well he should. After all, I did insinuate that the deputy prosecutor committed mass murder during the trial. It was his fingerprint on my Maserati that gave me license. He's since admitted that he'd spotted Miss Hawaii getting out of the Maserati with me at Chip's and he'd considered confronting us in the lot when we returned to the car. Oahu really is too small an island sometimes.

"To hell with Luke Maddox," I say. "We'll face each other again in open court and at the end of the day we'll see which lawyer's left standing."

In the play for Kerry Naikelekele, however, it is neither of us. Word on the street is, she's currently dating a native Hawaiian, who also happens to be an Ultimate Fighting champion.

Standing just outside the courtroom door my B & E client, whose name I can't quite remember, waves to me. As I rise I apologize, tell Sherry time's up, I've gotta go.

"Just a couple more things, Kevin," Sherry pleads as she gets to her feet. "Two more things, then I'll let you go."

I hold up my arm and motion for the client to wait inside the courtroom for me.

"Go ahead," I tell her.

"You killed a man, Kevin."

I look her in those big brown eyes, pretty, even today, even in the murky hallways of the criminal courthouse. "In self-defense," I say.

"Still, it changes people. *A lot,* I've been told. How has it changed you?"

I exercise my jaw. "To be honest, this is the first time I've given any thought to it at all."

Her eyebrows lift to meet her bangs. "So killing a man hasn't changed you even a whit?"

I tell her it's something I'll have to think over. "And the last?" I say.

"It's about Luke Maddox again," she says, timidly. "I've read the transcript for the Erin Simms trial over and over again."

"And?"

"And when you had Josh Leffler on the stand . . ."

I knew the kid was harboring a secret. A *big* secret. He'd told me as much as he pet Grey Skies on his lap on my lanai. I just hadn't been listening at the time.

Somehow the conversation stuck with me, just as it did the day Josh took me to his old house on Ke Iki Beach. *"Over there,"* he'd said, pointing out the window at some rocks jutting out of the ocean. *"That's where they say my mommy died."*

Not "That's where my mommy died," but "That's where *they say* my mommy died."

Then Josh plucked a pair of binoculars out from beneath a floorboard in his closet. At first I didn't even consider the fact that the binoculars were hidden. But why would a kid hide a pair of binoculars—unless he'd seen something with them that could come back to haunt him?

Add that to all his talk of secrets and lies and it became clear to me that he had witnessed his mother die. And that it was no accident; it was murder.

Until then it had never occurred to me that Josh could have been the target of the arson. The evidence was there. I'd even pointed most of it out to the jury during my cross-examinations: the point of origin; the open door; the puddle of accelerant on the floor of the adjoining suite; the pennies in the hall. All of it, right in front of us.

Gently, I say, "What are you asking me, Sherry?"

Thanks to the information I received on Luke Maddox from Milt Cashman & Company, I'd had Baron Lee run the unknown print found on my rented Maserati against those of all state employees. The arrest of Luke Maddox for domestic violence in L.A. was bullshit. A pissed-off ex-girlfriend filed a false report and was later prosecuted for it. The domestic violence charge against Maddox was dropped and the case sealed. The rumor that Maddox had been investigated for obstruction of justice while working the sex crimes unit in L.A. County was just that, a rumor. But it was enough to justify digging deeper. More embers for the flames.

When Baron Lee called Flan and told him he'd finally discovered a match for the unknown print found on my rented Maserati, everything changed.

Why the hell would Luke Maddox try to kill me? I hadn't even called him a cocksucker to his face.

Then I thought of Kerry Naikelekele and what she'd told me the day we went snorkeling at the Kupulupulu Beach Resort lagoon. When I told her I spotted Maddox surfing off Ke Iki

Beach, she wasn't the least bit surprised. In fact, Maddox had mentioned to her that he surfed there sometimes, that he used to date a woman who lived there.

That woman was Katie Leffler.

"Kevin," Sherry says again, unable to look me in the eyes, "I don't know quite how to say this." She pauses, takes a deep breath and exhales. "When you had Josh Leffler on the stand . . ."

"Yeah?"

"You cut him off." Her eyes finally meet mine. "You cut the kid off immediately after you got what you wanted."

"He had answered the question I asked," I say.

"But we know now that what Josh meant was that Maddox had come over for pizza that night. Maddox had come over and left. Josh was about to say that on the stand and you stopped him."

"I didn't know what words would come out of Josh's mouth next."

"But you knew they'd be the truth."

"The truth?"

"You *knew* it wasn't Luke Maddox," she says. "Josh didn't see *who* it was that killed his mother, just that *someone* did. It was too dark. There were no lights behind the house. It could've been anyone."

"It could have," I agree.

But juries don't accept shadows, I want to tell her. They don't acquit when you try to feed them ghosts. They want names, they want faces. They want to know that someone is going to be punished for what's been done.

"You *knew* it wasn't Luke Maddox," Sherry says again. "You didn't know who it was that killed Katie Leffler, but you *knew* it wasn't Luke Maddox."

I stand silent, my eyes shooting past her down the long sallow hall.

"But whoever killed Katie," she continues, "could be fingered for the murder of Trevor Simms and the arson targeting Josh Leffler. You needed someone specific to point to. So you gave them Maddox. You went after Luke Maddox with no regard for the truth."

"The truth," I say again with the slightest smirk.

I'm a lawyer, Sherry, I want to tell her. My objective in a criminal case is to create reasonable doubt. When all of the evidence points to my client, the best way to accomplish that is to find someone—*anyone*—to point to in order to create that doubt.

"You knew it wasn't Luke Maddox," she says again.

I'm a *lawyer*, Sherry, I want to tell her. My objective is *not* to solve crimes or track down killers. I'm a lawyer, Sherry. I'm not a cop.

Once I turned down the mistrial, once I decided to go for a verdict, I decided I would do anything it took to win an acquittal, even if it meant burning someone else in order save my client. I decided I would do anything it took to save Erin Simms.

And I did.

"Are we done?" I say.

Sherry nods and backs away as though I'm someone to fear. Maybe I am.

"Send me a copy of the book when it's published?" I call over my shoulder as I stride toward the courtroom.

"Sure," she says.